# After the Rain

# Jo Watson

**HEADLINE**
ETERNAL

First published in Great Britain in 2018
by HEADLINE ETERNAL
An imprint of HEADLINE PUBLISHING GROUP

1

Cataloguing in Publication Data is available from the British Library

ISBN 978 1 4722 5774 1

Typeset in 11.55/16.25 pt Granjon LT Std by Jouve (UK), Milton Keynes

Printed and bound in Great Britain by CPI Group (UK) Ltd, Croydon, CR0 4YY

HEADLINE PUBLISHING GROUP
An Hachette UK Company
Carmelite House
50 Victoria Embankment
London EC4Y 0DZ

www.headlineeternal.com
www.headline.co.uk
www.hachette.co.uk

*I think this book needs to be dedicated to all the colourful Stormy-Rains out there. The ones that don't fit into moulds and conform and follow the pack. Stay crazy and colourful and yourselves. And to GP, DM and WP!*

# After the Rain

# THE BIG ONES

⌒

*The universe is full of questions.*

*Big questions.*

*Strange questions.*

*Wondrous, marvelous, magical questions that don't have easy answers.*

*Like . . . Who are we? Where do we come from? Where are we going? How did it all begin? Is there such a thing as destiny? Fate? What happens when we die? What are the Kardashians really famous for? Did ancient aliens really build the pyramids? And why did the chicken cross the road?*

*Well, that's what this story is all about. Trying to answer the big questions. And by the time you read that final word, turn that last page, you'll believe it all. (Perhaps not the thing about the aliens.)*

*Because there's just no other logical, rational explanation for it. For how the hell it could have happened. How could two people like Marcus and Stormy-Rain have ever come together?*

*And who are Marcus and Stormy-Rain, I hear you ask? Why, they are contradictions. Opposing opposites. Yin and yang. True and false. Night and day.*

*Two people from completely different worlds brought together on a freakish collision course, in the strangest of ways, in the strangest of places and under the strangest of circumstances (there's a lot of strange in there—but you'll soon see why).*

*Yes, this is a story about the hand of Fate. About crazy kismet and creeping karma. Inexplicable happenings and uncanny coincidences. Finding sense in the nonsensical. Enigmatic enigmas and everything you never thought possible. But it's time to believe the unbelievable, because this is a story about how the universe works in mysterious ways.*

*Very, very, very mysterious ways . . .*

*P.S. We'll probably never fully understand the Kardashian thing, but we'll deal with that another time. Let's deal with Marcus and Stormy-Rain first, they're far more interesting . . .*

# CHAPTER ONE

# IF HUMANS WERE MEANT TO FLY

Stormy

"*L*illy, that's totally tubular!" Stormy-Rain was probably the only person outside of the 1970s that still used the word "tubular." And when she wasn't using words that hadn't been uttered in decades, she was making them up. A couple of months ago she'd tried to get the word "Funkyliciously" circulating. For some reason, it hadn't caught on.

"Yayness, I'm so happy for you guys," Stormy said excitedly. "So, when's the big day?"

But as the words were out of her mouth, the phone's speaker delivered a loud, angry hiss. This was an all-too-familiar sound that always forced her to run to the other end of her room while waving her phone in the air. But when the hissy crackle continued to drown out their conversation, she resorted to sticking her head out the window of her tiny third-floor apartment.

Her cell phone reception was dodgy at the best of times, which possibly had something to do with the fact that her phone was a prehistoric relic from the nineties, complete with jam-jar size buttons and an aerial that could easily take out someone's eye—as everyone was always so fond of pointing out. Not that she gave three continental hoots. Besides, she just didn't understand everyone's obsession with having the world at their fingertips 24/7, and on a phone of all things! Phones were for phoning. Not for Googling and FaceSnapping and You-Tweetering—such technological things were simply beyond her comprehension.

"The wedding will be on the twentieth of September," Lilly was shouting over the ever-increasing crackle. Stormy climbed out of the window and balanced dangerously on the rather rusty fire escape.

"Wait! What's Damien's star sign again?" Stormy shouted over the growing hiss, and a street vendor looked up at her curiously. She waved at him happily, careful not to lose her grip on the railing in the process.

"Leo!" Lilly screamed back at the top of her lungs.

"Okay, hold on, I need to check something quickly. Call me back in exactly five, I'm running out of airtime. Peace out." Stormy hung up, jumped back inside and raced across the room, almost tripping over her pet tortoise Elvis as she went.

Once at her bookshelf, she pulled out her large, well-thumbed astrology book and reached for her reading glasses. They were the only reading glasses she'd ever owned, and well over ten years old—the cracked lens and wonky arm that had been sellotaped back together attested to that. But her philosophy was simple: why throw something away when it could still be used? Besides, she couldn't afford new ones.

She flipped the book open with a flourish and ran her neon-purple nail down the wordy index column. "Leo, Leo, Leo, where are you . . . ? *AH-HA*, page twenty-two," she said triumphantly.

Stormy scanned the words on the page, "Uhm-ing" and "Ah-ing" as she went. She pulled out a pink pencil, which had been sharpened to within an inch of its life, and began scribbling some numbers and notes down on the back of an old envelope she'd fished out of her dustbin.

The phone rang again just as she'd happily finished her important calculations.

"Hey, Lil, it's okay, you can have the wedding on the twentieth, the numbers say it's a good day," she reported seriously. Astrology and numerology were no laughing matters.

"Well, that's a relief, I'll let Damien know," Lilly said with a slight smile in her voice.

The hiss and crackle were finally gone, so Stormy flopped down onto her pink beanbag. A few tiny polystyrene bits burst through the torn corner that she'd been meaning to staple closed. "So, where's it going to be . . . *no wait*, don't tell me, let me guess. Some fancy-pancy place like the Winelands, or the Midlands maybe? Or maybe a beach in the Cape? That would be beautiful, but you'd have to watch out for the wild penguins . . . *Hey*, I wonder if you could train one to bring the ring up the aisle?" she asked thoughtfully.

But Lilly didn't answer Stormy's question. Instead, there was a long, loaded pause on the other end of the phone, and Stormy's psychic senses started buzzing.

"Okay," Lilly started slowly, "please don't hate me, but . . ." Her words were tentative and cautious, but their effect was immediate.

"No!" Stormy exclaimed, grabbing her chest as if she was in physical pain. "It's not . . . ? You wouldn't . . . ?"

"I'm so sorry, Stormy. But it is," Lilly admitted.

Stormy took a long, deep breath, trying to quell her sudden agitation. *Out with anxiety, in with love, light and fairy dust*, she chanted in her head, but she was failing dismally as her heart involuntarily started beating at double time.

"Where?" she finally asked.

"Prague—it's really beautiful—and you'll love it there," Lilly said.

"But, Lilly, you know I can't fly," she wailed, repeating her internal mantra again, *Out with anxiety . . . in with, with . . .* But it wasn't helping in the slightest.

"Please, Stormy, I need you there, it wouldn't be the same without you," Lilly pleaded. "Besides, who's going to help with our mother when she gets drunk and falls off a table, or worse—gets up to make one of her famously inappropriate speeches?"

Stormy and Lilly had technically only been stepsiblings for a few months, back when they were teenagers, during a rather short-lived and tumultuous marriage between their dysfunctional, dramatically inclined, drug-addicted parents that had ended in an impromptu bonfire and a near police riot. Still, Stormy thought of Lilly's mother Ida as her own, since she was the only one she'd ever known. Stormy's real mother had abandoned her just hours after giving birth to run off with a hippie cult called Children of the Moonbeam. True story!

Stormy snapped back to reality as Lilly issued another loud and rather long plea. "*Pleeeaaaassseee?*"

"But, but, but . . ." Stormy was in the grip of full-blown panic and twirled her hair around her finger frantically, something she'd done since childhood whenever she felt anxious—which had been very often. She winced a little as the tip of her hair-entwined finger started going slightly blue and tingly.

"It's been proven that it's more dangerous to drive than to fly," Lilly offered in a calm, soothing tone.

Stormy stopped twirling and smacked her hand down on the beanbag, causing another puff of white stuff to fly out of the corner. "And I suppose you read that on Google?" she asked sarcastically, adding a breathy scoff to the end for added emphasis.

"Yes," Lilly admitted tentatively and with a twinge of expectancy in her voice.

Stormy rolled her eyes dramatically, even though there was no one there to appreciate the theatrical gesture, and let out her famous *do-I-really-have-to-explain-this-to-you-again* sigh. "Lilly, when are you going to realize that the world government is controlling us with fake information on the World Wide Web? I mean, next you'll be telling me that you think they really landed on the moon!"

"Didn't they?"

"Of course not," Stormy said. She had it on good authority that the photos of the lunar landing had been faked. It was all in the shadows, or lack thereof!

"Please . . ." Lilly was really begging now. "With a hundred cherries on top and stuff like that. And besides, they've already all been bought and paid for."

Stormy swallowed hard. She could almost taste the bitter panic as it rose up from the pit of her stomach and into her mouth. Planes were not safe! If humans were meant to fly, they would have been given wings, not arms. Planes were dangerous things.

"But . . . but . . ." Stormy stuttered, the words getting caught in her tight, panic-strangled throat.

"Stormy, there's nothing to worry about, I promise. Plus, Damien's cousin Marcus will be on the same flight, so you wouldn't be totally alone."

"Like that's supposed to be comforting. It's not like I know the man from a bar of Adam . . ." Without even trying, Stormy also had this uncanny ability to confuse every idiom that had ever been created. But she'd never cared much for rules anyway.

Stormy ran the options through her mind a few times. Maybe it wouldn't be as bad if there was someone else on the flight with her. At least she would have someone to talk to. "What's Marcus's star sign? If you find that out, at least I'll be more prepared to meet him."

"So you're coming?" Lilly squealed excitedly.

"I can't miss your wedding."

"And what about a plus one—do we need to get you another ticket, or has that last guy reached the three-week mark?"

"The street magician? No, *noooo*, he passed the three-week mark two weeks ago."

Stormy had a very strict relationship policy: she dated men for exactly three weeks and then broke it off. To date, no one had ever made it past the three-week cut-off. But oh, how she loved those three weeks! Those blissful days spent wrapped up in the delicious honeymoon phase, delightfully ignorant of each other's foibles and flaws. By ending it then, she was ensured of happy relationship memories that never ended in pain, suffering, animosity and—in her father's case—the odd death threat. She knew all too well that long-term relationships just didn't work—her four bitter ex-stepmoms could attest to that.

"I'm so excited, Storm! It's all going to be perfect with you there! I've got to go now, I have wedding invitations to attend to."

"Okay. Kiss kiss, love and light, Lilly." She hung up the phone and then sat there for a moment. A feeling was starting to niggle deep inside her. *A bad feeling about flying.* A feeling that sent a shiver down her spine and all the way into her toes.

At least she wouldn't be flying alone. That was her only consolation.

# CHAPTER TWO

## SOME STRANGE NEBULOUS FEELING

~

Three months later
Marcus

*T*he last thing Marcus wanted to do was babysit an anxious woman on a plane—but he'd made a promise to Damien, and he was a man who always kept his promises.

Who the hell was afraid of flying in this day and age anyway? And while he was contemplating the whole *who the hell* thing, who the hell was named Stormy-Rain? His mind boggled at the possibilities.

He wasn't looking forward to this flight, at all, and he didn't even know what she looked like. When he'd asked Damien how he'd recognize her, Damien had gotten a strange tone in his voice and said, "You'll just know."

*What the hell was that supposed to mean?*

Marcus made himself as comfortable as possible on the hard metal benches that snaked around the boarding gate. The flight was due to board in forty-five minutes so he opened the *Business Day* and flipped to the stock reports. Playing the stock markets was a little hobby of his, one that had made him quite a bit of pocket money over the years. Not that he needed it—his recent promotion to partner at his law firm had come with a few extra zeros on his pay check, along with some other enviable benefits.

Marcus scanned the paper and was just about to pat himself on the back for yet another shrewd investment when his phone buzzed. He pulled it out of his pocket and a wave of discomfort washed over him when he saw the message.

It was from his ex, Emma. She was supposed to have been his date to the wedding but they'd broken up several weeks ago. The break-up had completely blindsided her, or so she'd claimed. But after two months together, Marcus had realized that she just wasn't right—and by that, he meant that she simply wasn't wife and mother material. She had not met enough of the requirements of Marcus's carefully thought-out list. Over the years, Marcus had put together a very thorough Excel spreadsheet that accurately scored all his partners on eligibility. Something his friends and cousin Damien thought was completely odd. Damien was always going on about how you couldn't apply rules and logic to love. He was always talking about "that feeling" you get when you meet the right person. But when Marcus had asked Damien to explain and qualify this so-called feeling further, he couldn't.

Well, Marcus wasn't going to rely on some strange, nebulous feeling. He would rely on facts and his checklist. Because Marcus was looking for someone very specific. Someone stable, dependable and mature. And most importantly, someone he could settle down with. He was thirty now, after all, and successful enough to provide a good home for his future family—a family he wanted more than anything, perhaps more than he would ever admit out loud. Since he'd barely had one growing up.

Unfortunately, Mrs. Right was proving to be rather elusive thus far. And when he'd explained all this to Emma in a very calm, meticulous manner, she'd called him a cold-hearted bastard. He didn't see it like that, though. He was simply relaying the facts to her, it was nothing personal. Besides, they'd only been together for a month. He briefly glanced at her message.

*Please give Damien and Lilly my best on their wedding day. I would do it myself . . . only I'm no longer invited.*

He shook his head, put his phone away without responding and turned back to the paper. But just as he'd started a highly informative article about the pros and cons of investing in Bitcoin, his focus was once again shattered, this time by a rather loud ruckus on the other side of the departures area.

"Excuse me." A high-pitched sing-song voice seemed to cut through the chatter of the room.

"Sorry, zipping through," it said again.

"Thanky-thanks!"

"Scuse moi!"

Feeling irritated at the disturbance, he looked up—and that's when he smacked eyes on her.

She was small, thin and rather waiflike, but despite all this, the noise emanating from her was monumental. She was also wearing a hideous dress that looked like it had been purchased at a charity store from an aged hippie. It was a cream-colored creation, splashed with a loud, canary-yellow sunflower print. He ran his eyes down the length of the dress until he found his gaze transfixed by the ugliest pair of shoes he'd seen in a while—old, worn brown sandals that seemed too big for the dainty feet they were strapped onto. And to top the whole atrocious ensemble off: a massive pink scarf that almost hung to the floor with bright-yellow pom-poms dangling from it. He cringed.

"Just squeezing through. Cheers, cheers!" The voice was getting louder and coming closer.

But it wasn't only the loud jet of words flying out of her mouth that was responsible for the public disturbance—it was also her bangles. Chunky wooden things and purple plastic junk with pink feathers and large shells dangled from her slender arms and clanked together as she minced. Because she didn't simply walk—*oh no*—she sort of flapped about as if she had no control over her limbs. Her arms and legs seemed to veer off in random directions, knocking the odd person as she went. His eyes moved up for the first time and his gaze settled on her face.

*Her hair!*

It looked like a rainbow had exploded on her. Pink, purple, blue and orange radiated from her scalp. The colorful strands were braided together into a plait that hung over her shoulder and was fastened at the end by a giant purple flower. He'd never seen anyone with rainbow-colored hair before; in fact, he'd never seen anyone so utterly bizarre-looking. And then it dawned on him . . .

*This must be Stormy-Rain.*

# CHAPTER THREE

## Whatever Floats Your Duck

⌒

Marcus

*M*arcus heaved a resigned sigh as he got up, straightened the cuffs of his crisp polo shirt, and walked over to her.

"Stormy-Rain?" He couldn't believe he was actually calling anyone by that name, let alone saying it out loud for the whole damn world to hear.

"Marcus!" she exclaimed brightly, as though she were genuinely happy to see him. *They'd never even met.* "It's just Stormy, or Rainy, or Rain, or even Rainbow—that's what people usually call me. But if you want to call me Stormy-Rain, that's also okay. Whatever floats your duck."

"Boat," Marcus corrected her instinctively without even thinking.

"Where?" Stormy asked, swiveling her head around as though she were really looking for a boat.

*What the hell?*

Marcus blinked several times as he tried to make sense of what had just happened. In the few short moments since he'd clapped eyes on her, he'd already taken measure of her personality. And she was utterly ridiculous. She obviously had verbal diarrhea. Add that to her overly saccharine disposition, and an obvious tendency towards confusion—she was just way, *way* too much.

"Um . . . where do you get Rainbow from?" he asked, wanting to change the subject away from boats but already grappling to find some common conversational ground between them.

"They come after the stormy rain!" She swooshed her arms around and swayed from side to side. She was so cheerful it unsettled him.

"Huh?" He felt his brow furrow as he tried to figure out what she was talking about.

"Rainbows. They come out after the rain . . ." She stuck out her wrist to show Marcus a garishly colored rainbow tattoo. "I've always loved them."

Marcus looked her up and down. "Mmm, I can see that," he muttered.

"And you're Marcus. Aries." Without warning, she grabbed his hand and started shaking it violently. Her bangles knocked about again, making a noise that he imagined must be reminiscent of some kind of tribal drumming circle. Perhaps that was the intention.

Marcus pulled his hand away as the overly enthusiastic handshake threatened to turn into a full-blown fist-pumping session. "Not Aries. My surname is Lewis."

"No, no." She burst out laughing as if he'd just made the world's funniest joke. "Your star sign is Aries. I did some research on you, just to check out our compatibility vibey-vibes."

*Vibey-vibes?* Saccharine, verbose, confused, overenergized and nonsensical. His mind continued to boggle.

"And what did you discover?" he asked, playing along out of sheer curiosity.

"Well, we're very, very, *very* sexually compatible," she reported seriously. She seemed to emphasize the word "very" rather a lot. He wasn't sure he liked it. "We're both fire signs—I'm a Sag. But we wouldn't be good in a relationship. Too fiery. Too stubborn, too many arguments and differences of opinion. But we could become friends," she concluded with yet another overly eager smile.

Despite himself, Marcus had to admit that he agreed with some of what she'd said. He could never be in a relationship with her, that was obvious. He was also stubborn, he knew that. Argumentative—yes. Fiery—most definitely. They were qualities that made him a great lawyer.

But there was one thing he vehemently disagreed with: there was no way, no way, *no way* (he was placing much emphasis on the "no way" here), they were sexually compatible. She wasn't his type, *at all*. He usually liked women whose hair didn't remind him of a toddler's colorful finger painting. He wouldn't sleep with her if she was the last woman on the planet, and he suspected the feeling was mutual. He probably wasn't her type either—he clearly didn't have dreadlocks, wear tie-dye clothes and play the didgeridoo, or whatever else her ilk was up to these days.

But the flight that day was eighteen hours long. Seven and a half to Doha, with a seven-hour stopover, and then another six to Prague. So despite their glaring differences, he would have to make nice.

"Here, why don't you sit down?" Marcus asked as he moved his briefcase off the chair next to him. Stormy smiled and tossed her bags down on the floor with a loud thud as she flopped down next to him. He glanced down at her carelessly discarded luggage, and once the literal dust had settled, he tried not to recoil in horror.

Exhibit A was a strange-looking embroidered handbag that had been decorated with pins and badges and looked like it had then been dragged through a swamp, and Exhibit B was none other than an old brown guitar box covered in tattered stickers and black-marker scribbles. He quickly shifted his foot and nudged his pristine leather briefcase a little further away from her bags. Sudden thoughts of sterilizing her belongings popped into his head. But since he couldn't do that, he pulled his soapless disinfectant out and gave his hands a quick, refreshing wipe. The gesture clearly didn't go unnoticed by Stormy, who looked at his hands and then gave a strange scowl he wasn't sure how to interpret. It wasn't that he was a germaphobe, he just liked things to be clean and neat.

Marcus sat back down in his seat and then turned back to his newspaper . . . Where was he before being so abruptly interrupted? Oh, yes, the benefits of investing in Bitcoin . . .

He was just starting to regain his focus when he felt a sharp blow to his ribs.

"*Ouch!*" he winced out loud.

"Sorry." Stormy smiled apologetically as Marcus turned to see her trying to cross her legs on the narrow chairs.

"What are you doing?"

"I'm just going to do some meditation before taking off." He watched in fascination as she fluttered her eyes closed, made some strange humming sound and then let her hands come to rest in a kind of praying position. She was like an alien creature. She might as well have come from another planet. It was a miracle they even spoke the same language, breathed the same kind of air.

Deciding to ignore her, he turned back to his paper. But her deliberate, wheezy breathing was driving him mad, and his years of training as a lawyer meant he couldn't keep quiet when he had an objection. "Do you mind?" he finally said.

Stormy turned to look at him. "Mind what?"

"Your breathing is very loud. I'm trying to read the paper."

Stormy smiled broadly. There was absolutely no sign of fear or offence on her face, which was the type of reaction he was used to eliciting when using that specific tone. "Someone's a grumpy grump," she replied in a lively tone, and then, much to his absolute horror, poked his shoulder.

If there was one thing he hated, it was unnecessary touching. Especially from strangers. But it only got worse, as the poke turned into a squeeze, which then turned into a rub. "Mmmm, I see," she said, nodding her head knowingly while kneading his neck.

Marcus pulled away quickly. "See what?"

"You carry a lot of tension in your shoulders. In fact, some deep-breathing exercises would really help to unblock your throat chakra—I think that's probably the cause of it."

"My shoulders and chakras are fine, thanks." Shifting as far away from her as the narrow seat would allow, he flipped the paper open again and held it close to his face, trying to create a barrier between them.

But clearly Stormy wasn't taking the hint and she peered over the top of his paper. "Fine, suit yourself, but it's going to start giving you back pain and headaches. Don't say I didn't warn you."

"I'm sure I can handle it," he hissed at her as she smiled and disappeared back behind his paper.

## Stormy

Even though she'd only just met him five minutes ago, there was no doubt in her mind that Marcus was one of the most blocked people Stormy had ever encountered! And she wasn't just referring to his throat chakra and severely knotted shoulders. It was the weekend and he was wearing a terribly claustrophobic-looking long-sleeved shirty thing with big buttons and tight cuffs, *and what did you even call that color*? It wasn't quite white, it wasn't brown, it wasn't grey . . . *beige*? She cringed. He had a starched-looking black jacket over that, as well as equally stiff-looking pants on. He looked like he was going to a funeral, not a destination wedding. And what was all that disinfecting about anyway?

But right now, she had bigger concerns than his throat chakra and those ridiculously shiny lace-up shoes that were so highly polished you could see your reflection in them. She glanced up at the board above their gate: ten minutes until they started boarding, and she was starting to freak out. She could feel the anxiety bubbling up inside her. She'd drunk an entire pot of chamomile tea before leaving for the airport, and when that hadn't helped, she'd practically inhaled the contents of the bloody teabag. But she was still terrified. Because on top of her usual fear of flying, there was something else too. A feeling she hadn't been able to shake for months.

Something bad.

Something terrible.

Something truly frightening.

She'd run all the numbers. She'd checked the cards, three times, and even called on her spiritual guide, and they all said the same thing.

*Today was not a good day to travel*. At all.

The signs were all there, and they were flashing. Her horoscope had explicitly stated that today was *not a good day for any kind of travel*. There was going to be some kind of *big incident*, the cards had said, and a string of *fateful events*, the numbers had confirmed. But she'd promised Lilly that she would be at the wedding. So, there was nothing she could do other than arm herself with some sage and amber stones for protection, and hope for the best. And by the best, she meant that they didn't plummet to their grizzly and possibly very fiery deaths.

She'd been practicing her deep-breathing relaxation and it had been working. That is, until a few minutes ago, when Mr. Grumpy-Tight-Shirt had interrupted her. Now she felt even worse. She'd only flown once in her entire life, and it had been a total disaster. Granted, she'd taken some kind of hallucinogens prior to the flight, and that's probably why the roof had looked like it was melting and the floor had grown tentacles. It wasn't her fault, though, she'd been at a forest trance party communing with nature and the man who'd offered her that delicious-looking cookie had seemed so nice—and she was starved.

"Flight E579 to Doha is now boarding at gate twelve." A tinny announcement broke her train of thought. The voice sent chills down her spine.

"Come." Marcus was already on his feet, picking up his bags and heading for the gate.

Stormy froze as the fear and panic seized every muscle in her body and turned all her joints to slabs of cold concrete. She couldn't do this. Every single one of her six senses knew that this was a bad idea. She could taste it. Hear it buzzing in the air around her, and even smell it.

Something bad was about to happen. And there was no way she was going to be able to get onto that plane today.

# CHAPTER FOUR

## BOUNCING BABY PANDA BEARS

～

Marcus

*M*arcus only noticed that Stormy wasn't behind him as he was handing his ticket over. He turned to discover (to his irritation) that she hadn't moved. Not an inch. She looked like a mime artist who'd frozen mid-position. Marcus huffed as he put his ticket back in his pocket and broke away from the queue. The flight hadn't even begun and she was already acting like this!

He shook his head, trying to dislodge at least some of his building irritation, and moved towards her. But as he got closer, he saw nothing but sheer terror flashing in her eyes. For the first time since meeting Stormy, he allowed himself to make eye contact with her, and he was both startled and very unsettled. She had the greenest eyes he'd ever seen—not a light, insipid green, but a rich, dark emerald green that was intensified by her pale, porcelain skin. And right now, those green eyes were wide and glassy with terror.

"Are you coming?" he asked, pointing at the boarding gate behind him, trying not to sound as angry as he was quickly becoming. He liked things to happen timeously. He liked things to go smoothly and perfectly, and having Stormy freeze up like this wasn't part of the plan. "Well, are you?" he asked again when she didn't respond immediately.

Stormy blinked several times and were those . . . ? *Yes*, tears had welled up in her eyes. Was she seriously *crying*? Over a *flight*? This was ridiculous. Stormy was clearly way too sensitive. Just another thing to add to the list of her annoying attributes. *Saccharine, verbose, nonsensical and overly sensitive. (And possibly a mime artist.)*

"Stormy-Rain . . . um, Stormy, Rainbow . . . STORMY . . ." *Shit, this was confusing.* "There's nothing to worry about, flying is safer than driving."

But as those words left his mouth, almost as if on cue tears started streaming down her face. Marcus was not used to, nor did he like, displays of emotion like this, especially in public, and he automatically looked around to see if anyone was looking. *What would people think?*

"If we were meant to fly, we would have been given wings," Stormy said in between slightly breathy whimpers.

"What?" Marcus was shocked. This was the worst logic he'd ever heard. "If we were meant to travel across the sea, we would have been given gills or would be able to breathe under water—" he started to counter her argument, only he wasn't expecting what came next.

"We can breathe underwater. In utero," she returned.

Marcus stared at Stormy, trying to figure out how on earth

she'd arrived at that rebuttal. But there was no time to try and figure out how her brain worked—and anyway, even if he had the luxury of an entire decade, he would probably never figure *that* out. It was clear that she operated on another page—*no*, perhaps an entirely different *book*. The gates were closing in five minutes and if he did not get her on the flight, Damien and Lilly would be very disappointed. Not to mention he would have failed at the task he'd been given. And Marcus *never* failed.

"Okay," he whispered softly, hoping that his best attempt at a calm voice would reassure her. He walked all the way up to her in a slow and steady manner, so as not to startle her any more than she already was. "What can I do to help you?"

Stormy immediately extended her hand to him. "Hold my hand, please."

"You want me to . . . *what*?" Marcus couldn't believe that this total stranger was asking him to hold her hand. But before he could object, she reached out, grabbed his hand in hers and intertwined their fingers.

Marcus shuddered and had to force himself not to let go. Her hand was tiny and her wrists were like small twigs. He ran his eyes up her arm and they settled on her neck and chest area; her collarbones protruded through her pale skin and looked so delicate that they could be snapped in a strong breeze. She was just so *petite*, there was no other way to describe her.

Suddenly, Marcus remembered a baby bird he'd rescued as a child. It had fallen out of its nest. He'd picked it up so gently and had cradled it in his hands as if it were the most breakable thing in the world. He'd run home and lined a shoebox with soft towels and laid the helpless creature down. He'd tried to feed it, but it had refused. He'd sat up with it all night hoping it would survive. And when it didn't, he'd been crushed. He hadn't thought about that bird in years.

Marcus gave Stormy a little tug and started walking back towards the boarding gate, but midway, she stopped him.

"Wait!" Stormy bucked against his hand. "I need my bag and guitar," she said in an almost-whisper.

Marcus glanced over at her haphazardly discarded things on the floor. The last thing he wanted to do was carry them, but if it was going to help get her onto the plane, then he was prepared to brave whatever bacterium they were probably carrying. He picked up her bag and slung it over his shoulder and put the guitar under his arm, highly aware that it would probably leave a massive dust smudge on his perfect, recently dry-cleaned suit.

"Okay, let's go." He extended his hand for her to take this time, and she did. They resumed their walk to the boarding gates when she bucked against his hand once more.

"I can't do this." She sounded almost hysterical.

"Well, you have to!" Marcus said, deciding to go for a more direct approach with her. "You don't have a choice, unless you want to miss your stepsister's wedding?"

"No, I don't." She shook her head and then suddenly, without warning, slipped an arm around his waist and squeezed. This time he did flinch. His entire body tensed, especially when she wrapped her other arm around him and pulled him into a bear hug. He opened his mouth to protest, but she cut him off.

"Thanks," she said, looking up at him from the crook of his arm and smiling gratefully.

"I . . . I . . . Sure," he stuttered, which was very unlike him.

## Stormy

Stormy felt strangely safe with her arms wrapped around this pecu-
liar Marcus person. He was big, and her arms were barely able to
reach around him completely. He was clearly a large, macho, muscly
man. She'd never had her arms wrapped around such an exotic
creature before; his type was totally foreign to her. She tightened her
grip as they got closer to the gate and felt him flinch in reaction.

*Blocked, grumpy and uncomfortable with touching.* His list of
not-so-nice attributes was growing rapidly, she thought with
slight amusement.

Stormy could feel them getting closer to the gate and she was left
with no choice but to close her eyes tightly and go to her happy place.
It was an imaginary realm she'd created as a child that had let her
escape from the harsh realities around her: rainbows and fresh
spring rains, bouncing baby panda bears rolling down green hills. A
place where Bambi's mother had lived and fairy tales *did* come true.

She kept her eyes tightly squeezed shut and let Marcus lead her
up to the boarding gate, down what felt like a very long passage,
and finally onto the plane. She only knew they'd arrived when
Marcus finally came to a complete stop. She opened her eyes
slowly, removed her arms from Marcus and found herself standing next to her seat.

They were unlike any seats she'd ever seen before, they looked
like something out of a science-fiction film. She could only
imagine what tickets like this cost. Luckily, she hadn't paid for
them, otherwise she might have been broke for the rest of this life,
and all her other lives that were still to come.

This was not an environment she was accustomed to, let alone agreed with. Millions of people in the world were starving, and the price of one of these seats could probably feed an entire village for a year. This was capitalism at its worst; she didn't like to be around injustices like this at all.

She stood there for a moment, unsure of what to do with herself. She glanced behind her, the door to the plane was being shut and her window for escaping was quickly closing . . . *no, closed*. Officially. She watched the air hostess turn the handle on the door and heard it lock with a loud and frightening click. The click reverberated through her entire body, making the hairs on the back of her neck prickle, as if a ghost had just walked past her. Perhaps this was some kind of premonition—meeting her future ghost self when this plane inevitably fell out of the sky and crashed.

She looked over at Marcus and watched with curiosity as he seemed to be packing and unpacking the overhead storage compartment vigorously. He was lining up their luggage in a pedantic manner, making sure they were all dead straight in the compartment before closing it. When he'd finished he turned and looked at her.

"And? Are you going to sit down?" he asked.

"Uh . . . okay . . . I guess." She lowered herself into the seat and tried to fight back the tears that were welling up in her eyes again.

# CHAPTER FIVE

## BLOCKED CHAKRA ALERT!

～

Marcus

*"The emergency exits are being pointed out to you now, and in the case of an emergency, floor lights will illuminate your way to the nearest exit."*

The air hostess was giving the usual demonstration, but Marcus had seen it so many times before that he was already reading his newspaper. Once again, though, he was interrupted. This time she hadn't held back and had stuck her entire head over the top of his newspaper and stared at him.

"What if the lights don't come on and we can't find our way to the exit, then what?" she whispered fearfully.

"It's a plane, a cylinder," Marcus answered dryly. "There are only two possible directions—that way," he pointed up the aisle, "and that way," he pointed down. "Trust me, you won't get lost on the way to the emergency exit, it's impossible."

Stormy nodded and looked satisfied with his answer, so he raised his paper again, only to see a small white hand reappear moments later.

"But what if the emergency doors get jammed, because we crash into snow, like those people did on the Andes? Lilly told me about this program she watched and they had to eat each other to stay alive. Raw." Stormy shuddered dramatically.

Marcus found himself blinking rapidly again—it seemed to be the involuntary reaction he had to her outlandish statements, a combination of shock and confusion as he found himself at a loss for words. He was *never* lost for words.

"Um . . ." He was still searching for the words. "Um . . . well, I . . . I'm sure we won't have to eat each other," he offered lamely.

"Goddess, I hope not. I'm a strict vegan."

"I'm sure you are." Marcus was unable to hide the bemusement in his tone. Of course she was a vegan. It made perfect sense. And he was very sure that soon she would be telling him all about her vegan ways.

"What's that?" Stormy jumped as the plane started moving, once again snatching Marcus's hand without his permission. This handholding thing of hers was becoming a bit of a bad habit. And like all bad habits, it needed to be broken. If not, this was going to be the most torturous few hours of his life.

"It's just the plane moving," he replied impatiently, trying to free his hand from her surprisingly strong grip. But as soon as he tried to pull away, her fingers tightened like a vice around his.

"Does it have to go so *fast*?" Stormy sounded frantic now.

"Yes, it needs to gain enough momentum to lift itself into the air. Have you ever flown before?" Marcus asked.

Stormy nodded, and with her free hand started twirling some hair around her finger. "But I don't really remember all the specifics. I was accidentally on drugs."

"What?" Marcus stared at her, shocked. "You don't have any illicit substances on you now, do you?" he whispered urgently, looking around to make sure none of the crew or passengers had overheard. "Because it's illegal. You could be arrested for that, you know."

Stormy swung around and looked at him with genuine surprise. "Absolutely not. I don't do drugs."

"But you just said—"

"That was the first and only time, and it was the worst experience of my life, thank you very much, so you can stop being so judgey."

But Marcus was skeptical and it clearly showed on his face.

"You don't believe me?" Stormy said, sounding genuinely angry.

"To be perfectly honest . . . no," he responded matter-of-factly, and he could immediately see this pissed her off even more.

"Why not?" She sounded indignant.

"Well, no offence, but look at you."

"What?" Stormy glared at Marcus, widening those already huge green eyes at him. They were so piercing that they gave him a little chill.

"Grumpy-grump and judgmental," she hissed over the loud rattle of the engines.

"Well, you have to admit it, you're not exactly . . ." He paused, looking for the right words. He didn't want to offend or upset her. He wasn't a *total* bastard. "Well, you don't exactly embody normality, Stormy," he finished more gently.

"Well you know what they say about *normality*," Stormy scoffed.

"No . . . ?"

"It killed the cat." She let Marcus's hand go and pointedly faced the front, turning away from him.

"That was curiosity," Marcus corrected.

Stormy nodded. "That too, Marcus. That too."

## Stormy

Stormy wasn't sure she liked Marcus. Which was unusual for her—she liked everybody. Even the grumpy bank manager who kept sending her rude letters. Although she did appreciate the way he decorated them with the big red pretty stamps.

Marcus was judging her and that wasn't very nice. And she certainly didn't need to be in his negative energy field as this giant metal capsule was about to unnaturally catapult itself into the air.

And the plane seemed to be gaining an awful lot of speed. She looked out the window and the lights were going by in streaks. So *not* natural. She reached into her bag and pulled out a piece of amber and a handful of sage that she'd brought from home. She placed them carefully on the armrest next to her and couldn't help but notice that Marcus shot her a sideways look as she did. She knew what he was thinking: it was written across his face. It amazed her that two people from the same family could be so different. His cousin Damien was a free thinker, a true free spirit, and this guy was a closeminded, grumpy douche box.

"Aaaahh . . ." Stormy let out a series of nervous squeaks as the plane started lifting. She shut her eyes tightly and clutched onto her chunk of amber for dear life as she felt her stomach and possibly all her internal organs falling to her feet.

The tilt of the plane was getting more dramatic as it lifted higher and higher into the sky. Stormy willed herself to think happy thoughts again: rainbows, daisies, cuddly puppies and colorful butterflies . . . *tumbling out of the sky and plummeting to their painful deaths!* Her happy place was no longer happy, and the angry roar of the engines was getting even louder as the plane climbed steadily.

They were going to crash. She was sure of it. And if she died next to Marcus—the bearer of bad energy—Goddess only knows what she would reincarnate as.

*Ding-ding.* A noise rang out over the slightly quieter engines and the plane seemed to level out slightly.

*"Please note that the seat belt signs have been turned off."* The voice over the intercom sounded very calm, which helped to relieve some of Stormy's concerns, and she heaved a sigh of relief.

"Do you mind, now?" Marcus suddenly asked loudly as she felt someone pulling at her fingers. She finally opened her eyes and looked down to see that one of her hands was gripping his thigh so tightly that her knuckles had turned white. *How had her hand landed up there?* She'd thought she was holding onto the armrest.

She quickly removed her hand, after giving his thigh a final investigative squeeze—*he was very muscular.* "Sorry. I didn't mean to." She looked up and met Marcus's gaze, but instead of looking irritated with her, there was another expression on his face. She couldn't quite make out what it was, and as she scrutinized him, he dropped his head quickly and cleared his throat. (Blocked chakra alert! He'd be complaining of a headache next, mark her words.)

"Sorry, would you mind moving your bag, please? I want to go to the restroom." His voice was overly polite and stilted, and he was suddenly refusing to make eye contact with her . . . *and who called it a restroom anyway?* It made it sound so formal and fancy, a total euphemism for what it really was.

"Sure." Stormy got up nervously to drag her bag to the side. She felt a little unsteady on her feet, especially when she imagined what lay beneath them—absolutely nothing! The vast, empty nothingness of thin air.

"Thanks," Marcus said politely as he walked off up the aisle. He stopped suddenly and turned back to her. "Can I get you a drink on the way back, Stormy?"

"No, thanks," she said, feeling somewhat confused. Strange muscular man—polite one second and rude to her the next. It was a miracle he actually went to the "restroom," what with that blocked chakra of his!

So why the hell had she felt *that* ?

*What, exactly?* Well, she wasn't quite sure, to be honest. But it had been the slightest ting-tingle as he'd brushed past her. Their shoulders had touched briefly, and yet she'd felt a tiny electric zip and now something inside her was fizzing. Curious!

She sat back down and continued to watch him as he walked up the aisle. She didn't like clean-cut, close-shaven, bright-white-Colgate-smiling, collar-shirted, smarty-pants-wearing, neat-haired guys. He wasn't her type, *at all*—but the tiny fizz inside her belly seemed to be saying something else. It was ever so slight, and if she wasn't a person totally in tune with her body, she might have even missed it.

But she hadn't missed it. And she wondered if Marcus had felt it too.

# CHAPTER SIX

## EATING EACH OTHER IN
## THE ANDES?

⌒

Marcus

*H*e didn't need the toilet. He just needed to get away from her. Everything about her was driving him absolutely mad. Her hair—the color, the length, the way it hung, the way she incessantly twirled it around her finger. Her whimsical hippie clothes, especially that eye-offending scarf, her old filthy handbag, the way she had attempted to turn their seats into a rockery garden. And especially the things she said: eating each other in the Andes? Normality killed the cat?

But more than anything, he hated the effect she'd just had on him when she'd gripped his leg. He'd immediately felt a surge of something run up his thigh and into a place it really shouldn't have gone.

And even though the feeling had been very fleeting, it had been enough to completely unsettle him. Not to mention confuse him, especially since he didn't find her attractive, at all. He'd noticed a burst of bright pink hearts at the base of her neck, for heaven's sake. She reminded him of one of those My Little Pony toys that all the girls had at one stage.

His ex, Emma, was stunning. A real Jessica Rabbit, with long red hair and curves in all the right places. Stormy was her total opposite in looks, and yet when he thought about her right now, his pulse suddenly started to race. He shuffled uncomfortably around the tiny bathroom cubicle for a few minutes and then splashed some water on his face, bringing himself back to reality. Regaining his sense of control. Finally, when he was feeling himself again, he left the pokey bathroom and walked back to his seat.

As he approached it, he was relieved to find that she seemed to have wandered off somewhere. But when he got closer, he saw that she hadn't left the seat, in fact she was only bending down to search in her bag. He gazed down at her and that's when he realized with shock that he could see all the way down the top of her dress—and she was not wearing a bra. *Who doesn't wear bras?* He almost gasped but quickly swallowed it down. He tried to pry his eyes away, but for some really inconvenient reason, couldn't.

And then suddenly Stormy turned and looked directly at him. She met his gaze with those emerald eyes of hers. For a moment she looked at him as if she was wondering what he'd been staring at, and then her eyes widened and she gave him a small, knowing smile followed by a quick casual shrug . . .

Shit! He'd been caught in the act. Staring down her dress.

## Stormy

Stormy never wore bras. She didn't believe in them fundamentally. Bras were designed to repress, and now that she thought about it, had probably been designed by a man. Because no sane woman would ever have thought to wear pokey pieces of wire under their most delicate parts! She also didn't believe in hiding her body. She'd never been a prude when it came to that. She wasn't a flaunter, but she couldn't care less if someone saw her topless on the beach or in a changing room. It was a body. Everyone had one. Made up of muscles and meat and bones. Why be embarrassed or ashamed of your body parts? Besides, a boob was almost exactly like a knee, just with a nipple.

*But Marcus was definitely embarrassed.*

She could see he'd been looking down her dress. She couldn't really blame him—the dress was old and the neckline gaped, but she loved it and had chosen it especially for the flight. It reminded her of a field of bright sunny sunflowers, which was a happy thought she wanted to hold onto during this nerve-wracking journey.

She didn't mind that he'd seen her boobs, though. But it looked like he *did* mind, because he'd gone the most bizarre shade of red that really didn't suit him. It made him look like one of those cartoon characters whose head was about to explode.

"I . . . um, sorry . . ." Marcus mumbled and stuttered, averting his eyes and turning even redder, if that was even possible.

"Oh, it's okay!" Stormy smiled breezily. "It's not like you've never seen a boob before."

"Shhh," Marcus hissed, looking panicked now. His eyes darted around to see if anyone had overhead her. "Do you have to say such inappropriate things in public?"

Stormy giggled at him. She couldn't care less who overheard them. "Does the word *boob* make you uncomfortable, Marcus?"

"Sssshhh. *Please* stop it." Marcus slid sheepishly into his seat and looked around once more. But the other passengers were too absorbed in what they were doing to notice what was going on, so she decided to push him a little further.

"Breast, boob, tits . . ." she teased playfully, almost laughing to see him squirming in his seat before turning to glare at her. She threw her hands up in resignation. "So I guess you wouldn't like it if I said *ass*, either?"

"You are the most inappropriate person I have ever met!" Marcus hissed under his breath.

"And you have the most blocked chakras I've ever seen." She was still amused by Marcus's dramatic reaction.

"Well, it's a good thing I don't believe in chakras, then."

"Well, they believe in you, Marcus," Stormy countered. "They believe in you."

"You know that statement of yours makes no sense?" His tone suddenly had a sharp edge to it and she didn't like it.

"Hey, I'm just teasing you. No need to be a snapper-dragon," she shot back.

"Snap!" The word came out a little too loudly and nastily for her liking. "It's a *snap*dragon," he said.

"Snip snap. Snipper, snapper. Snap, crackle, pop . . . *whatever*," Stormy retorted.

"No, it's not whatever actually," Marcus continued.

"Geez, sorry," Stormy shot back sarcastically. "I didn't know I was traveling with the grammar police." She crossed her arms, starting to feel a little put out by this conversation too.

"I'm not the grammar police. I just like things to be right," he bit back.

"Fine," Stormy said. This conversation was getting ridiculous—even by her standards. Not to mention the fact that she never fought with people, and she didn't like it one little bit. Fighting was a waste of energy. But something about Marcus rubbed her up the wrong way. And he was clearly used to fighting with people—he did it for a living.

They stared angrily at each other for a moment, before breaking away at the same time and then sitting in silence for what felt like forever until a perky air hostess appeared at their side.

"Hello there. Can I offer you chicken or beef?" she asked with a toothy smile.

"Do you have anything vegan?" Stormy asked.

"Um . . . we have a vegetarian option. A lovely vegetable lasagna."

"Mmmm. It has cheese in it, doesn't it?" Stormy tilted her head to the side and was about to launch into her *do-I-have-to-tell-you-about-the-tragedy-of-animal-slavery-and-the-evil-antibiotics-they-add-to-dairy-these-days* speech when the air hostess spoke again.

"Unfortunately, it does." The toothy smile flickered and it was clear that the air hostess was irked. "I could remove the cheese and just pick out the veggies . . . ?" she offered, slightly sourly, but trying her best to hide her obvious irritation.

"That would be fabu-delish. Thanks so much." Stormy heard Marcus sigh next to her and decided to ignore him. Perhaps ignoring him was best.

The air hostess smiled politely and turned to Marcus. "And you, sir? Chicken or beef?"

Marcus leaned over towards Stormy and raised his voice deliberately. "Beef, please. Very rare."

Stormy cringed at the image and once the air hostess had disappeared with a swish of her crisp linen skirt, she turned to Marcus. "Do you know that when an animal is killed, they experience intense fear and produce a surge of adrenalin, which is still in the meat when you eat it? So it's basically like eating negative emotions!"

He blinked rapidly at her. She hated it when he did that, which seemed to be pretty often. But then, he did have nice eyes, she had to admit. She'd only recently noticed them. They were rather big and a deep, rich brown with a splattering of caramel in the center. Stormy liked caramel. But not enough to keep looking at him, so she broke eye contact and looked away.

They sat in silence a little while longer waiting for their food to arrive. At least eating would kill some time and give her something else to do with her mouth—other than fight with him. But as soon as the food arrived and they started eating, Stormy became even more uncomfortable. The way he was slicing into that meat, the way the blood was oozing out onto the plate and the way he was mashing it between his molars—she couldn't hold back any longer.

"That cow probably had a mother and someone that loved it, you know." Stormy pointed her knife at his offensive plate.

"What about that mushroom?" he countered smugly, pointing at her meal with his bloodied fork. "I think I read an article recently about how plants can hear themselves being eaten and get defensive when attacked." His tone was snippy and sarcastic.

"You're making that up," Stormy said.

"No. I'm actually not." Marcus stared straight back at her. His eyes were deadpan and there was no sign of lying on his part. "It's possible that you're the one who's eating negative emotions," he added smugly.

Stormy looked at Marcus for the longest time before speaking again. "I don't think I like you, Marcus, you know that. And I like most people." She held Marcus's gaze while trying to hide her building guilt as she considered what Marcus had just said.

"Well, I'm not exactly mad for you, either, Stormy-Rain." Marcus swallowed his last mouthful, pushed the dish aside and tossed his napkin down all rather dramatically.

"Then I guess we understand each other," Stormy replied huffily.

"I guess we do."

Stormy glared in the opposite direction for a few moments, stewing over Marcus's rudeness, when the plane suddenly started shuddering. "What the hell was *that*?" She jumped in her seat.

"It's just turbulence." She could practically hear him rolling his eyes. She hoped it was painful.

The plane bumped again and her stomach dropped. "Something's wrong, something's wrong," she fretted out loud. And despite her current intense dislike of him, she found herself clutching onto Marcus's thigh again.

"Nothing is wrong, trust me. There is always some turbulence on a flight." He started trying to peel her fingers off him, but she intensified her grip. People always looked at Stormy and completely underestimated her strength. But she had an orange belt in karate, something most people didn't know about her. She was no wallflower, even though she was very fond of flowers.

"Are you sure?" Stormy was still petrified. The words from her horoscope were ringing in her ears, and she was more convinced than ever of her imminent and untimely demise. Death by airplane crash. She hoped it would be into the sea, at least—smashing into the ground would surely not be fun. Not that smashing into the sea was a picnic in the park either, but at least she'd die by drowning and not incineration.

"I fly all the time and have never been on a flight where there isn't some sort of turbulence. And we always land safely. It's fine." Marcus was still trying to pry her fingers off him.

Stormy looked around at the other passengers. No one else looked even vaguely perturbed, and the air hostesses were relaxing as they chatted happily. She took a deep breath and tried to steady her nerves.

"Try to get some rest. We have a long flight ahead." And with that, Marcus extricated himself from her grip, put his chair down into a full reclining position and lay back, pulling the covers over him.

Stormy *did* feel tired. The stress that she'd been experiencing over the last few days leading up to this flight had been exhausting. So she did the same, lowering her seat into its full reclining position and then pulling the soft blanket up around her and soon drifting off to sleep.

## Marcus

Marcus woke with a fright as the plane felt like it dropped a few feet in the air. Everyone around him jumped. A few passengers let out shocked gasps. Marcus was wide awake now. He turned to see that Stormy was looking at him with a frightened expression plastered across her face.

*Ting-ting.*

The sound of the seat belt signs being turned on rang out through the cabin, and everyone around them started scrambling in their seats just as the plane did another gut-wrenching drop. This time, it felt like a lot more than a few feet. Stormy grabbed Marcus by the hand again and looked at him in sheer terror. This time he didn't mind. He felt a responsibility to keep cool, calm and collected, so as not to send her into full-blown hysterics. But truthfully, he was struggling to keep a lid on his own sense of alarm. He had to admit that he'd never felt anything quite like this.

And it only got worse as the plane suddenly felt like it was being tossed around in the air like a ragdoll. The engines roared and made a loud grinding noise as they struggled against what sounded like gale-force winds. People were screaming now, and the overhead storage compartment burst open, tipping some hand luggage out into the aisles.

Stormy grabbed Marcus tightly, eyes now wild with terror. "We're . . . going . . . to . . . die!" The words came out in short, sharp frantic bursts. Marcus was just about to open his mouth and protest when the captain's voice rang out.

"Ladies and gentleman." He sounded calm . . . *or was he just pretending?* "As you've noticed, we are experiencing some rather severe turbulence. A storm that we were tracking has suddenly changed course and is now directly in our flightpath over Kenya. We have just received word to make an emergency landing at the Jomo Kenyatta airport in Nairobi. They have requested that all planes in the area be grounded."

"Shivering Shiva! I knew it! I knew it!" Stormy was practically on top of Marcus now, straining against her seatbelt as she crawled into his lap and squealed hysterically in his ear. The sky outside looked like the interior of a strobing nightclub as the lightning split the air around them, causing the plane to shudder even more. The overhead lights flickered and failed, plunging the cabin into darkness. A rogue catering cart clattered past them down the aisle as the nose of the plane tipped precariously.

*Shit! Holy crap!*

Panic finally gripped Marcus, and a realization hit him: he was going to die. He was going to die in the arms of this strange woman, this Stormy-Rain. How appropriate, in a way, considering they were currently engulfed in a storm.


## Stormy


A terrifying thought hit Stormy: she was going to crash and die in the arms of Marcus. The stars had been right, Goddessdammit. She'd broken into a sweat and the nausea was rising and falling in intense swells as the plane was buffeted through the air.

"Please keep your seat belt buckled and do not leave your seat."

The pilot was shouting to be heard above the roaring engines and pounding wind. "Hold on, this is going to be a bumpy landing, but don't worry—I will get you on the ground safely." Stormy couldn't help wonder if she'd detected a hint of doubt in his voice.

The turbulence got even worse as they began their descent, and the engines sounded like they were about to blow up and fly off the plane at any second. The grinding sounds coming from them grated against Stormy's already shattered nerves. The plane felt like it was bouncing up and down on a trampoline—one minute they were dropping and the next they were rising. The tray tables started to shudder and all Stormy could do to stop herself from screaming was clutch onto her amber and to Marcus for dear life. Her eyes were tightly shut and her head was buried in his chest. She felt him reach up and wrap his arm around her shoulders and pull her closer. Even in her state of wild panic stations, she felt a little reassured by the strength and solidness of his body.

Stormy forced her eyes open and looked up at Marcus. His eyes were wide and glued to the seat in front of him, and his mouth was set in a grim, hard line.

"Marcus," she managed to whisper through the nausea. "I don't really hate you. I'm sorry I said that."

Marcus's eyes met hers and he forced a tight, fleeting smile. "Me too. Sorry I said that, too."

And then, without any kind of warning, *it happened*. The most strange and inexplicable thing to have ever happened to her in all her lives . . .

*They were kissing.*

It was fast and frantic and furious and frenetic. Stormy gasped loudly as Marcus buried his tongue in her mouth with an audible groan. Suddenly, Stormy needed him. She needed him more than anything she'd ever needed in her entire life. The need was so great that it quickly drowned out her pulsing fear. She couldn't get enough of him as she opened her mouth wider and wrapped her hands around the back of his head to pull him even closer.

It was clear Marcus felt the same way and Stormy gasped against his mouth once more as she felt him slip his hand down the front of her dress and squeeze her breast. She squirmed in his lap as he bit down not-so-gently on her lip. Stormy responded, arching forward and pushing her body into him. His mouth left hers and traveled to her ear, and a shiver shot up her spine as he bit down on her earlobe and ran his tongue down the length of her neck.

*This. Was. Crazy.* She knew it, but she didn't care.

She reached under the blanket that was still draped across his hips and ran her hand over the front of his jeans. He was rock hard. And got even harder as her fingers ran the length of him through his pants. Her fingers quickly found his zip and she started tugging at it urgently. They grabbed at each other as the world around them totally disappeared. They were completely unconcerned that they were about to plummet to their deaths and totally oblivious to the fact that they were surrounded by people. They were caught up in their own storm right now.

"We're about to land, please assume the brace position." The pilot's strained voice finally broke through their frantic groping, and they let go of each other as the plane thundered towards the runway. Stormy grabbed Marcus by the hand as the plane finally hit solid ground with a heart-stopping thud and seemed to skid across the wet runway for what seemed like for ever.

Finally, the plane came to a stop. There was a brief moment of deathly silence and then cheers and applause rang out through the cabin. Some passengers burst into tears from the sheer joy of being alive and strangers hugged each other. But Stormy didn't move. She froze. Dead still and silent. Out of the corner of her eye, she observed Marcus fixed in a similar pose, still locked in the brace position with his eyes down.

Slowly, as the minutes ticked by and the passengers around them started to gather up the hand luggage strewn down the aisle, she stuck her head up like an ostrich out of the sand and came face-to-face with Marcus. They stared at each other in absolute shock.

"Um . . ." Marcus finally spoke, his voice sounding shaky and uncertain. "We should probably get our . . . um . . ." It looked like he'd just lost his words, which was confirmed when he pointed to the storage compartments above their heads as if he'd completely forgotten what they were called.

"Bags?" Stormy offered.

"Yes. Bags," Marcus echoed. "We should get them. Our bags." He began to stand up, but as he did Stormy gasped.

"What?" Marcus looked down at her as she sheepishly pointed a finger in the direction of his crotch.

He looked down, his zip was undone.

"Shit!" He sat back down in his seat again, pulled the blanket onto his lap and dressed himself under it. When he was done he shot her a brief look. He was looking at her face at first, and then his eyes drifted down to her chest where they widened in what looked like shock.

"What?" Stormy asked, following his gaze. And that's when she saw it.

"Oops," she said, clutching at her top as she realized that one of her straps had slipped down and her breast was almost on display.

*What the hell had just happened?*

# CHAPTER SEVEN

## THERE'S NO SUCH THING AS VAMPIRES

~

Stormy

*T*he Jomo Kenyatta airport in Nairobi looked like a marketplace. It was packed and buzzing with activity. Dozens of planes had been grounded due to the storm and frightened passengers had been herded into the cramped airport terminal like cattle. Some were still green around the gills and wobbly from their landings, while others were bruised and scraped due to falling luggage, but all of them had one thing in common: *relief.*

Everyone looked relieved to be alive, and despite the chaos of the airport, it was filled with an overwhelmingly positive energy. The happy chatter of people talking, people phoning home to let their loved ones know that they were okay. Honeymooners making out, parents hugging their children and strangers shaking hands. No one cared that they'd been diverted or inconvenienced; they just cared that they were still alive. The atmosphere buzzed and hummed with a happy, joyous energy.

But Stormy felt anything but happy and joyous right now as she glanced over at Marcus. She was confused. *Very.* It was clear Marcus felt the same way; that look of agitation on his face that had caused his brow to furrow seemed like a dead giveaway to her.

Stormy and Marcus stood there in the middle of the cheerful commotion, but neither of them moved, or said a word. Stormy was still desperately trying to process what had happened.

She could almost wrap her head around the idea that her plane had practically nose-dived from the sky, what she was struggling to wrap her head around, though, was what she and Marcus had been doing while the plane had been nose-diving. Her skin still tingled from where his hands and lips and tongue had been. She could still taste him and smell him. She turned to Marcus and was just about to open her mouth to say something, anything that would break this bone-crunchingly awkward silence between them, when Marcus deliberately took several steps away from her and firmly planted himself next to a big concrete pillar.

Stormy took offence at this and walked after him, closing the gap between them by depositing herself right in front of him. She folded her arms and glared at him.

"What?" Marcus asked, not looking directly at her. He was avoiding eye contact as if she was Medusa and looking at her might cause something horrific to happen.

"What are you doing?" Stormy asked.

"Leaning against a pillar, is that okay?" He looked down at his foot and shuffled it across the floor.

"Are you trying to get away from me?" she asked.

"Honestly?" Marcus finally looked up at her. "Yes," he said bluntly.

"Why?"

"I think you know why." Marcus's tone was sarcastic and he met her eyes for the first time since disembarking the plane. Her skin felt like it flushed from head to toe.

"Yes, well, that." She stumbled over her words.

"Yes. *That!*" Marcus reiterated. "That indeed."

"Well, it's not going to happen again, if that's what you're worried about," Stormy said quickly, trying to quell all the flushing rushing over her.

"Oh, I'm not worried about that," Marcus quickly pointed out. "I know it will *never* happen again. *Ever.*" He folded his arms as if he was trying to block her.

"Finally, we agree on something." Stormy took a step closer to him and Marcus seemed to react by stiffening his body and moving closer to the pillar.

"Finally," he echoed, looking back down at his shuffling feet. They fell into another long uncomfortable pause.

"So now what?" Stormy asked, gazing around at the general airport chaos.

"Well," Marcus looked down at his big shiny watch—*why did his watch need to be so big? And so bloody shiny? It was practically luminescent. It could blind people.* "We have a wedding to get to in Prague. We have a pre-wedding family lunch, final fittings, bachelor and bachelorette parties and then the rehearsal dinner followed by the wedding." It was clear Marcus had studied the wedding agenda that Lilly had sent out with the invitations. "We have four days to get to a wedding and we are currently stuck in a country almost on the other side of the world, with a massive storm in progress."

"Goddess! Do you think we'll miss the wedding? We can't!" The thought of missing Damien and Lilly's wedding made Stormy feel sick—she had to be at that wedding, come hell or hot water.

"That might not be in our control," Marcus said looking around. "It doesn't look like any of us are going anywhere fast. That's for sure."

"I swear to Buddha, I knew I shouldn't have flown today, the stars and the numbers predicted this. I *knew* it!" Stormy started wrapping her hair around her finger frantically. She felt like she was going to wig out at any second. She turned to Marcus, hoping for some kind of reassurance, but all he did was roll his eyes at her.

"I don't know how you believe in all that crap." Marcus shook his head. "That stuff is about as real as things like aliens and vampires."

"What!" Stormy gasped. For someone who seemed so worldly, Marcus was woefully ill-informed. "Aliens built the pyramids. Don't be so close-minded."

"And vampires?" he spat sarcastically.

"Oh, don't be silly." Stormy stopped twirling her hair now and faced off with him angrily. "Everyone knows there's no such thing as vampires."

"Really?" Marcus blinked rapidly at her again. "I just don't get you." He looked her up and down again.

"I don't get you, either. One minute you're kissing me and the next you're insulting my belief system," she spat back, feeling riled.

"Hey." Marcus sounded angry. "I could say the same for you. It's 'close-minded' to only believe in one thing and not open your mind up to the possibility that you could be wrong, too!"

Stormy looked at him, trying to size him up, but failing dismally. "So we still don't really like each other even though we . . . *you know*?"

"Look," Marcus said slowly, "it was a stressful situation, we thought we were going to die. Things like that happen under unusual circumstances like that . . . I think."

Stormy considered this for a moment. "That's one explanation. The other, of course, is that the stars were right—we're just fiery-crazy sexually compatible."

"Well, you know what I think about your star signs, so I'll go with the near-death experience theory." Trust Marcus to look for the logical—and *boring*—explanation.

They fell into another silence. It was bizarre. It was as if they couldn't communicate like normal humans. Whenever they tried to have a conversation, they fought.

"I guess we might as well get comfortable, since no one seems to be telling us what's going on," Marcus said, looking around angrily. Every single chair in the airport was full and most of the floor was too. He let out a long sigh as he looked down at the floor. He reached into his briefcase and took out a packet of disinfectant wipes. Stormy watched as he cleaned a little patch to sit on. Now it was her turn to roll her eyes.

Stormy flopped down without a second thought and sat there

cross-legged watching Marcus adjust uncomfortably to the hard surface he was now sitting on.

## Marcus

He needed to move away from her. As far away as possible. His fingertips were tingling, his lips burned, his heart was racing a million miles an hour. He took solace against the cold, hard concrete pillar hoping that it might bring his internal core temperature down somewhat. Or that it would ground him, bring him back down to earth from wherever it was that he was currently existing. Floating around above his body, or something bizarre like that. Because the Marcus he knew, and had known for the past thirty years, didn't do the kind of thing that he'd just done in the plane. And certainly not with someone like Stormy-Bloody-Rain.

But no matter how far away from her he was, he still felt it. That inexplicable mix of sheer irritation, and the desire to touch her again. He sat on the floor—not before disinfecting it, though; he wouldn't go into the germ count to be found on a public floor right now, suffice it to say, it was a lot—and tried to relax. But he also hated not knowing what was going on with the flight, and right now, no one was saying anything. Situations like this did not agree with him, and he started to feel his sense of control slipping rapidly.

*Were they meant to stay here? What about their baggage? Could they leave the airport? What the hell was happening?*

With all these questions driving him completely mad, he was about to get up, find the person in charge of this circus and demand to know what was going on and threaten to sue them if the issue wasn't resolved, when his attention was pulled in the other direction. A guitar note filled the air and he looked up to see where the sound was coming from.

It was Stormy. In the few minutes that she'd been sitting on the floor, she'd managed to strike up conversation with the family next to them and was now strumming the guitar and starting a sing-along in the middle of the bloody airport.

He cringed as he watched her and the others start singing. *What the hell was next?* A camp fire, marshmallows and kumbaya? He shook his head and tried to look away from the ridiculousness, but something inside him couldn't.

She was smiling from ear to ear. Her green eyes were wide and the color seemed intensified by the overhead lights. She was bobbing her head from side to side, her colorful plait rising and falling as she did. Her guitar-playing was absolutely awful, and every time she strummed, her bangles clanked together and let out that goddamn terrible sound that grated against him like fingernails down a blackboard. But she clearly didn't care. In fact, she looked like she was having the time of her life, and before long, more and more people had gathered to join in this public display.

He shuffled on the floor, this was making him so uncomfortable that he wanted to climb out of his skin and crawl away. The crowd was growing, as was the noise and singing and clanking. He pulled out his phone looking for a distraction and decided to send Damien a message, updating them on the situation. He was just about to press send when an even louder noise caught his attention. He froze. Finger hovering over the "Send" button, he looked up.

"Come on!" Stormy was looking at him, smiling.

"Huh?" He looked from her to the others; everyone's eyes were on him, all beckoning him to join in the sing-along. God, this was embarrassing, not to mention totally unnecessary.

"Come on," Stormy said, strumming the guitar expectantly and waiting for Marcus to . . . *what*? Was she serious? As if he would ever consider joining such a ridiculous public display!

"Sing with us," she urged. "It will help pass the time, and it's fun." Her smile grew.

"I think our definitions of fun are somewhat different." He shot up from the floor and straightened his shirt. "I'd rather do something constructive, like see what's going on around here." Marcus turned away from all the expectant faces and walked away.

"Suit yourself," she called after him. "Music therapy is very good for your *you-know-whats* though." He heard a giggle behind him and was glad she hadn't actually said the word "chakra" out loud, otherwise he wasn't sure what the hell he might have done.

God, she was so infuriatingly enthusiastic! She was so ridiculous and over the top and way too fond of public displays and a terrible musician and . . . and . . .

He stopped walking and looked back at her colorful bobbing head.

*And . . . he'd never wanted to reach out and touch anyone more in his entire life.*

# CHAPTER EIGHT

## TWIRLS AROUND ON POLES WEARING NIPPLE TASSELS

~

### Stormy

*S*he knew he wasn't about to join in the singing. In fact, she knew that asking him would probably wind him up the wrong way, but goshness it was fun winding him up. And so damn easy too.

Stormy had settled in and was making the most of a bad situation, making friends with the other stranded travelers and finally pulling her guitar out for a sing-along. She loved sing-alongs, in fact, she'd always thought that the world would be a much better place if people sang and danced more. She'd often imagined her life as a colorful musical, especially as a child. In musicals, people sang and danced through fights, even enemies. And when the curtain dropped, you could be sure of a happy ending. She'd always wished real life was more like that. But alas, she knew better. Besides, her life had been so disastrous that no amount of catchy songs and choreographed dance moves would make it any better.

But why dwell on all that when she could live in the here and now and sing a song with a bunch of happy strangers?

After a few songs with her new friends she finally looked up, trying to find Marcus in the throng. It didn't take her long to locate him, he was head and shoulders taller than most people. She hadn't realized how tall he was until now, he was the kind of guy you'd never lose in a crowd. She watched him for a few moments as he elbowed and pushed his way through with what looked like determination and purpose. He was jostling his way to the front of the queue that had gathered around the airline desk and was now talking with a rather frazzled-looking woman.

She tried to turn her attention back to the people in front of her and their request for another song, but her eyes kept drifting off towards Marcus, who was now standing a little way away from the queue, pacing and talking into his phone. His shoulders were tense under normal circumstances, but she watched with interest as he tensed them even more, raising them so high that they looked like they were attached to his earlobes. His entire body language suddenly changed as everything seemed to seize and stiffen. His posture screamed anger and she was worried about what might be going on.

She got up, bid her new friends farewell, and walked over to him just in time to hear what he was saying.

"What do you mean, you only have one room?" Marcus said, sounding angry. "But you don't understand," he beseeched. "There are two of us." He was unaware that she was now standing right behind him. There was a pause as Marcus listened to the person on the other end of the line and then started shaking his head rapidly. "No. Absolutely not." He said it with such conviction. "It would be a very, *very* bad idea for us to share a room. Trust me."

"Why?" Stormy asked. Marcus turned and when he saw her standing behind him, his face contorted into a shocked expression.

## Marcus

Marcus was struck by an unfamiliar bolt of panic—he didn't panic. What would happen if he and Stormy shared the same hotel room? Look what had happened when they'd just been sitting next to each other on the plane, surrounded by other passengers! His bolt of panic only intensified when he suddenly found her standing behind him, staring at him.

"Fine. Fine," Marcus hissed down the phone, "book it." He hung up quickly. "It's rude to creep up on people and listen to their phone calls," he said, walking past Stormy.

"Hey, where you going?" She had to jog to keep up with him as he made his way to the luggage carousel. Now that he'd learned they could leave the airport and he'd managed to book a hotel room for the night, he had a sense of purpose. Before he'd felt like he was in purgatory, waiting in limbo for something to happen. And when nothing had happened, he'd decided to make it happen himself. And he was not spending a night in this crowded airport.

"Going to get our luggage. We're leaving this place," he said over his shoulder, not slowing down for Stormy who he could see was struggling to keep up. The sooner they could be out of here, the better.

The baggage carousel was utter chaos. So many flights had converged on this small airport that bags had piled up all over the place. Confusion reigned supreme, with people pushing and shoving each other in an attempt to find their bags.

Marcus knew they had to hurry. The woman behind the counter had pointed out that although he could leave the airport—South Africans did not need a visa here—he would probably be hard pressed to find a taxi willing to drive them around in the storm.

Marcus scanned for his luggage. It was easy to find. His pristine Louis Vuitton suitcase stood out immediately; Stormy's generic duffel bag, however, did not. And he was getting more and more annoyed by the second as he watched her clumsily look for it. She'd tripped at least twice, trying to step over a bag on the floor, but seeming to misjudge the size of it. She'd then bumped into someone as she'd started walking backwards, without thinking to look behind her first. And then when she'd started helping other people find their bags, instead of focusing on finding hers, he knew he needed to step in and put an end to it.

"That's it!" He clapped his hands together and she swung around. "Can we just focus on getting *your* bag, and not trying to be the bag Samaritan of Nairobi! We don't have time for that."

"There is always time to be nice to people," she said, hands on hips now. She was looking even more disheveled from the physical exertion of searching for her bag. Her hair had fallen out of its plait, her face was glowing with a fine layer of sweat and her cheeks were flushed from the activity.

Marcus sighed. "Let me help you."

"I don't need your help, Marcus," she quickly snapped back.

"Oh yes you do," he made a beeline for one of the piles of luggage and started going through it, "or else we'll never get out of this airport."

"Fine." She seemed to resign herself to his suggestion, and then both continued to wade through the never-ending piles of luggage. Marcus riffled through the bags and jumped when a chicken suddenly stuck its head out of one of them and clucked at him angrily.

"Found it!" Stormy suddenly screamed—way too loudly in his opinion. He looked up, she was jumping up and down excitedly, clapping her hands together as if she'd just discovered a lost pirate treasure. *He could never get used to this exuberance of hers.* She grabbed the bag and slung it over her shoulder with a smile.

"Check it's yours before you just take it," Marcus said walking towards her.

"Marcus," she stopped and rolled her eyes at him, "do you think I don't know my own bag?" She squinted over at his bag and tutted loudly. "Just because it's not a fancy Loo Veeton, doesn't mean I can't recognize it."

"That's Louis," he said sarcastically over his shoulder while hurrying for the exit.

The weather outside was severe and Marcus hadn't fully appreciated it while inside the safety of the airport. But now that they were standing outside he could really get a sense of the storm's fury. Sheets of water were pelting down and the winds were whipping the water around in a manner that made it look like it was coming from every direction at once. And although Marcus wasn't one for histrionics, he couldn't help but think of one of those post-apocalyptic films where the world as everyone knew it was annihilated.

Marcus took in his surroundings. There was only one taxi there and it looked like it was about to pull away. Without giving it a second thought, he threw himself off the pavement and made a dash for it. Within seconds, he was completely soaked. He banged on the window, and after some hesitation, it finally came down.

"I'm off duty," the man inside the taxi shouted at him through the sound of the rain hitting the car roof. It was reminiscent of hammers banging nails into steel.

"Please, we need to get to our hotel, it's only a few kilometers away," Marcus shouted back at the man, water spitting from his lips with every word.

The man shook his head. "Too dangerous." He started winding the window back up.

But Marcus knew what would solve this problem. It was the currency that solved most problems. He pulled his wallet out, it was thick with cash, and held it up to the man.

"I'll pay you double," he said, not waiting for the man's response and already opening the back door.

He glanced across the road; Stormy was still standing on the pavement.

"Come on," he bellowed at her.

She gave Marcus a quick thumbs-up, before jumping off the pavement into the cold rain. She didn't try to run or cover her hair, like most people would have done. Instead, she deliberately jumped into a massive puddle on the way across the road and at one stage actually stopped, held her arms open and looked directly up at the sky, allowing the water to wash over her. She reminded him of a child, jumping through puddles as if she didn't have a care in the world. Even though they were in the middle of a (bordering on) natural disaster.

He held the door open for her and she climbed in, pulling her luggage onto her wet lap. Marcus climbed in next to her and did the same, trying not to glance over at her; he was now acutely aware that her wet dress was clinging to her breasts like a second skin. The sight of this made his temperature rise, despite the fact he was shivering from the cold. His fingers tingled at the thought of touching her. The corners of his mouth twitched as he tried very hard not to imagine what kissing her *there* would feel like.

He needed to stop thinking about her in this way. He needed to be out of this taxi. He shook his head, sending a few drops of water flying across at Stormy. She giggled as they hit her on the side of the face and turned to smile at him. He quickly averted his eyes and looked out the window. He *really* needed to be out of this taxi.

Luckily, a few minutes later, after the driver had negotiated the perilously flooded streets, they arrived at the five-star hotel that Marcus had managed to get the last available room in. Marcus felt a lot better when he thought about the warm shower he could soon take and the plush linen he'd be sleeping on—preferable to a hard airport floor.

And he wasn't disappointed when he saw the room; it was spacious, tastefully decorated and most of all at this stage, warm. The only catch was the solitary double bed. Marcus quickly decided that he'd sleep on the comfortable-looking sofa in the corner—the more distance he could put between him and Stormy, the better. This wasn't like him at all, but he just didn't trust himself in her presence. He liked to think of himself as the master of control, but there was something about this woman that was causing him to lose his grip. This was uncharted territory—not a comfortable position for someone who was used to dictating the rules and following the letter of the law.

"Wow," Stormy said, standing in the center of the room looking around. "This room is bigger than my entire apartment." She dropped her luggage down with a wet thud. "And that bed!" She moved towards it and looked like she was just about to climb onto it.

"Don't do that!" Marcus said, raising his voice. "You're wet. You'll leave a wet patch."

"It's just water," Stormy said before she climbed onto the bed and gave it a small bounce.

Marcus shook his head. "Do you have to do that?"

"What?" she asked innocently. "It's not like I'm jumping on it. I'm just giving it a little bounce. To see what it's like."

"But you're wet." Marcus watched as she bounced on the bed once more.

"Fine, fine," Stormy finally conceded and climbed off. "Party pooper."

"Why don't you have a shower, or a bath, or something. You'll get sick if you leave those wet clothes on." Marcus was feeling irritated that he was even having to point this out to her. "And I'd like to also get something to eat."

"Yes, Dad!" Stormy teased, before picking her bag up and walking off in the direction of the bathroom. She closed the door behind her and Marcus breathed a sigh of relief. She was driving him mad. What grown woman bounced on the bed, and in wet clothes no less?

Marcus began peeling his wet clothes off and had put some dry ones on, when he heard a panicked yell from the bathroom.

"Oh my Shiva!" Stormy screamed; it sounded like she'd hurt herself.

"What's going on? Are you okay?" Marcus jumped up and hovered by the door, not sure whether he should go in.

"No, I am *not* okay!" She stuck her head around the bathroom door. "This isn't my bag."

"Are you sure?" Marcus asked.

"Yes! I must have picked up the wrong one."

Marcus was about to open his mouth and give her an *I told you so* when she spoke again.

"It's a stripper's bag!" she whispered at him.

"What do you mean?"

"Exactly what I said! It's a stripper's bag."

Marcus felt amusement. Clearly, she was blowing things out of proportion, as usual. "I am sure it's not a stripper's bag."

"I'm telling you, the woman that owns this bag twirls around on poles and wears nipple tassels."

"I doubt it very much," Marcus snorted.

"Fine, if you don't believe me, I'll show you."

Stormy disappeared into the bathroom again and Marcus sat back down on the bed, caught between amusement and exasperation at her histrionics. "Stripper clothes" probably meant modern clothes. Clothes that did not look like they came from a charity store in the sixties smelling of old cigarette smoke and mothballs. She was overreacting.

*Only, she wasn't.*

# CHAPTER NINE

## WHAT THE HELL WAS HE DOING?

~

Marcus

*T*he bathroom door opened again and Stormy walked into the room.

She was wearing a tiny pair of bright-purple hot pants. The tight fabric clung to her body; he could see the outline of everything, *perfectly*. They were not only short, but also low, and the top of them barely covered her. He noticed that she had a belly ring and a tiny pink star tattooed on her protruding hipbone. Her stomach was as flat as a board and her legs were short, but shapely. She was also wearing a tiny, tiny, tiny—did he mention *tiny*—shiny bikini that barely covered her breasts. She twirled in a circle for him, exposing her bum that was poking out of the shorts. A small, perfectly round bum. The high Perspex heels she was wearing seemed to round the whole ensemble off nicely.

"Um . . ." Marcus was speechless.

"See? Would you like me to give you a lap dance? I could use some spare cash," she said.

Marcus's mind ran away with him; images of her on his lap, in that outfit, twirling and grinding and swirling . . . He quickly crossed his legs out of sheer necessity. "No, no . . ." He swallowed hard. "No lap dance, thanks. No need for that."

"You sure?" she asked, doing another twirl. "I could really do with the extra cash. In fact, I'm sure if I took these back with me and stood on the corner of Oxford, I'd make a better living than I am now."

"Jesus! Do you have to keep saying stuff like that?" Marcus threw a hand in the air. "Who talks about standing on a street corner?"

"I'm just joking, Marcus." Stormy put a hand on her hip. "Just pulling your arm."

He shook his head. "Pulling my leg."

"If you say so." Stormy placed another hand on her hip.

"I do say so," he hissed back, thinking a whole array of inappropriate things he really shouldn't be thinking. He needed to end this conversation, and more importantly, he needed to get her out those clothes and into something else. "Is there anything in that bag that would be appropriate for dinner?" he asked.

"No! But you're welcome to look for yourself." Stormy pulled the bag out of the bathroom and tossed it on the bed.

Marcus looked through it and was met with lacey, barely-there crotchless panties that were doing nothing to quell the feeling in his pants.

"What about this?" He reached for a satin dress that seemed to be the most conservative thing in the bag. It was shimmery red, and had no back, but it was vaguely acceptable. (Well, not really, but it did look like the item that would cover the most flesh.) "Is your other dress too wet?"

"Soaking," Stormy replied.

"I could lend you a T-shirt?" he offered.

"And wear it with what?" She pulled out another pair of lurid hot shorts and some tiny cut-off denims and waved them at him. "The bottoms in this bag are worse than the tops. I'll go try this on." She took the red dress from him and disappeared back into the bathroom.

A few minutes later, she reemerged in the skin-tight dress. It wasn't as short as the others, but the halter-top squeezed her small breasts into some rather impressive-looking cleavage. She turned, exposing a low-cut back that tied in the middle with a diamante string (classy) and dipped all the way to the small of her back, where he noticed another rainbow tattoo between the two perfect dimples just above her bum. She looked even sexier in this outfit than the other one. Her rainbow hair was wet and piled up on her head, and for the first time since meeting her, he vaguely appreciated it. In some strange way, the colors made her skin seem even paler and more porcelain-looking.

"I can give you a jacket to cover yourself a bit more, if you want," he suggested, pulling one out of his bag.

"Sure, that would be good."

A few minutes later, once Marcus had also had a shower, they were ready to leave for dinner. But as they walked to the door, Marcus noticed that Stormy was barefoot. "You can't go down without any shoes on."

"Well I'm not wearing *those*." She turned and pointed to the rather offensive Perspex things, which actually had water and glitter in the eight-inch heel. "And my sandals are drenched."

"This is a five-star hotel, you can't go barefoot," Marcus insisted. What would people think if he went traipsing into the dining room with a shoeless woman?

"Fine," she said, slipping on the Perspex shoes and the jacket that Marcus had given her. It was longer than the dress and she buttoned it up to hide the outfit—or lack thereof—beneath it.

But as she walked (sort of hobbled) down the corridor in front of him, Marcus realized that he'd made a huge mistake: wearing the jacket made the whole thing so much worse, because now she just looked like she was naked underneath it, especially with those heels.

Stormy pressed the button for the elevator, and they waited in silence again. When they weren't arguing, they seemed to have absolutely nothing to say to each other. The elevator door finally opened with a *ting* and they stepped inside.

But as the door closed again, something started to happen. The air around them felt hot and the space felt smaller and tighter than it really was. He began to feel a strange pull, as if an invisible magnet was exerting a force on him and he wasn't able to escape its magnetic field. He moved to the other side of the lift, away from Stormy.

*Don't look at her, don't look at her* . . . He repeated it like a mantra in his head, over and over again.

But then more disaster struck: the lights flickered and then went off, plunging them into total darkness, and the elevator stopped with an unpleasant grinding, thudding, moaning sound.

"What's happening?" Stormy's panicky voice rang out through the darkness.

"Power failure probably, must be the storm." Marcus felt a hand come out and touch him—she had made her way over to his side of the elevator.

"Small spaces freak me out." She sounded genuinely frightened.

"We'll be out in no time, don't worry."

But he *was* worried. Her hand was on his chest, and he felt a burning sensation where her palm rested against him. He tried to stop himself but couldn't. He slipped his hand over hers.

*What was he doing?*

Their fingers intertwined and he felt her body pressing up against him in the darkness.

*What the hell was he doing?*

He slipped his arm around her waist and pulled her closer. She let out a breathy moan. He felt her other hand come up and brush against his neck, and he leaned forward, looking for her lips . . .

*What the fuck was he doing??*

# CHAPTER TEN

## THE WIND MUST HAVE RIPPED OUR CLOTHES OFF

~

Stormy

*T*hey were like two puppets being controlled by some unseen force. And that unseen force had one objective, by the look of it!

All feelings of panic and fear were forgotten as Stormy felt Marcus's lips on her. Her back came into contact with the wall as he pinned her to it forcefully. In the darkness, her other senses seemed heightened, which just made the whole experience that much more intense. His touch was electric and hot, and the woody smell of his aftershave was inebriating. He tasted like toothpaste, and she could just make out a slight salty taste coming from the tiny beads of sweat that were gathering on them both.

Stormy reached up, and without a second thought to what she was doing and the consequences it might have, ripped his very beige shirt off. The buttons fell to the floor and she heard them bounce across it. For the first time she was free to run her hands over his bare body. She traced the lines on his chest and dug her nails into his stomach and squeezed. Yes, he was muscular and hard as a fricking wall, just as she'd suspected.

He picked her up and pushed her higher against the wall. She dug her nails into his back and pulled him closer, wrapping her legs around his waist tightly. Stormy wiggled out of her jacket and within seconds Marcus responded by frantically pulling at her halter neck straps to expose her breasts.

Marcus ran his tongue over her body, down the side of her rib cage, across her stomach and then her nipples. She moaned loudly as he took one between his teeth and gave it a soft bite. She grabbed the back of his head and coaxed his mouth over to her other breast—he was only too happy to oblige her. She slipped her hands between them and began pulling at his belt, trying to free him up for her to touch. But it was taking too long, so Marcus helped her, pulling his belt off in one swift movement, tossing it to the floor and then moving into a position that allowed her full access.

He moaned as her hand slipped into his boxers and she gripped him firmly, feeling him grow even harder in her palm.

"Wow." She hadn't really meant to say that out loud, but she had and it had only caused Marcus to moan even more as he bucked his hips forward and thrust into her hand. Suddenly, he pushed her hand away and moved his between them, grabbing the top of her thigh hard and pushing her legs open even more.

Only one thought penetrated Stormy's dizzy mind as he bit at her earlobe now, while digging his fingers into her thigh: she wasn't wearing underwear. Hers had been wet from the rain, and the others in the suitcase . . . *well*, she would hardly class those as underwear, besides she also drew the line at wearing another person's knickers.

Marcus was running his hand up her inner thigh, right now—and he was about to find out that she was going commando! She trembled with anticipation as his hand worked its way higher and higher and—

"Ooops," she breathed as she felt Marcus touch her there, and then heard the loud breath that came rushing out of his mouth when he realized that there was nothing between them. He didn't waste any time running his fingers over her. She threw her head back with a bang and let go of him as he held her to the wall with one hand and teased her with the other.

Everything was clumsy in the dark, which made the whole experience so much hotter. It gave it an urgency that made them giddy. They both fumbled hungrily with each other, completely lost in the moment.

So lost, in fact, that neither of them registered that the lift had finally started moving again!

So lost that they didn't notice the lights had come back on.

And so bloody lost that they didn't hear the doors go . . . *ting!*

"AAAAHHH!"

A high-pitched scream rang out behind them and they both jumped in fright. Stormy was almost topless, Marcus was shirtless, and his pants were undone and lurking somewhere around his ankles. And suddenly, they were no longer alone.

An elderly couple clung to each other in terror and a mother rushed away with her teenage son—who was smiling from ear to ear.

"What's wrong?" A hotel security guard and what seemed to be the manager appeared out of nowhere.

Stormy felt Marcus's arm come up and cover her breasts, which she felt was oddly touching, considering there were now multiple pairs of eyes either gawking at them, or deliberately trying to avoid them.

The manager looked at them in blatant disapproval for a few seconds before opening his mouth. "OUT!" he screamed, pointing at the door of the hotel lobby. "Get the hell out of here."

Marcus stepped forward, placing himself in front of her protectively. "I'm so sorry, I can explain." Stormy could hear from the tone of his voice just how utterly mortified he was. And quite honestly, there was no explaining this. What excuse could Marcus come up with? *The wind must have ripped our clothes off, little clothes-stealing elevator gnomes bust in and attacked us . . .*

"There is nothing to explain here." The manager stuck a finger out and pointed at Stormy. She was about to start nodding in agreement with the man when . . . "And we certainly don't welcome *her kind* in here. You need to leave."

"Whoa! Hello!" Stormy felt her temper flare and stepped around Marcus. Not caring that she was practically topless, she placed her hands on her hips in a defiant pose. The elderly man started coughing loudly and his wife hurried him off to a nearby chair, clucking indignantly as the guy looked like he was about to have a coronary.

"What does that mean? *My kind*?" she asked aggressively.

The manager looked Stormy up and down with contempt. "Working girls."

"Hey, hey!" Marcus stepped forward again as Stormy spluttered furiously. "She is not a prostitute! This is blatant defamation of character."

The manager glared at them for a moment, before speaking in a strangely calm tone. "And this is public indecency. You have five minutes to get your things and get out before I call the police."

"Wait, let's just talk about this," Marcus tried to reason with him. "There is a storm and all the hotels are booked up, and—"

"You should have thought about that before you engaged in public indecency, sir," the manager replied coolly.

"I'm *not* a hooker!" Stormy screamed at the man so loudly that people started to gather around the elevator. "Not that I have anything against hookers, in fact, there's a really nice hooker, Brooke, that lives in my apartment building and I often go over to borrow milk from her and she—"

"Stormy!" Marcus hissed between his teeth. "Stop talking. You're not helping."

"OUT!" the manager shouted back. "Or I will have security drag you out!" The color was rising rapidly in his cheeks, and the vein in his forehead looked like it was about to explode.

"Okay." Marcus threw his arms in the air. "We'll leave, just give us a few minutes to get our bags."

And so five minutes later, Stormy and Marcus were standing outside the hotel in the pouring rain once more, clutching onto their bags.

But Stormy wasn't thinking about being kicked out of a fancy hotel for public indecency . . .

Once again, she could still feel the sting of his hands on her body. The wetness of his mouth on her stomach and the burning trail his fingertips left when they climbed up her skirt. Suddenly, despite the cold outside, she felt blazing hot.

# CHAPTER ELEVEN

## WHAM-BAM-THANK-YOU-MA'AM

~

Marcus

*N*o! No! No!

*How?*

Marcus couldn't believe he'd just done that. *Again.* And in an elevator! If those doors hadn't opened when they did, he might have actually taken it all the way. This was not like him and he barely recognized the person he was suddenly turning into. God, he was so embarrassed, nothing like this had ever happened to him. Not even close. He was a law-abiding citizen, for heaven's sake.

He could still taste her, even as the wind and rain whipped against his skin. Marcus wasn't sure what his next move should be, so he simply stood in shocked silence as the rain washed over him—hopefully washing her scent away, too. Stormy seemed to be doing the same thing. They must have looked like a real pair of lunatics, he thought, standing in the rain, doing nothing.

It took him a few moments to snap back to reality and realize what a shit storm they were now in: no taxis in the vicinity and in the middle of a full-blown real storm. The only thing Marcus could think of was that they needed to take shelter somewhere, or find a hotel and hope that they would have a room. He reached into his jeans and pulled out his cell phone. Shit, it was wet and wouldn't turn on. *Nothing* seemed to be going right today.

"Is your phone dry? I want to look for the nearest hotel." Marcus turned to Stormy, raising his voice against the wind and finally breaking the silence between them.

"How will you find a hotel on my phone?" She looked genuinely confused.

Marcus looked at her as if to say, *duh*. "Google maps, the internet."

Stormy shook her head and shouted through the rain, "I don't have the internet on my phone."

"What?" He couldn't have heard her right. It must have been the noise. "What?" he asked again.

"I said, I don't have internet on my phone." At this, Stormy reached into her bag and pulled out a giant, brick-shaped creature with an aerial that had been sellotaped together. Marcus took it and stared down at it with a mixture of disdain and curiosity. Not only was it shockingly primitive, but she'd also stuck rainbow stickers all over it, and was that . . . *yes*, a feather had been glued to the top of the aerial. *Why?* He'd never seen anything like it in his life.

"*This* is your phone?" he asked.

Stormy nodded.

"Your *current* phone?" he continued, still not sure he was able to accept this, even from someone like Stormy.

She nodded again. "I had one of those smarty phones once, my friends bought me one, but I didn't get a good vibe from it. Besides, it didn't have buttons." Marcus shook his head and then tried to shelter it from the rain. He squinted down at the screen. It was still working, but not for long—it looked about a hundred years past its expiry date. Suddenly, a massive bolt of lightning lit up the sky. The sound of the thunder was deafening, like an atom bomb exploding next to them, and the ground felt like it shook.

Marcus instinctively jumped and Stormy screamed.

"We have to go!" Marcus grabbed her by the arm and started pulling her away.

"Where?"

"I don't know. We have to find shelter."

They ran across the road, splashing through deep puddles as they went.

"I told you! I *told* you! Not a good day to travel!" Stormy shouted over the rain.

"And I told *you*, I don't believe in that stuff!" Marcus screamed back, his eyes looking from left to right, trying to find them shelter.

"Well, how on earth do you explain all this?" she shouted back at him.

"I'd rather not get into some esoteric debate right now." He continued to pull her through the puddles, running from one spot of cover to the next; a bus stop, an overhang, a large tree. He wasn't sure they were going to make it. Or even where they were going to land up. But ten minutes later, Marcus and Stormy found themselves miraculously standing in the reception of a small motel.

Marcus looked around the reception area, utterly disgusted. He wasn't accustomed to this level of—he couldn't quite find the words—this level of filthy cheapness. This was a roadside dive. He saw the irony of it all, of course: kicked out of their fancy hotel, accused of solicitation, and then landing up in a motel that probably charged by the hour and had condoms on the bedside tables.

It was filthy; the carpet was peeling in all four corners of the room, an old Persian rug with holes in it lay on top of that, as if it had been discarded carelessly. He looked up at the wall above the reception desk, a holographic silver and gold picture of a lion shimmered back at him and next to that, a framed certificate: *Glory Lodge*. A one-star motel.

There was certainly no glory here, and he was sure they had received that star by accident. But this was no time to be a snob, he realized that. It had been the nearest, and possibly only place to take shelter. They were drenched and Stormy was covered in mud from tripping, breaking a Perspex heel and falling into a puddle. Marcus had been forced to carry her the rest of the way. He hadn't wanted to be in such close proximity with her body since their latest *incident*, but he'd had no choice. She'd been as light as a feather, and with her in his arms like that, his desire to find shelter and protect them had only intensified.

The room was nothing like the previous one. It was small, dark, damp and dingy. The floor was tiled with bright white tiles that were cracked in several places and made the room look more like a prison cell. The bathroom was pokey, with a shower that was so small you could barely fit into it. And the worst part, there was a small, solitary bed pushed up against a wall of peeling pink paint. The maroon-colored curtain that hung from the one tiny window looked like it had been nibbled on and was covered in spider webs, which made him nervous. His skin physically itched just looking at the place and he was desperate to get his antibacterial wipes out and give this place a lashing.

He suddenly felt slightly short of breath; this place reminded him too much of his childhood and he wanted to turn and run. It reminded him of every bad thing that had ever happened to him and he felt an overwhelming desire to start cleaning, which had been the only way to deal with all the chaos that had surrounded him as a child. He closed his eyes quickly, took in a short, sharp breath and composed himself. There was no way he would be able to relax enough to sleep here.

Stormy tossed her bags on the floor, dripping large puddles of water onto the tiles. Instinctually, Marcus picked her bags up and rushed them off to the corner of the room, where he stacked them as neatly as possible. There was hardly any floor space as it was, no need to clutter the place even more. He hated clutter. When he was satisfied that the bags where were they should be, he turned and came face to face with a completely naked Stormy.

"We need to have sex! Now!" she declared in a matter-of-fact tone that caught him completely off guard.

"What? Huh . . . uh . . . WHAT?" he spluttered nervously, not sure where to look.

"We need to have sex and just get this thing out of our systems."

Marcus could barely think straight as he gazed at her in

absolute awe. She had a small birthmark below one of her breasts which he hadn't noticed before, and at the right angle, it was almost heart shaped.

"So?" she prompted, snapping Marcus back to reality. "Are we going to do this or what?"

"Uh . . . um . . . uh . . ." He was still speechless.

"Bat got your tongue?" she asked, looking at him as if she wasn't even vaguely fazed that she was standing in front of him in her birthday suit.

"Cat," he replied quickly, still not sure where to look.

"Whatever!" Stormy rolled her eyes. "You're going off the path now. We *need* to have sex!"

"Do you really think that will work?" he finally managed to utter as he forced himself to pry his eyes away from her body.

"Yes. We just need to shag each other and then all this sexual tension will disappear and we can go back to not liking each other and not groping in public."

Marcus wanted nothing more than to "shag her" (who *said* that these days?), but he wasn't so sure this was the best solution to their problem. "What if we have sex and then want to have it again?"

Stormy shook her head. "No, that won't happen. I've figured this whole thing out."

"Figured what out?"

"Why this thing between us keeps happening—other than the star sign thing, of course."

"Okay," Marcus folded his arms, "I'm all ears." He wanted to hear this. He was open to considering all options at this point.

"So . . . I'm probably very different from anyone you've ever been with, and you're totally different from anyone *I've* ever been with. So, I think a lot of this . . . *tension* is just curiosity. But if we do it, we'll totally satisfy that curiosity and then it can all go back to normal. And we can *not* like each other again."

Marcus thought about it; maybe she was right. There was a certain amount of logic to her argument.

"So?" she asked again, as if getting impatient.

"Fine," Marcus said, peeling off his shirt and tossing it to the ground. "Let's do it."

"Good. Good. Let's go for it." Stormy clapped her hands and readied herself. He couldn't help but notice how her breasts shook as she moved. She was obviously very comfortable with her body. It showed—and it made her even sexier. *Fuck*, if that was even possible.

"Yes, let's do it." Marcus was loosening his belt now and pulling his pants down.

"Abso-mundo," Stormy agreed, appearing fired up and ready to go. She jumped from side to side, almost like a cheerleader with pom-poms. "It doesn't have to be this whole long thing, or anything like that. So don't worry about all that foreplay stuff. Just a quickie. Just a *wham-bam-thank-you-ma'am* to get it out of our systems."

"You're right! No big deal. Just a quickie." Marcus had pulled his clothes off and was also completely naked now. He couldn't help notice how Stormy's eyes moved over his body, lower and lower, and settled on his . . .

"Mmmm," she mumbled out loud.

"Mmm, what?" He felt a bit sheepish now under the intensity of her gaze.

"Mmm, not bad!" Stormy replied with a small smile.

"Uh . . . yes, you too," Marcus responded awkwardly.

But as he gazed at her, and she gazed back, as they looked from each other's eyes to naked body parts and back again, the whole thing started to feel *very* awkward. The silence stretched between them, and neither one made a move.

"Okay," Stormy said a little less enthusiastically, shuffling a bit. "So, let's do it." She fist-pumped the air. "Let's go!"

"Yes! Okay. Let's go for it," Marcus responded enthusiastically, almost as if he were trying to convince himself.

Except neither moved. They both stood dead still.

"I can't just *do it*, just like this. We need to . . . you know, kiss first or something," Marcus finally said, painfully aware that although there was a naked woman in front of him, his body was simply not responding in the way it should have been.

"Okay." Stormy moved closer to Marcus. She tilted her head to the left to go in for a kiss—just as Marcus did the same thing.

"Sorry," he mumbled as they bumped noses. He tilted his head to the opposite side. But Stormy did the same thing.

"Um . . . you go left, and I'll go right," Marcus said, pointing in the different directions.

"Don't tell me which way to go, what happens if I like right?"

"Okay, whatever, then go right and I'll go left." Marcus was getting frustrated now. This wasn't exactly how he'd imagined them having sex. It felt completely wrong and forced.

"I didn't say I *wanted* to go right, I just said that *maybe* I wanted to." Stormy placed her hands on her hips again in that defiant pose that he was becoming quite familiar with. It was her signature move.

Marcus sighed. "This isn't working, is it?"

He looked her in the eye and he could see the relief. "No, it's not."

Admitting defeat, they both turned away from each other and went back to their wet, sticky clothes.

# CHAPTER TWELVE

## ACTUALLY-SMACKTUALLY

~

Stormy

*A*fter pulling the wet stripper dress back on, Stormy walked over to the bed and sat down contemplating what had just happened.

"Maybe we're over it?" she offered quietly and thoughtfully.

Marcus nodded. "Yeah, maybe we are."

"Well that's good news, isn't it?" she asked.

"I guess it is."

Stormy turned towards Marcus and his dark eyes met hers. She tried to hold his gaze, she wanted to look inside him and figure out what he was thinking, but he quickly looked away.

"We need to change into dry clothes. Why don't you go shower first?" he said.

"Sure." She got up and walked into the bathroom and straight into the tiny cramped shower.

The warm water felt amazing as it rushed over her freezing cold, muddy body. She thought about Marcus sitting there in the other room alone, naked just a few minutes ago. What *was* this thing between them? It was volatile and clearly dangerous, since it had gotten them kicked out of a hotel and caught in a storm. But obviously the sexual tension between them had finally fizzled out. Maybe the incident in the elevator had beaten it out of them.

Yes, that was probably it!

They were no longer sexually attracted to each other. Stormy breathed an enormous sigh of relief and started humming happily to herself. Her world had returned to normal once more. Well, a Stormy version of normal.

## Marcus

Marcus was relieved that they were finally over it.

It had gotten them kicked out of a hotel and into a deadly storm. Imagine what could have happened if they hadn't found this motel? Mind you, finding it may yet result in catching some dreaded disease, from the look of that bed.

That bed!

Another issue.

One bed.

Two people and nothing but cold tiles to sleep on.

He looked up as he heard a happy humming coming from the shower. And, for some reason, he found himself smiling as he listened to it. Stormy was definitely one of a kind and he'd never met anyone like her before.

"Your turn!" Stormy said cheerfully, coming into the room wearing nothing but a towel.

Marcus jumped up fast—he'd never wanted a shower so badly, and he didn't want to be in the same room as a towel-wearing Stormy for too long.

The cascade of hot water was exactly what he needed, and he emerged from the tiny shower cubicle feeling like a new man; relaxed, revived, refreshed. They had been traveling for almost twelve hours now, and it had been an exhausting day.

He wrapped the towel around his waist and walked into the room, where he was almost knocked off his feet. Stormy was wearing his shirt. That part he didn't mind; but what he *did* mind was that she looked so damn hot in it. It was way too big and hung off her like a tent. There was something so intimate about wearing his shirt, like she'd stayed the night and they'd had sex, and she'd woken up and slipped it on.

"Hey." She swung around. "Sorry, do you mind?" she asked a little awkwardly, gesturing down at the oversized rugby top.

Marcus shook his head. "Not at all." He noticed that the green rugby jersey made the color of her eyes even more intense.

"I've never worn a rugby jersey," Stormy said, running her hands over it. "In fact, I've never watched a rugby match. It's such a barbaric sport."

Marcus gave her a knowing smile. "Of course you haven't. What sport do you like?"

"I don't believe in sport!" Stormy stated emphatically.

Marcus laughed out loud at this statement. He was starting to get her. Anything that was normal, and mainstream and that most people liked or took part in—she did not. "Why not?" he asked.

"It brings out unnecessary aggression and competitiveness in people."

"Competition and aggression are what helped the human race survive. Imagine if our ancestors had sat around in their caves all day doing nothing."

"Maybe. But it's not okay in this day and age. Our society is already way too aggro, there's far too much competition and capitalism already."

Marcus was the epitome of all those things: aggressive in business, fiercely competitive and an unashamed capitalist. He liked making money and he wasn't embarrassed of that fact—he worked hard for it.

"So, tell me, Stormy, what is it that you actually *do*? Damien mentioned acting and something with crystals?"

Stormy shot him a cynical look. "You don't really want to know what I do, you just want to mock me."

"No, seriously, I do. No mocking intended. We have a whole night ahead of us in a pokey motel room. Might as well get to know each other, since we may be stuck here for a few days."

Stormy looked startled at this. "You think? But the wedding . . . ?"

Marcus walked over to the window and looked out again. "It will be a miracle if this is over by morning. And as you can probably guess, I don't believe in miracles."

"We need to be at that wedding though." She joined him at the window and looked out bleakly.

"We might just make it to the wedding, but I doubt we'll make it to the wedding rehearsal and the bachelor and bachelorette parties. Unfortunately, it's out of our control."

"Mmmm. Grant me the serenity to accept the things I cannot change, the courage to change the things I can, and the wisdom to know the difference," Stormy murmured, wiping away some of the condensation that had gathered on the window.

"Huh?"

"The serenity prayer from Alcoholics Anonymous," Stormy explained, making an elaborate drinking gesture. "My dad. He likes a few whiskeys."

"Yes. Damien told me."

Stormy nodded. "And you? What about your family?"

"No alcoholics. And my dad's dead." Marcus said it quickly, like he usually did when people asked him about his family.

"Oh no!" Stormy grabbed her chest and turned to him. "I'm so sorry," she said, looking genuinely concerned.

"It's fine, it was a long time ago." Marcus looked away and could tell she was still looking at him, as if she was waiting for him to say something else. "My mom is a kind of addict, I guess," he said softly, not really sure why though. He never shared personal information with people but it seemed to slip out under the intensity of her gaze.

"See, there!" Stormy said brightly. Marcus turned to look at her. Her face lit up with a smile and she clapped her hands together. "Finally, we have something in common: Parentalholics!"

"I suppose we do, then. That, and we share the same basic human anatomy," he quipped sarcastically. He was feeling so much more relaxed around her now that the sexual tension had melted away. She wasn't even irritating him that much—at the moment anyway.

"I bet we're not all that different. I bet if we got to know each other, we'd find we have lots in common."

"Well, it looks like we've got a lot of time for that," Marcus said. "But first, I need to put some clothes on. Can you turn around for a second?"

Stormy shot him an amused look. "It's not like I haven't seen it before."

"Exactly, so there's no reason to see it again. Turn around," Marcus commanded, making a circle gesture with his hands, and Stormy obliged.

"Just so you know, if you're embarrassed, you have no need to be," she said over her shoulder.

"Stormy!" Marcus exclaimed loudly. If he wasn't embarrassed before, he was now. She had an uncanny ability to say the most inappropriate things.

"I'm just saying, it's very attractive."

"Jesus! Do you have to say stuff like that?" Marcus felt his face growing hot.

"But it's true. You have very good proportions and a good shape. You know, sometimes they can be very strange-looking. Especially when they're all narrow and then way too big on the top, like a giant mushroom cloud. Or what's worse, is when they're smaller at the top and bigger at the bottom, like a pyramid. Or when they veer off the left and you're like, 'how is this going to work?' and when they're—"

"OKAY! Stop it!" he cut her off, exasperated. "I can't believe the stuff that comes out of your mouth sometimes. I've never met a person who says the things that you do."

"I say what I say and mean what I think," she replied tartly.

"I think you mean, *you say what you think and mean what you say.*"

"Same thing," she shrugged.

"No, it's not."

"Of course it is!"

"Nope."

"Who says?"

"Um . . ." Marcus said, pulling on his pants and shirt. "Just about every literature or English teacher in the world."

"Well, have you ever thought that maybe *they're* all wrong?"

"I doubt that, Stormy," he sighed. "You can turn around now."

But as she turned around, he saw that she was striking her signature pose, hands on her hips and looking like she was ready for an argument—which she clearly was.

"I bet you think you're right a lot," she accused.

"I usually am, actually."

"Well, I *actually* bet it's not as often as you *actually* think it is, *actually*, Marcus!" she spat.

"And I think you've just overused the word 'actually' in a sentence," he replied, feeling his pulse rise a bit.

"Actually-smacktually," she shot back at him.

"Oh my God, that makes no sense again!" Marcus was getting riled up now too. She was driving him crazy again.

"Sense is what you make of it, Marcus."

"No! No, it's not." He felt a wave of overwhelming exasperation wash over him.

"Who says?" She sounded like a petulant child and cocked her head to the side.

*God!* She looked utterly ridiculous and yet totally adorable in his rugby jersey. Head off to the side, waggling her angry little finger at him with that disapproving look on her face. She looked like she was getting ready for an argument, and all he could think about was what the quickest way of ripping her shirt off was . . .

# CHAPTER THIRTEEN
## THE GENTLE FLOWER WHISPER

~

Marcus

"Oops," Stormy said when they finally got their bearings and caught their breath. She was naked and bent over the bed, and Marcus was lying on top of her, his breath coming rapidly.

"Big oops," she said again, with a huge sigh.

Marcus shifted against her. Her hair was wet and strands were sticking to his face and chest. He was in shock from the sex they'd just had—it had been mind-blowing. It had all happened so quickly that the details were a blur, but he could see flashes of it.

At one stage she'd been dangling off him—literally. One minute, he was standing and she was wrapped around him, and the next she was bent over backwards and hanging. She was so light and flexible that he'd been able to do exactly what he wanted with her—and he had. No woman had been so uninhibited. Mind you, no woman had hung from him upside down like a bat, either.

Thank God this pay-by-the-hour dive *did* have condoms next to the bed.

Although she was small and delicate-looking, her fragile build was deceptive. Very. That thing she did with her leg twisted like that—he'd never seen it before. Perhaps she'd just invented it.

They lay there. Not moving. Not talking. Just catching their breaths.

Marcus eventually got up. He didn't know quite what to do now—most women wanted to be held and cuddled at this stage, but Stormy was not like most women. And despite their sexual gymnastics, they didn't *really* know each other. There'd been nothing emotional or intimate about what had just happened either—it had been nothing more than lust. Pure, unadulterated lust.

He got it now—why it hadn't happened earlier when she'd offered herself to him on a virtual platter. They had to be arguing, or in some kind of life-threatening situation, like a plane crashing or a lift getting stuck.

He got off and walked away. He wasn't really sure what else to do. He needed a moment alone to think. Hopefully his rational brain would soon return from the time-out it seemed to be on.

## Stormy

Stormy was shaking from head to toe and finding it hard to breathe under the weight of his body, but she didn't care. She was still shell-shocked. It had been the wildest sex she'd ever had. Normally she was into burning candles and incense, listening to Mayan chanting, setting out crystals and doing some slow tantric breathing vibes, followed by intricate poses called "The gentle flower whisper" and "Two lilies blow in the warm breeze." But this had not been like that.

To tell you the truth, she wasn't exactly sure how it had happened. There had been some intense staring across the hotel room and then all of a sudden she had been on the floor, against the wall and bent over the bed. She remembered ripping his clothes off as quickly as possible and tearing the neck of his shirt as she had tugged at it. He'd thrown her rugby jersey across the room and he'd taken charge. And it had been amazing—the best sex of her entire life.

The stars were right—they were *very, very, very* sexually compatible. Oh yes indeedio.

*But now what?* What the hell were they meant to do after sex like that? Pillow talk and bedroom chatter seemed totally inappropriate— besides, the pillows here looked more like flat pancakes. After sex like that, it would probably be appropriate to bite his head off and eat him, praying-mantis style. She suddenly felt Marcus's body lifting off her and then heard the bathroom door shut.

She got up and Marcus was no longer in the room. Instead, she could see his feet shuffling back and forth under the bathroom door. She glanced around, looking for her clothes, eventually finding them strewn on opposite sides of the room. She rubbed her hip and looked down, seeing a red mark. It looked like it was going to leave a bruise. How had she gotten that? *Oh yes*, the wall . . .

She bit her lip thinking about it. The wall. The hard, cold wall against her hot, sweaty body. Him, behind her, hands around her waist, thrusting into her furiously at that angle that had caused her to scream over and over again . . .

She sat down on the bed and waited for Marcus to come out of the bathroom. They needed to talk about this. *Didn't they?* But the minutes passed and he didn't reappear. It felt like he'd been in there for ages. Eventually, she got up and approached the closed door.

"Marcus," Stormy called softly, knocking on the door.

"Mmm," a quiet moan of acknowledgement issued from the tiny bathroom.

"Are you okay in there?"

A pause.

"I'm not sure . . . are *you* okay?"

"Ummm, I think so."

Another long pause. Stormy tentatively opened the door and peeked round. Marcus was sitting naked staring at the wall opposite him with a somewhat shocked look on his face.

Stormy sat down on the other side of the door and peered at him through the crack.

"What was that?" he finally asked, looking at her.

She shook her head. "I don't quite know."

"Did I hurt you, with the wall and . . . ?" He sounded agitated.

"A little bit."

Marcus sighed loudly and put his head in his hands. "Shit. I'm so sorry!"

"No, no!" Stormy pushed the door open wider. "In a good way . . . *a very good way.*"

An awkward silence fell over them again and dragged on for far too long. "It can't happen again, though," Marcus finally said. "I mean, you and I . . . it would never . . . it's insane . . . And I don't do this kind of thing!"

"Goddess, no!" Stormy exclaimed. "Never. It won't happen again."

"So we agree?" Marcus asked.

"Oh yes," Stormy nodded.

"So this will never happen again, and we should just try and forget about it?" Marcus continued.

"Absolutely!" Stormy said loudly. "Besides, I'm sure we've gotten it out of our systems now."

"You're right," Marcus agreed. "It's out of our systems, so we won't want to do it again."

"No. No," Stormy said. "We won't."

"Great. Shake on it?" Marcus stuck his hand out of the crack in the door.

Stormy took it and they started shaking.

Bad idea . . .

# CHAPTER FOURTEEN

## MAYBE THERE'S A SELF-HELP GROUP FOR IT

Stormy

"*D*ouble oops," Stormy said, this time with her back pressed up against a hard metal towel rail on the bathroom wall.

They peeled themselves off each other with a squeaky sound, once again both reeling from what had just happened. *Again!*

Stormy was almost positive she remembered doing something that might have resembled an actual cartwheel at some stage. Possibly even a headstand and a pirouette.

"I don't think *double oops* quite cuts it, Stormy," Marcus said, wrapping a towel around himself. "We've got a serious problem here," he added crisply, walking out of the bathroom hurriedly.

"Maybe there's a self-help group for it. We could get a sponsor and a key ring," Stormy joked flippantly as she followed him out.

"Sex addicts anonymous?" Marcus suggested in jest.

Stormy shook her head. "Nah, this only happens when I'm around you."

"Really? I doubt that." The sarcasm in his tone instantly rubbed Stormy up the wrong way, and—still naked—she assumed her hand-on-hip pose.

"What are you trying to say? That I'm some kind of girl that randomly sleeps with strange men at the drop of a cap?"

"Hat."

"What?"

"Drop of a hat."

"Same thing!" she said, stamping her foot and feeling utterly exhausted by his irritating habit of correcting almost everything that came out of her mouth.

"*Not* the same thing. Crap, put some clothes on, why don't you." He pointed at her while deliberately averting his gaze.

"Fine!" she huffed. She turned back into the bathroom and found the rugby jersey dangling from the light fixture . . . *how the hell had it gotten there?*

"By the way, you wear both on your head. Caps and hats. Same thing," she called out from the bathroom as she pulled the shirt on.

"Fine," Marcus conceded. "I don't want to argue about head apparel. Can we just talk about this thing that keeps happening between us?"

"What is there to say? We keep having sex. Clearly there's an attraction between us and it's very powerful and we can't seem to control it. It's in our stars."

Marcus sat on the bed and held his head in his hands. "You seriously never do this with other guys?"

Stormy shook her head as she emerged from the bathroom again, this time fully dressed. "Never. And never like *that*!"

"Like what?"

"Well, it wasn't exactly very calm sex, was it?"

"No, I guess not," Marcus responded.

"I mean, it wasn't exactly *gentle*."

"No."

"It was rather hard and fast and very, very vigorous actually and rather—"

"*Okay*, okay, you can stop now! I was there too, I know what kind it was." He cut her off.

There was a pause in the conversation and Stormy was thinking about what had just happened between them.

"Me too," Marcus finally spoke. "I never do this either. I don't really sleep with women that I'm not in a relationship with and if I do, I don't do it like . . . well, like *that*."

The wind outside had gotten louder and the sound of the rain pelting against the window forced them to raise their voices over it. "Why is it such a bad thing?" Stormy eventually asked. It was something that had just dawned on her. They were two consenting adults, after all—what was so wrong with them having sex?

Marcus looked up at her. "Well, you and I . . . We just wouldn't . . . and—"

Stormy interrupted him quickly before he got the wrong idea about her. "Hey, I'm not looking for a relationship with you, if that's what you're thinking. Not at all."

"No, no, of course . . ." Marcus said quickly. "Me neither."

Stormy plonked herself onto the bed and nudged him playfully with her shoulder. "Anyway, remember what the stars said: 'not good in relationships.'"

"So . . . what are you trying to say then?" Marcus sounded tentative. "That we should, just, keep having . . . um . . ."

"Sex?" Stormy offered.

"Yes. Sex," Marcus said. He sounded somewhat coy and Stormy thought it was rather adorable that this grown man was getting all blushy over the word, especially since he'd just ravished her against a wall—*twice*.

He seemed to think about this for a while. He looked very serious, as if he were measuring their behavior against some kind of checklist that he had—mind you, knowing Marcus the way she did already, she could imagine him as a list guy.

"I don't think so," Marcus finally said. "It's just not a good idea."

"Why?" she asked, not quite sure if she was feeling relieved, or disappointed by his reply.

"Well, it's not going to lead anywhere, and it clearly keeps getting us into trouble and . . ." He paused as if he was grappling to find a third option. Stormy decided to cut him off before he found it.

"You're right," she said. "We won't do it again then."

"Good." Marcus breathed a sigh of relief. "Thank God!"

"Well, it doesn't have to be like *that*," Stormy was strangely offended by his statement. "I mean, it's not like it was bad sex," she offered. "In fact, it was rather good, and very surprising, not to mention quite a workout."

"Can we just stop talking about it?" Marcus got up from the bed and started looking around. It was clear that conversations like this made him very uncomfortable, and that made her want to talk about it even more, just to watch him squirm. But she dropped it.

"I'm tired. I'm going to sleep on the floor." And with that, he grabbed one of the tiny pillows and a towel and laid them down on the hard tiles. He walked around the towel a few times, as if trying to decide something; she had no idea what that was, though. Finally, he sat down on the towel and then went about trying to make himself comfortable on a surface that looked anything but.

There was nothing else Stormy could do but retreat to the bed, even though she wasn't even vaguely tired.

The atmosphere in the room was strangely tense. Not the usual atmosphere you would expect from two people who've just had sex. It was as if they were both retreating to their own private corners, as far away from each other as possible. They certainly hadn't been retreating a few moments ago. That thing he'd done with her when her ankles had been somewhere around his ears and—

"A-choo!" Marcus suddenly sneezed loudly. "A-choo! A-choo! A-choo! A-choo!" It sounded like he was having a full-blown sneezing fit now.

"Are you okay?" Stormy asked, leaning over the edge of the bed and looking at him.

"I have . . . *A-choo!* . . . dust . . . *A-choo!* . . . allergies, the tiles . . . dust . . . *A-choo!* . . . it's . . . *A-choo!*"

Of course a man like Marcus had allergies. It made perfect sense. "Fine, I'll take the floor, you take the bed."

"I could never do that . . . *A-choo!* . . . still a gentlemen . . . *A-choo!*"

Stormy sat in silence, contemplating the solution. "Okay, get up here, we'll sleep head to foot."

Marcus squinted up at her through red-rimmed, puffy eyes that were starting to water.

"Fine," he sighed.

But the bed was tiny and trying to fit both of them on it head to foot was proving impossible. She practically had a toe up her nose, and every time either of them moved, they were assaulted by a heel in the head.

"This isn't working," Stormy finally said after feeling his foot grinding up against her forehead. "Just get up here. You can sleep on top of the blanket and I'll sleep under it, if you want."

Marcus looked at her nervously for a few moments, but finally agreed. "Fine."


## Marcus

The bed was so tiny that their bodies were pushing up against each other, but at least she was under the blanket and he was on top of it. They lay there in silence, listening to each other's breathing and the rain whipping against the window. Eventually, he heard Stormy's breathing getting longer and softer as she fell asleep. He couldn't seem to drift off, though, and found himself lying in the darkness, staring at the ceiling. He didn't know how long he'd been lying there like that when suddenly Stormy turned over and her arm flopped across his chest.

He squirmed uncomfortably, trying to shift it without waking her, but when she stirred she only tightened her grip and her head came to rest on his chest.

He froze, stiff as a board, as she cuddled into his side. But then Marcus surprised himself as his arm came around her and he surprised himself even more when he moved a little closer to her, stuck his face into her hair and inhaled her smell.

# CHAPTER FIFTEEN

## WAS IT WORN BY A
## SERIAL KILLER?

～

**Stormy**

*S*tormy dreamed that she and Marcus were kissing. Not the kind of kissing they'd been doing—the hungry, messy, desperate kissing—but the other kind.

The soft, gentle, slow kind. The kind loaded with meaning and feelings.

In her dream, they were lying in bed, holding each other like lovers who'd spent the night together. The sun was streaming through the window and onto their faces, and it felt like they could lie there for an eternity. Their eyes were closed and she felt his hands come up and pull her shirt off over her head. She reciprocated, pulling his off too, and their chests were bare, naked and pressing into each other. There was no frantic urgency this time—it was slow, delicious, gentle. And then she opened her eyes and—

"WHAAAA!" Stormy screamed and went tumbling backwards out of the bed.

"WHAT?" Marcus woke with a start and scrambled out of bed too.

"What the fricking hell!" Stormy screamed at him as she pulled herself up into a sitting position.

"*What?*" Marcus looked confused and frightened.

"You took my shirt off! *And* you kissed me!"

"I didn't kiss you!" Marcus objected, touching his lips. But Stormy saw a look of surprise cross his face as he realized that he tasted her.

"That was real . . . It wasn't a dream?" he asked.

"NO! You kissed me and tried to undress me while I was sleeping."

"Excuse me," Marcus protested angrily. "You were kissing me back, and I'm not wearing a shirt either. You took it off."

Stormy paused, her eyes slipping down over his now very naked chest. "Okay. Good point. So we both took advantage of each other," she admitted.

"Jesus, this is crazy, you know that? We can't even control ourselves when we're unconscious," Marcus said, sounding exasperated. She watched as he started rummaging under the blanket for their shirts and tossed Stormy's back to her.

She nodded and slipped the rugby jersey back on. "It is." She touched her mouth, a sudden and rather horrifying thought striking her. "Eeew, I can't believe we kissed with morning breath."

Marcus shrugged. "I can't believe we kissed at all."

Stormy suddenly realized that the room was much quieter

than it had been the night before. As if reading her mind, Marcus climbed out of the tiny bed and opened the curtains. Bright sunlight streamed in.

"Well, at least there's some good news—the storm seems to have passed. Maybe we can catch a flight out of here today after all," he said, gazing out. Stormy couldn't help but notice how the sunlight played off the natural highlights in his hair and accentuated that golden color in his eyes. He also did have really nice lips; full and kissable. And as for those big manly hands that were both hard and demanding and soft at the same time, not to mention his . . .

"Mmmmm." She quickly put her hands over her mouth when she realized she'd said that out loud.

"What?" Marcus asked, turning to her.

"Mmmmm, so glad the storm is over," she quickly corrected. She got up and walked over to the window. Even though the sun was out, there were signs of the storm everywhere. The streets were littered with garbage and a few more unusual items—a rogue garden chair, a grocery trolley and a mannequin, which looked very disturbing, sprawled on the curb in an oddly contorted pose. A few palm trees had bent and some had even fallen over. Huge puddles filled the road and water was gushing like raging rapids out of drainpipes.

"What's the plan, then?" Stormy finally asked.

"Go to the airport and see if we can get a flight out of here."

"You know I can't afford to pay for a flight, right? Or this room for that matter."

Marcus nodded. "Don't worry about it. I've got it."

"Thanks. I really appreciate that," Stormy said, feeling

somewhat uncomfortable with this, but knowing that she didn't really have another option.

"We should hurry, I still need to buy a new phone, too. If we leave now, we'll definitely make the wedding, and might not even miss any of the pre-wedding celebrations."

"Careful what you say—don't tempt Fate," Stormy said, rapping her knuckles against the wooden window frame superstitiously. "And then what should we do about . . . *you know*," she added, turning to him with a pointed look as she tried to convey the real meaning of her question telepathically.

"Oh!" Marcus finally clicked. "*That.* I don't know."

"Well, we have two options, really," she declared, holding up her fingers to count them off. "One, we keep doing this. Two, we put an end to it immediately, and make a pact that it will not happen again. A real pact that we stick to this time, not like before." Marcus looked at her like he was considering the options. "Well, we've both agreed that we'd never work in a relationship," he said finally.

"Never." Stormy nodded in agreement.

"And I don't want stuff to get complicated between us."

"No!" Stormy repeated. "Especially because we're almost related."

"What?" Marcus exclaimed in shock.

"Well, your cousin is marrying my stepsister," she replied. "So that makes us . . . us . . ." She searched for the words but couldn't find them. "Something with an 'in-law' and a 'twice-removed,' I think," she concluded.

"That's hardly related," Marcus quickly corrected and cleared his throat nervously. "In fact, that is not related, at all!"

"Whatever you say, Marcus."

"I do say. Because it's illegal for people who are related to have, *you know*?"

"Sex." She filled it in for him, since he always seemed to be so uncomfortable saying it out loud.

"Yes," Marcus said. "So let's put an end to this thing. For real this time."

"I can deal with that," Stormy replied.

"So it's a deal: no more kissing and touching, and definitely no more sex."

"Right—let's shake on it," Stormy said, extending her hand. Marcus looked at it hesitantly, and Stormy had a sudden flash of what had happened last time their hands had touched—five seconds later, she'd been straddling him and his hands had been on her waist, grinding her into him, over and over and over and ov . . . She quickly pulled her hand away. "Um, how 'bout we give that a miss—no touching, starting now."

"Okay. No touching," he agreed.

* * *

An hour later, they were at the airport, receiving some more bad news.

"What do you mean, no flights today?" Stormy could see that Marcus was getting worked up. In fact, she'd noticed that whenever he got worked up, a little crinkle appeared between his eyebrows.

"I'm sorry, the runway has sustained damage from the storm, and we have some communications knocked out," the battered-looking desk clerk explained. She looked like she had spent the morning being yelled at by frustrated tourists—which she probably had, Stormy thought. Her aura was giving off a distinctive dark non-glow glow. Stormy felt sorry for her.

"I'm sorry, sir, there is really nothing we can do," she apologized again.

"We have a wedding to get to in Prague." The line in Marcus's brow crinkled even more and she wondered if he was even aware that it happened. She stood back and watched him curiously. Apart from when he'd fucked her—that was the only way to describe it; a crude term, but effective and apt in this situation—other than that, when he'd been totally free and uninhibited, he was completely tense. His shoulders were always pulled high, brow wrinkled, lips pursed and as for his chakras . . .

"May I make a suggestion?" the desk clerk asked. "The airport in Mombasa is operational, and there are international flights taking off from there. The drive is nine hours and if you leave now, you'll get there before it's dark. I'm sorry . . . We just don't know when we will be operational again."

Marcus sighed. He was rather fond of sighing too, she noted. He went back to talking to the desk clerk and Stormy wandered away from the counter—after closing her eyes quickly and sending some positive vibrations to the woman behind the desk.

People were still camped out on the floor and on chairs, and many of them looked like they'd slept there the night before. She adjusted Marcus's tracksuit pants, hitching them higher up her waist—they were far too big for her, but she was tired of looking like a stripper, so she'd rolled the legs up and fastened the front with a belt. She was also wearing another one of his shirts. A few small kids rushed past her playing with each other; children always found the best in a situation. This was probably like a giant sleepover for them, she thought. Suddenly, she saw some waving arms and familiar faces. They were her friends from yesterday. She stuck her hand in the air and, without thinking about it, yelled out to them.

"*Assalamu alaikum*," she shouted across the airport at the top of her voice. The group of Middle Eastern travellers had taught her how to say hello, and why not practice it? She was sure her pronunciation was terrible, but so what? She loved learning new things.

"Sssshhh." She heard Marcus come up behind her. "You can't scream across the airport."

"Why?" Stormy turned around and looked at him.

"Because it's not appropriate." The little line in his brow was back.

"Why do you care so much about what other people think of you, Marcus?" she asked.

"I don't, I just don't like causing public scenes."

"Mmmmm," she muttered as she looked him up and down. "I think you're just a scaredy crow." She folded her arms and looked at him challengingly.

Marcus shook his head. "There is so much wrong with that sentence that I can't even address it right now. What I will address, though, is that there is a flight to Prague leaving from the airport in Mombasa tonight," he reported. "If we catch that, we'll make the wedding and most of the pre-wedding celebrations too. I've arranged a rental car and we should leave in exactly half an hour, but in the meantime, let's buy a phone and get you some clothes."

"But what about my bag?"

"There's no time to go looking for it—the airline knows it's missing and they promised to get it back to us."

"Oh," Stormy said, "but I don't have the money for new clothes."

"Here." Marcus slid an extraordinarily shiny credit card out of his wallet and offered it to her.

"I'm not taking your money," Stormy said, folding her arms across her chest.

Marcus shook his head. "Stop being so stubborn. Take it. Buy yourself a few outfits."

"No! What I'm wearing is fine, thanks."

She felt Marcus eye her up and down. "It's swimming on you, those pants are about to fall off. And if that happens . . . it might just land us in more trouble." He shot her a knowing look and she understood what he was trying to say immediately.

"Oh, I see what you mean. Fine," she conceded. "I'll see what I can do." She took the card from his hands, careful not to brush his fingers with hers, because Goddess knew what would happen again if their body parts connected.

"The pin is five, two, eight, three," Marcus said.

"Five, two, what, what?" Stormy asked; she'd never been good at numbers, and certainly not at remembering them.

"Eight, three," he repeated.

"How am I going to remember that?"

His brow crinkled again. "Uh, say it to yourself a few times."

Stormy tried to repeat it, but only succeeded in confusing herself even more.

"I know," she said, "five is easy, that's one full hand of fingers," she held her hand up, "and twenty-eight is easy to remember because its Angel Number meaning is a message that your positive affirmations and optimistic outlook will manifest wonderful blessings into your life and then three is a full hand of fingers minus two, like if you had cut two off in an accident cutting cucumbers or something painful like that." She smiled triumphantly at Marcus as the numbers fell into place in her mind in a neat series of pictures.

He seemed to stare at her blankly for a moment or two and then . . . *was that . . .?* Yes, it was. His lips twitched, his eyes began to crinkle up, not in a stressed way, and he started laughing. It was small at first, just a chuckle and then the chuckle began to grow and grow until he was standing there laughing.

"What?" she asked, unsure of what he was finding so funny.

He shook his head as the laughter finally tapered off. "You," he said, shaking his head even more.

"Me what?" She was confused.

Marcus looked at her for a while, as if he was trying to figure something out about her. "I don't actually know." He gave her a smile, and then much to her surprise, gave her a strange awkward pat on the shoulder. "I'm going to buy a phone, and some food and drinks for the journey. Meet back here in precisely twenty-four minutes."

"So specific." Stormy nodded and skipped off to the nearest store. She hated shopping, but luckily on this occasion, it was easy. She walked into the first shop she saw and was met by a rack of summery dresses, a few T-shirts and pairs of shorts—all on sale. She grabbed a few items, as well as a toothbrush and toothpaste, and hauled them over to the register to pay. She watched the screen light up with numbers as the attendant punched in the prices and when she saw how much the final amount was, she gasped.

She'd never spent that much on clothing in her entire life. In fact, she didn't really believe in buying new clothing. As soon as you wore it, it started aging anyway. Besides, she loved the idea that everything she bought had a story and a history to it. She'd often wondered about some of the dresses she owned; did a care-free hippie wear it to Woodstock? Did this belong to a young girl in love, and once, was this worn by a serial killer? (She'd thought that spot on the last cardigan she'd bought was blood, turned out to be a bit of food coloring though.) And then there was some-thing else about this whole scenario that struck her as very odd; a man had never bought her clothes before either. Ever.

It was a bizarre concept to her; not even her own father had provided for his family. That's probably why she'd landed up in three foster homes over the years. Her foster families had been sort of okay (not really). It hadn't been easy.

When she was sixteen, she'd gone looking for her mother, driven by a naïve childhood fantasy that maybe she could have a life with her. But that dream had soon been shattered, and she'd been left heartbroken when she finally tracked her mother down to a colony on the Transkei coast.

Stormy had been surprised when she'd arrived. It was nothing like she'd imagined. Where were the melodic sounds of wind chimes blowing in the warm coastal breeze? The sense of ashram-zen as you walked barefoot through the beautiful organic veggie garden? The place looked less like an informal hippie colony and more like one of those dusty compounds you might see in a pro-gram on the reality TV channel about a strange religious leader with ten wives and seventy-five children. Her mother was also not what she'd spent so many of her childhood hours imagining. For starters, she was bald. In Stormy's imagination, her mother's hair was long and thick, the color of bright golden sunshine. Her clothes too were nothing like the colorful, flowing pink thing Stormy had imagined her ethereally wafting around in while strumming her guitar. Her outfit looked more like a silver astronaut suit.

"Hey, aren't you my daughter?" her mother had said to her upon meeting. She talked particularly slowly and flatly, with no emotion in her voice whatsoever. "I've seen a picture of you." It was bizarre. Almost robotic.

And when Stormy had asked if she could stay with her and get to know her, her mother had basically said that she wasn't mother material. "This parent thing is just not for me." That was all she'd gotten.

Rejection. Abandonment of the cruelest kind.

She'd gone back to her foster family feeling utterly heartbroken and more alone and worthless than she'd ever felt in her entire life. But when her father had married Lilly's mom a few months later, and Stormy had moved in with them, things had finally started looking up. She had a sister for the first time, someone who she loved and cared for, and those feelings were reciprocated. She had finally dared to hope that she would know happiness and stability in her life. But it'd been short-lived, and a few months later they were divorced and Stormy was on her own with her deranged father again. But she hadn't lost Lilly, at least—they would always be sisters as far as they were concerned, and that's why she had to get to her wedding celebrations, no matter what it took.

Stormy walked out of the shop holding the bag of clothes in her hand. She hated thinking about that stuff and didn't have anything bright and colorful on hand to distract her from the dark thoughts. Trying to shake herself out of her weirdish mood, she went to the bathroom, put on one of the new pairs of panties she'd bought, slipped on one of the dresses and tied her hair back. It was a simple white dress with no patterns or colors—not her usual style. But it was strangely pretty. Fresh, and clean. She could almost imagine herself running through a field of white daisies wearing it. But it did need a little something to make it better.

She started digging through her bag. Luckily she still had her colorful bangles on hand, *and what was that thing at the very bottom of her handbag . . . ?* She dug a little deeper and pulled it out; an old, red ribbon that she'd kept from a balloon she'd gotten handed on the street as part of some sales promotion. The deflated balloon was still clinging to the end. She ripped it off and then proceeded to tie the ribbon around her waist like a belt. She looked at herself in the mirror. At least the tiny red ribbon gave the dress something.

She fiddled with her hair a little more, it was wavy and messy from being wet one minute and dry the next and she was unable to wrangle it into its usual plait, so she piled it all up on the top of her head and kept it in place with a yellow pencil she'd also dug out of the bottom of the bag.

She glanced at herself in the mirror one more time and then walked out.

## Marcus

Thank God for modern technology, Marcus thought. The guy at the electronics store had shown him how to sync his new phone with the cloud and his shiny new device had instantly populated with all his contacts, emails and photos. It was like having his old phone back, and it made him feel a lot more in control again. In fact, with his phone firmly back in his palm, he felt such a sense of relief wash over him.

Pocketing the phone, he looked up at the exact moment that Stormy started making her way towards him across the crowded airport terminal, and he found himself blinking rapidly. And his blinking was not for the usual reason. When she wasn't drowned in all those loud, distracting clothes and ridiculous scarves she was—uh, he didn't know if he could even think this word, but it was true—*she was gorgeous.*

He took a deep breath and steadied himself. Because suddenly he was feeling rather unsteady. They were going to be in a car together for the next nine hours, an entire working day, he needed to get a grip. But she was looking better than he'd ever seen her before; in fact, the stripper clothes might have been preferable to this simple white dress she was wearing right now. He could see she'd incorporated some pops of color to it, which was so Stormy, but its simplicity showed off her beauty.

"So, road trip!" Stormy said brightly, handing back his credit card.

"Road trip," Marcus echoed vaguely, still enthralled with her.

"So, what do you think?" Stormy asked playfully, twirling around so her dress lifted just a bit above her knee.

He nodded and smiled, trying not to betray what he really thought. "Much better."

"Thank you so much," Stormy said with a sweet, sincere smile that made her look even more beautiful. "No one has ever bought me clothes before."

He watched her as she swept her hands over the dress and swayed from left to right. She smiled up at him again, and Marcus felt something tug inside him.

# CHAPTER SIXTEEN

## FAITH IN SAMMY

~

Marcus

The two of them walked out of the airport together. Stormy was a little way ahead of Marcus and he took the opportunity to watch her closely.

She seemed to prance, not walk. She stopped and picked a single flower that was growing through a small crack in the concrete and tucked it into the hair at the top of her head. Even like this—a totally downplayed version of herself—she was still totally unique, different in every way. She certainly didn't need all those other adornments that seemed to swallow her completely. Sometimes the things she wore were so distracting that it was hard to see the person below them. He wondered if that wasn't the point?

She stopped walking again, kicked her new sandals off and stuck her foot into one of the many puddles and splashed the water. There was something so innocent and childlike about her demeanor, in one respect. And then in another, she was an absolute demon in bed . . . *well*, against the wall, the floor, on his lap and . . .

*Shit!* He quickly shook his head. *Stop thinking about that.* He mentally scolded himself.

They finally reached the car rental place and yet another disaster was awaiting them. The only car available was an old, manual Beetle from God knows what decade. No aircon, no electric windows, and a missing hubcap. It was an absolute miracle that this car was still working—*or maybe it wasn't?*

But it was all they had. Marcus felt his sense of control slipping again. This car looked terribly unreliable. He didn't like unreliable. At least he'd managed to get himself a new phone with GPS, so there was no getting lost.

He watched Stormy walking around the car curiously, her hand trailing over the roof and then down onto the bonnet. For a split second, he found himself fascinated by her once again. By the way she moved and the way her fingertips left a trail across the car's dusty bonnet . . .

Stormy dusted off her hands and stood beside the car, nodding approvingly. "Good car. It has a good vibe."

"And how do you get that?" he asked.

"Mmmm," she intoned, patting the car's bonnet as if it were a dog that had just done a good trick. "Sixth sense kind of thing-thang."

Yet again, she was demonstrating her unusual talent for leaving him completely speechless and bewildered. "You know, Stormy," he said as he loaded the bags into the car, "I just don't know what to say to that."

Stormy looked confused. "Why not?"

"I feel obligated to point out to you that cars don't give off good vibes."

"How do you know?"

Marcus opened his mouth to respond sarcastically, when he remembered—whenever they argued, she landed up naked and pinned underneath him. It was far safer not to argue! "You're right. I don't know. Maybe they do give off vibes," he conceded.

Stormy turned and pointed at him enthusiastically. "See! You're coming around to the many impossible possibilities of life!"

"Mmm-hmm," he responded vaguely. What he really wanted to say was "NO." But he just couldn't afford to argue with her.

"I'll drive," Stormy said, holding out her hand for the keys.

"I don't think so. I'll drive," he retorted rather sharply.

"But I love driving!" she cooed. "And I never get a chance to, since I don't have a car," she continued.

"You don't have a car?" Marcus was shocked for a second or two before thinking, *Of course she doesn't have a car.* "When did you last drive?"

"A few years ago, maybe."

"And how do you get around?"

"I catch taxis, hitch rides with people."

"*Hitch rides?* In South Africa? Are you crazy? Do you know how dangerous that is?" He didn't know why, but he was suddenly overcome with great concern for her safety.

"It's not *that* bad, I've only had my bag stolen once."

"What! How can you keep doing that then? I mean, what's next?" He threw his hands up in annoyance. He knew he was coming across as way too firm, but he couldn't help it. "Why would you keep putting yourself in danger like that?"

"Why are you so angry? It's not like it was your bag." It was obvious that Stormy was confused by his sudden outburst. Not that he blamed her—he was confused too.

"I'm driving. End of story," he insisted, pushing all other thoughts firmly out of his mind.

"You're bossy," she snapped back at him. "Has anyone ever told you that?"

Marcus ignored her last statement, climbed into the car and turned on the ignition. The old car chugged to life with a puff of smoke from the exhaust pipe, a strange rattle from the undercarriage and a loud humming sound from the bonnet.

"Great, let's hope we get there in one piece." He suddenly imagined them marooned on the side of the road with smoke pouring from this rusty tin can masquerading as a car.

Stormy patted the dashboard as she climbed into the passenger seat. "Don't worry. I have faith in Sammy."

"Sammy?"

"It's her name."

"You've named this hunk of junk *Sammy*?"

"Shhhh," Stormy hissed at him. "Cars have feelings, too."

This time Marcus burst out laughing. "I'm going to refrain from pointing out how absolutely ridiculous that statement is."

"Fine." Stormy shrugged. "But if she breaks down, it will be all your fault because of all the negative vibrations you're giving off."

Stormy put her feet up on the dashboard. Her skirt slipped down, exposing a good portion of her thighs. Marcus had to force himself to tear his eyes away from her legs in order to concentrate again. She was driving him crazy, plus he would never allow feet on a dashboard—but this was not his car, and at least her feet were cleaning off a thick layer of dust from the windscreen that was threatening to make him sneeze again.

Stormy plucked the flower out of her hair and attached it carefully to the car's rearview mirror with a hair clip.

"What's that for?" Marcus asked.

"Just brightening up Sammy." She paused. "Yes, yes, I know what you're going to say—"

"No, you don't," Marcus cut her off.

"Oh really?"

"I was going to say it looks . . . *interesting.*"

Stormy turned and smiled at him, and something in him softened. "I can work with 'interesting.'"

*Oh God, what was happening?*

Was he coming around to the "quirky Stormy charm," as Damien had described it?

# CHAPTER SEVENTEEN

## BE SURE TO WEAR SOME LEAVES IN YOUR HAIR

Stormy

*S*tormy wiggled her toes together. They were dusty from the dashboard, but a bit of dust never killed anyone. It certainly didn't bother her. But Marcus, on the other hand . . . She could imagine him as one of those people who disinfected *everything*.

His house was probably the picture of order. Clean. Organized and perfect. He probably had matching scatter cushions, which in Stormy's opinion were the most pointless things that had ever been invented. He probably had one of those flat-screen TVs the size of a wall and big, beige corner couch. He was by far one of the most uptight people she had ever met—not to mention a complete control freak. But on occasion he did surprise her, mainly when they were both naked.

She caught a glimpse of him out of the corner of her eye as he was fiddling with his new phone. Nothing irritated her more than phone-fiddling. These days, you couldn't go out with friends without them staring at their phones constantly instead of interacting with the people who were actually there in front of them. She'd just never understood it, this need that people had to exist in a cyber-computer world.

"What are you doing?" Stormy pointed at the glowing screen with disgust, as if it were some foreign creature—which to her, it was. *Where were the buttons, even?*

"Just sending an email to someone at work," Marcus replied distractedly, his fingers quickly gliding over the touch screen.

"Work!" Stormy scoffed loudly, unable to hide her contempt. "An email! Is that really necessary, Marcus?"

Marcus turned his head and met her eyes. He looked completely shocked and put out by her comment. "I beg your pardon?"

"Look around, Marcus. We're on holiday! An adventure. We're in a beautiful, exciting new country, and you're being all businessy businessy and sending emails."

"Businessy businessy?" he repeated.

"Yes!"

"Don't you mean business*like*?"

"Whatever." Stormy waved her hand dismissively. "The point is that you're missing out on what's in front of you in the real world, with your face buried in your phone like that. Plus, you'll get square eyes."

"Isn't that an old wives' tale about watching TV?" He sounded irritated now, and he wasn't doing a very good job of hiding it. "Besides, what else am I supposed to do to keep busy? We have a long drive ahead of us."

"You shouldn't fiddle with a phone while driving. It's dangerous."

"It's only dangerous when your car goes over twenty-five miles an hour," he responded quickly.

"Just put the phone down and look around you at the beauty that is this city!" Stormy waved her arms around. "Just look at it all."

"What am I meant to be looking at?" Marcus asked, momentarily looking up from his phone.

"At everything!" Stormy couldn't believe Marcus was even asking her that. Signs of the storm were still everywhere. Massive puddles the size of Jacuzzis covered the streets. There were broken tree branches on the sidewalks, rivers of brown water raced down the streets and into the drains, some of which were overflowing. But apart from all that, Stormy saw so much more. There was a hustle and bustle here. An energy that was so intoxicating and fascinating to watch. People walking, people running, people riding bicycles, weaving in and out of traffic, people cooking on the side of the road, a man riding a motorcycle with a chicken strapped to the back of it. Washing lines of colorful clothes stretched between retro-looking buildings, walls covered in bright graffiti and hundreds of hooting, flashing taxis jostling and pushing, *and wait* . . . was that a goat on the side of the road? And then in the middle of it, a shiny glass skyscraper surprised her. This place was the perfect mix of old and new. It was beautiful chaos, but there seemed to be an order to it too. A rhythm and a pace at which it moved and breathed and was absolutely, unequivocally, *alive*. This was Africa, after all. The place where it all began. Where it all started. It was the beating heart of everything, and Stormy could feel it. *Magical*.

"Okay, I've looked, now what must I do?" Marcus asked sarcastically, going back to his phone.

Stormy huffed. "I guess we could use this time to get to know each other. Have a real conversation. Using our mouths to make real words with our vocal cords . . . or have you forgotten how that works?"

Stormy wasn't sure her attempt at a joke had gone down well, because there was a sudden, long lull in the conversation. Maybe they had nothing to say when they weren't at each other's throats—or screaming out each other's names, drenched in sweat.

"Why is it that whenever we try to have a normal conversation, we argue?" Stormy asked, finally breaking the silence.

"I don't know," Marcus sighed, his tone much softer now, any signs of irritation gone.

"I never argue with people." Stormy took her feet off the dashboard and turned in her seat so that she was facing him.

Marcus turned to look at her momentarily, and to Stormy's utter amazement, he smiled at her and attempted to shrug his tense shoulders. Their eyes locked for a second before Marcus turned his attention back to the road. But it had been long enough for Stormy to feel a little tingle zip through her body.

This was ridiculous, she thought. Why was this man making her tingle when she didn't even like him?

## Marcus

Even her toes were ludicrous, Marcus noticed: each nail was painted a different color, and not normal toe colors like red or pink. Where the hell did you even get green and blue nail polish from anyway? Hang on, this wasn't the first time he'd seen her toes; an image of them on his shoulders suddenly popped into his head. He quickly pushed the thought out of his head and turned his attention back to the road ahead.

The road was long and fairly straight. His phone didn't indicate that they would be driving past anything particularly significant. They would be going through a national park, which was meant to be beautiful, but there was no time for stopping and admiring the view. He hoped Stormy understood that.

They'd been driving for a while now and the buildings and city began to give way to another landscape entirely. Marcus looked back down at his phone to make sure they were still on the right road, Mombasa Road. The further away from the city they drove, the less he could see of the storm. In fact, it looked dry out here, as if there hadn't been any rain at all. A thick band of bright-orange sand lined the sides of the crumbling, grey road. In the distance, green, undulating hills rose up in every direction. Dotted with massive power lines and broken up with thin, dusty-looking footpaths and roads, all of them crisscrossing like a massive spider's web. And then, as casually as ever, a zebra, languidly eating tall grasses on the side of the road.

"Look." Stormy almost took his eye out as her finger shot out and pointed at it.

"I can see it." Marcus pushed her hand away.

"I suppose you'd rather look at a picture of a zebra on the internet." Her tone oozed with sarcasm and he could sense her glaring at him. Marcus ignored her statement and went back to concentrating on the task at hand, driving. But a few moments later his concentration was broken my Stormy again.

*"If you're sailing to San Diego, be sure to wear some leaves in your hair."*

"What are you doing?" he asked, turning to look at her.

"Singing! Join me?"

"No, thanks."

"Why not?"

"I don't sing," Marcus said flatly.

"Maybe you should." Stormy gave him a very pointed look and he could almost hear those bloody words echoing in the car around them.

"It's *flowers*, by the way, not leaves," Marcus said quickly. Not even bothering to correct the rest of the very wrong lyrics.

Stormy paused and looked like she was taking this piece of information in. "Oh my gosh, that makes so much more sense. Thanks!" She smiled at him happily and then continued singing.

He let her sing. They'd probably argue if he asked her to stop, which might lead to her being pinned under him on the back seat or bent over the bonnet . . . Oh God, he couldn't stop picturing it . . .

Bonnet. Dress hiked up. Pinned. Hot.

"Stop, stop!" Stormy suddenly yelled as they approached what looked like a roadside market of sorts.

"No time," Marcus replied firmly. They had left the airport much later than he would have liked them to already.

Stormy swiveled in her seat and glared at him angrily. "Marcus, I command you to stop!"

"We are going to be late. We can't." He tapped his watch for added effect.

"What difference will ten minutes make? Look at it. We

should absorb the wonderful, colorful Kenyan culture while we're here."

"Kenyan culture, or any culture for that matter, is the last thing I want to absorb right now," Marcus argued back at her. "We are on a schedule! We have a deadline and we need to stick to it." He was getting angry now. Her total haphazard attitude towards time bothered him, immensely.

"I insist!" Stormy sounded determined and leaned over him. She grabbed the steering wheel, threatening to steer the car herself. The problem was that when she did, the close proximity made his body instantly react, and they were arguing again. Stormy obviously felt it too. Marcus couldn't help it; his fingers moved down, and involuntarily, he touched the back of her neck.

She let out a breathy whisper in response. "Marcus . . ."

His fingers moved even more, and suddenly he was tracing them down her exposed back, until . . .

"Fine, I'll stop the car." He skidded to a stop, pulled off his seat belt and threw himself out of the car at the speed of light. He moved away quickly, leaving Stormy to stare after him.

This road trip was such a bad idea. There was no way that they were going to get all the way to Mombasa without something happening between them. The prospect both excited him and scared the shit out of him. This thing between him and Stormy had totally blindsided him. He hadn't planned for any of it to happen, and he didn't like that.

He turned and looked at Stormy, who was still in the car, staring after him. She had a twinkle in her eyes—those big green eyes—and she was biting down on her bottom lip in a way that was making him crazy.

# CHAPTER EIGHTEEN

## BRING HOME THE BACON AND SARONGS

⌒

Stormy

*T*he market assaulted every one of Stormy's senses. For starters, it was boiling hot outside, and the air felt sticky and thick. Makeshift stalls had been set up along narrow, dusty paths and were selling everything from fresh exotic fruit and pungent fish, to huge bags of brightly colored spices and intricate beaded jewelry. There were just so many sights to take in; there was something new and interesting around every corner. And she was in her absolute element.

Intense smells filled the air—the sweet perfume of ripening fruit, the deep exotic scent of spices and the hearty aroma of corncobs cooking on fires. The biggest bunches of bananas that Stormy had ever seen lined the dusty walkways, alongside bright-orange mangoes and rows upon rows of handmade brown leather sandals.

But what really caught her eye were the rows of brightly colored fabrics that were blowing in the breeze, as well as the brightly dyed straw handbags. All were printed and decorated with the most beautiful traditional imagery she'd ever seen. It was culturally different from the African imagery that she was used to in South Africa—this was unique to Kenya. And she loved it. In fact, she wished she could buy some for Annie, her famous clothing designer friend, because she could see Annie's excitement as she morphed these fabrics into belts and hats.

One of the local vendors offered Stormy a slice of juicy mango as she went prancing past, which she took enthusiastically. But Marcus—or should she say the hygiene police—practically jumped on her from a few meters away and pulled her back by the arm.

"Hey!" he whispered urgently in her ear. "You can't eat food given to you by complete strangers on the side of the road!"

"Of course you can," she responded, popping it into her mouth. "People do it all over the world."

"Just because people eat street food all over the world, it doesn't make it right. Or healthy." He widened his eyes at her and that little line between his brows was back again.

Marcus grabbed the mango out from between her lips. "They probably wash it in unsanitary water. You don't know what germs you'll catch."

Stormy burst out laughing. "Oh Marcus, Marcus. You worry too much!" And with that, she swiped the mango back from him and ate it. It was so sweet and succulent that some of the juice escaped her lips and ran down her chin; she wiped it away with the back of her hand.

"Amazing," she muttered through her full mouth. "We have to buy some."

"I am *not* buying street food," he said adamantly.

"Aren't you hungry?"

Marcus looked hesitant as he thought for a moment. "I am, but I have some protein bars in the car."

"Protein bars!" Stormy scoffed loudly. Who ever heard of such a ridiculous thing? "You call that food?"

"They're perfectly nutritious," Marcus insisted. "In fact, they contain a list of essential nutrients and vitamins and just the right amount of carbs."

Stormy couldn't help herself, but she smiled at Marcus. It was hard not to when he was being so ridiculous. She reached out and touched the side of his face, "Oh, Marcus, Marcus, Marcus," she said, looking at him.

"Yes?" he asked, sounding tentative.

"Sometimes, you are just so misguided."

"Misguided?" He sounded shocked now. "How am I misguided?"

Stormy smiled at him again and shrugged, before walking away to sample more of the local fruits. She gave a quick glance behind her at Marcus, who looked utterly confused.

A few moments later, she came across a stall selling the most incredible-looking and -smelling vegetable kebabs. Her mouth watered as she watched the vendor take them straight off the fire, slightly charred.

"Very nice," the vendor, a regal, older-looking woman with a maze of deep lines in her face and a bright-purple headscarf, said as she held one out to Stormy.

"It looks amazing, but I don't have any money," Stormy said apologetically.

The woman smiled and pointed to one of Stormy's bracelets, a pink plastic thing that she'd picked up in a charity store years ago.

"You'll exchange?" Stormy's face lit up.

The woman nodded and Stormy quickly pulled off her bracelet. She walked off eating the kebab; it was delicious, and there was some kind of spicy sauce on it that she couldn't quite put her finger on. But again, the hygiene police pounced.

"Stop eating stuff here." Marcus sounded like he was bordering on panic. "Those things are probably full of bacteria." He pointed at the veggies.

Stormy eyeballed Marcus incredulously. "These are veggies, probably better than the ones we get at home, plucked fresh from someone's truly organic veggie garden, watered by loving African rains, warmed by the fat Kenyan sun and fertilized by falling leaves. Try it."

"I'm not trying it."

"I *dare* you." Stormy shot him a challenging look. Marcus stared back at her, she could see he was busy trying to make his mind up, and then suddenly, he grabbed the kebab from her hands and took a massive bite.

"Satisfied?" he asked, not looking particularly thrilled as he forced it down.

Stormy nodded and smiled. Maybe Marcus wasn't as far gone as she initially thought, maybe she could loosen him up after all. Mr. Uptight and In Control could do with some loosening, that's for sure.

They'd already been walking around the market for ten

minutes, a fact Marcus made sure to tell her by tapping on his big, shiny watch. She sighed loudly, but started walking back to the car. She had said ten minutes, after all—fair's fair. But on the way out, she couldn't help stopping at the fabrics stall to try one on. It was one of the prettiest things she'd ever seen: a bright, lime-green color, with what looked like hand-dyed dark-green flowers printed on it. There was a delicate blue stitch around the border coupled with a bold purple stripe. It was a sarong, but Stormy wrapped it around her shoulders like a shawl. The woman tending the stall indicated through gestures that the colors suited Stormy's hair.

"Buy it?" she asked Stormy.

Stormy shook her head. "I would love to, but I have no money."

Marcus walked up behind her. "How much?" he asked the woman, reaching into his wallet.

Stormy swung around and took the sarong off quickly. "No. I don't want you to buy it for me. You've already bought me clothes, I couldn't—"

"Don't be silly, Stormy."

"No." She shook her head emphatically.

"But I *want* to," he said with a look in his eye that Stormy was completely unfamiliar with. It was that whole, *I'm-a-man-let-me-provide-for-you-and-bring-home-the-bacon-and-sarongs* type of look. Still, it didn't sit right with her. She did not accept charity from people—ever.

"Okay. What about an exchange?" she asked, quickly thinking up a solution.

Marcus eyed her up and down. "Um . . . I don't think you have anything I want." Stormy couldn't help but notice his guilty expression as he quickly looked away, though, and realized that he wasn't quite being truthful. But that wasn't the kind of exchange she'd had in mind.

"How about I give you a Reiki crystal healing session, get those chakras unblocked?"

Marcus shook his head. "Absolutely not. There will be no massaging happening, Stormy."

Stormy rolled her eyes at him. "There's no touching involved. I'm just going to put some crystals on your throat and draw out some negative energy, that's all."

Marcus eyed her suspiciously. "Is that the only way you'll let me get it for you?"

"Yes. I don't want your charity."

"It's not charity—" he tried to argue.

She held her hand up to stop anything else coming out of his mouth. "Reiki healing vibes, or no deal."

"Fine." Marcus shook his head, pulling the money out of his wallet and handing it over to the vendor.

Stormy turned and extended her hand. "Deal. Let's shake on it. A business transaction."

Marcus shook her hand, dropping it quickly when they were done. She skipped off to the car happily, the bright fabric billowing out behind her.

## Marcus

She was like an excitable puppy with a squeaky toy. Marcus had never seen anything like it. She flounced around from one stall to the next; everyone who saw her smiled and made conversation. She had even kicked a ball back (very badly) to a few kids that were playing a game of soccer and had even scratched the head of a stray three-legged dog—which Marcus hadn't thought was a terribly good idea.

And the more he'd watched her move around, the more he'd realized how much like that one flower popping out of the crack in the concrete she was. There was something rare about her. Mind you, certain diseases were also rare, and that didn't mean you wanted them.

And then there was that other side of her, which was less excitable puppy and more sexual she-wolf. And when the mango juice had trickled down her chin, he'd actually had to fight the urge to lick it off, despite his misgivings about rancid water and exotic germs.

And when he'd seen her wearing the shawl, he'd been overcome with the desire to buy it for her. In fact, he would have bought her the whole damn stall if she'd asked. *Fuck*, he'd been so eager to buy it for her that he had agreed to some weird, hippie crystal ritual. He'd definitely try and wiggle his way out of that.

They finally climbed into the car and by this stage, Marcus *was* hungry. He reached over into the back seat and pulled out his bag of healthy snacks he'd bought at the airport. He took out one of the protein bars—it was a brand he'd never tried before—and started to open it.

He could feel Stormy's judgmental eyes on him as he raised it to his lips and was about to take his first bite.

"You know," she said, "that looks like someone chewed cardboard, then regurgitated it and squished it into a shape."

Marcus turned slowly and looked at her.

"And I bet it tastes like that too." She pointed at the bar, crinkling her nose up in a way that was, quite frankly, fucking adorable.

"It doesn't," Marcus countered. "In fact, they taste very nice." He bit into the bar and quickly tried to hide his true feelings. The thing tasted hideous. *Terrible.* It had clearly been sitting on the shelf for years and he wondered how far past its expiry date it was. But he wasn't going to give Stormy the satisfaction.

"Mmmm," he mumbled, "good." He forced himself to swallow and smiled at her. She shook her head and turned back to the front. When she wasn't looking, he stuffed the bar under the seat and turned the key in the ignition, ready to head off again.

He hoped there wouldn't be too many of these impromptu stops, because it would make them seriously late. She put her rainbow toes back onto the dashboard and her skirt slipped down her thighs again; thankfully, she laid her new sarong over them.

But something was niggling at him. "Do you often exchange services for things?" Marcus asked, trying to sound casual.

"Yup, all the time."

"Like what?"

"Well, I needed to have a pair of shoes repaired the other day, and I gave the man a neck massage—he had a knot that was giving him trouble."

Uneasiness shot through him. "You often give massages?"

"Not always, sometimes I'll do a Tarot reading."

"But you *do* give massages sometimes?" Marcus was harping, he knew he was, but he couldn't get that image out of his head.

"If you are trying to imply what you're trying to imply then your implications are way off what is implied," she said indignantly.

"Huh?" Marcus hadn't understood a word of that; once more she'd unnecessarily overused a word in a sentence to the point of it becoming nonsensical. Something he'd noticed she did from time to time.

"My massages do not have any kind of happy endings, if that's what you mean. Although I was offered a job like that once."

"You were what?!" Marcus swung round and looked at her.

"I didn't accept it, silly!" she said, brushing him off. "Besides, the guy who fixed my shoes, Luigi, is about a hundred years old. He was having headaches, and I wanted to help him. We exchanged services—simple. I often do it."

Marcus still didn't like it. He wondered how many men bartered with her just to get a back rub.

"There is nothing sexual about it!" Stormy added. "You'll see tonight when I work my magic on your chakras." She smiled at him innocently before putting her head back and closing her eyes.

It was boiling hot and extremely unpleasant in the car without aircon. Marcus rolled the window down and let the wind rush in. He hoped it wouldn't disturb her—she'd fallen asleep. He glanced over and noticed that a strand of bright-pink hair was blowing around in the breeze. He reached over and gently tucked it behind her ear so that it wouldn't wake her.

She stirred ever so slightly and he was about to take his hand away, when she grabbed it and held it next to her face. Still asleep, she tucked their hands together on her shoulder and rested her head on them.

Marcus's first thought was to move it, pull it away from her. But he didn't. He just left his hand there. He could easily steer with one hand and he found himself smiling softly as he fixed his eyes on the road ahead.

# CHAPTER NINETEEN

## SLOW AND STEADY
## WINS THE PRIZE

~

Stormy

*S*tormy woke up suddenly and realized that Marcus was no longer in the car. They were parked on the side of the road and the driver's door was wide open. Panic gripped her and she shot up. *Where was he?*

Alien abduction? That was very plausible; it often happened on long, deserted roads like this. But then again, it was daytime, and most abductions happened at night. But why would they have taken Marcus and not her? She was much more interesting than him.

She was just about to consider other, more drastic options (she usually never went for the most logical ones first) when she turned and saw him standing on the side of the road.

*Aaahhh*, nature was obviously calling. She was about to look away when she saw him bend forward and hold his head. Something was wrong. She jumped out of the car and ran over.

"Marcus, are you okay?"

He waved his hand for her to get back. "Fine. Fine," he sort of shouted-mumbled-choked.

"No, you're not. I can see something is wrong."

He waved his hand some more as she edged forward. "I just feel a bit nauseous. It's probably from that kebab you forced me to eat."

Stormy burst out laughing. "Nonsense!"

"You can't eat stuff off the side of the road. I *told* you. Look what happens!"

Stormy shook her head dismissively. "It's psychosomatic, Marcus. I'm totally fine. There was nothing wrong with—"

Marcus turned around and looked at her. He was positively green; his brow was wrinkled and his lips clamped together as he fought off the obvious urge to gag.

"Oh God! You really are sick."

Marcus gave a faint nod. "Just get back into the car, I'll be fine."

"I'm not leaving you here."

She approached him and his hand started flapping at her again. Clearly, he was the type of guy who didn't want anyone seeing him when he was sick and vulnerable—*typical*. But as she approached he threw up, and the arm waving became even more violent as he tried to shoo her away. Jolted by a stab of sympathy, Stormy ran up to him and rubbed his back.

"Stormy, seriously, leave me, I'll be fine," he choked.

"Marcus, will you stop being such a macho . . ." She put on a mocking, exaggerated manly voice. "*I'm-a-man-and-don't-get-sick-or-show-weakness-and-I-wrestle-bulls-to-the-ground-with-my-hands-tied-behind-my-back* kind of guy."

He ignored her jibe, wiped the back of his mouth with his hand and swigged down some water. She rubbed his back in large circles. "Do you know how many friends' hair I've held back when they've had too much to drink in a club?" she tried to reassure him.

"I don't really want to know that right now," Marcus bleated.

"I'm just saying . . . It's no big deal. You don't have to be embarrassed."

Marcus finally stood up and straightened out. He looked way less green but still a bit sick. Stormy reached out and laid her hand across his forehead to see if he had a temperature. He felt clammy.

"It's a good thing you've thrown up, actually. You got whatever was bugging you, probably that protein bar, out of your system," Stormy said.

"It wasn't the protein bar," he protested feebly.

"Okay. Whatever." Stormy smiled as Marcus walked off to the car again and climbed into the driver's seat. She eyed him worriedly; he didn't look well enough to drive.

"Why don't you lie down in the back and I'll drive?" she offered.

Marcus peered into the back. She knew what he was thinking, that there would be no space for his huge frame.

"I know," she said, "we could open the windows and you could stick your legs out." She reached inside and started struggling with the window, only to realize that the back windows didn't open.

"I know," she said again, "we could push the seat back and you could put your legs in the trunk." She started trying to wrestle with the back seats.

"The engine is at the back," Marcus said flatly.

"I know," she said again and then paused, realizing she didn't know at all. "Just climb in the back and try to relax."

## Marcus

Marcus hated this. He hated showing weakness of any kind and he hated not being in control and letting someone else take over. But he was still feeling a little sick and probably shouldn't drive. He was trying his hardest to get comfortable in the back, but even with the passenger seat pulled as far forward as it could go to give him more space, his legs were still cramped.

"Are you sure you can drive?" he asked nervously, watching as Stormy adjusted the rearview mirror ten times. "Do you even have a driver's license?"

She turned to him and smiled. "Don't worry, Sammy and I have an understanding," she said, as though he should be reassured by this. Which he wasn't.

"Just feel better," she commanded as she started turning the key in the ignition. Marcus couldn't remember the last time he'd ever had to stick a key into an ignition. His car didn't even need a key, it sensed the key and opened and closed for him automatically. The joys of modern technology. This car, however, had nothing that even vaguely resembled modern technology, or just plain technology for that matter!

As they pulled onto the road again, Marcus tried really hard to relax, but quickly realized that wouldn't be possible—Stormy was officially the worst driver he'd ever met. The car was moving at about ten kilometers an hour and every time she changed gears, the car sounded like it was going to explode and lurched forward for a second.

"It's okay, Sammy," she would croon every time the car made a noise. "Easy, girl, you're doing great!" And then she would proceed to pat the dashboard encouragingly. Thankfully, after several very, very long and terrifying kilometers, he was feeling a lot better.

"Okay, stop the car," he finally said, sitting up in the back seat.

"Why? Sammy and I are having so much fun together!" She looked at Marcus with a smile in the rearview mirror.

"Stormy, we'll only get there next year if I let you carry on at this pace."

"Remember, Marcus, slow and steady wins the prize," she said cheerfully.

"Please, just let me drive," he beseeched.

"Nope!" She shook her head.

"You're going to destroy the gearbox," he quickly added.

"Sammy's gearbox is perfectly fine, Marcus. And I'm happy driving."

Marcus sighed loudly. "Okay, how do I put this tactfully . . ."

"Put what tactfully?" she asked, clearly oblivious to where Marcus was about to take this.

"You are a terrible driver." He came out with it.

"What?" She sounded genuinely shocked by his statement.

"That's why I want to drive," he said.

"That is so rude!" Stormy turned around and glared at him, and the car momentarily veered to the left.

"Hey! Watch the road!" Marcus yelled. "Okay. That's it. Stop. Pull over."

"Fine, big macho man. Drive the car then!" Stormy swung the steering wheel wildly and the car swerved onto the shoulder of the road. She climbed out in a huff and went back to the passenger seat.

Marcus resumed his spot in the driver's seat and started the car up again. But he soon became acutely aware of the fact that Stormy was silently glaring at him with those piercing green eyes.

"What?" he asked, turning towards her.

"Just interested," she replied simply.

"In what?"

"In you, Mr. Marcus Lewis, Aries."

"What about me?" Marcus was feeling a little like he was under attack.

"You're an interesting person. Under that big, hard, powerful, in-control, macho exterior lies a vulnerable little person who hates to appear so," she informed him matter-of-factly.

"Oh God, are we really going to do this? This esoteric, touchy-feely crap?"

"It's not esoteric, it's factual. I mean, look at you—you would probably still insist on driving if both your arms were eaten off by wild, rabid lions. That's what a total control freak you are."

"Rabid lions?" Marcus was amused now. "Where do you come up with this stuff?"

"Stop trying to maneuver the conversation in a different angle."

"Direction," he corrected automatically again. "And I'm not, I'm just not comfortable talking about stuff like this."

"That's because you have a blocked throat chakra. It makes it hard to express your emotions or speak your truth."

"That has nothing to do with my fucking chakra." Honestly, if Marcus had to hear the word "chakra" one more time that day, he might actually go mad.

"Admit it, you're hiding the real Marcus under a mask. A big, smooth, shiny, perfectly disinfected, mask."

"What? That's the most ridiculous thing I've ever heard."

"Is it?" she asked. He could feel her green eyes boring a hole into the side of his head.

"Do we have to talk about this?" He was feeling very uncomfortable now. "I don't like talking about personal stuff."

"Marcus," Stormy tutted loudly, "we've had sex, *really, really, seriously, amazing sex*, twice—what could be more personal than that?"

Marcus swallowed. He really didn't need to be reminded of that, and certainly not how good it had been. His first instinct was to ask her "How good?"—and then show her that it could be even better (over and over again). But he resisted the urge.

"Fine! Then how about this, Stormy-Rain Rainbow Storm, Sagittarius: let me tell you something about *yourself*, since we are on the topic of masks."

"Sure!" she agreed, sounding perky and upbeat, as if she actually enjoyed such conversations. She probably did.

"I think that if anyone in this car has a mask on, it's you. A bright, crazy colorful one that hides someone else entirely inside." Marcus flashed her a look. "That deep and touchy-feely enough for you?"

"Really?" She was starting to sound slightly tentative now.

"Yes," he said. "You're already unique, you don't need to over-advertise it with all that glittery, fluffy crap and crazy scarves.

Your hair is growing on me, though, but you don't need all that other stuff. I mean, do you have any idea how beautiful you are without all that . . ." Marcus bit his lip, cutting off the rest of his sentence.

Shit. He *really* hadn't meant to say it out loud.

# CHAPTER TWENTY

## VLAD THE IMPALER

⌒

Stormy

*S*tormy smiled. *Beautiful.* He thought she was beautiful. Her stomach was doing a weird seesaw thing. She was used to being called many things, but she hadn't heard that one in a while. People usually referred to her as "colorful," "interesting," or her worst, "artistic," as if that was meant as some kind of a disguised insult. But beautiful? Nope, that she hadn't heard in quite some time.

"You like my hair?" she asked, twirling it around her finger, and not because she was agitated this time.

Marcus cast a sideways glance at her and shrugged. "Well, there's no one else in the world could pull it off. But that scarf and sunflower dress . . . truth be told, I'm glad your bag is lost, if those clothes you were wearing are any indication of what else there is."

"*What?*" Stormy screeched playfully and smacked him on the arm. "I can't believe you don't like Milly!"

"Who's Milly?" he asked, bewildered.

"My scarf."

Marcus shook his head and smiled. "Of course you named your scarf. Why wouldn't you? It makes perfect sense to name items of clothing and inanimate objects, like this car."

"Some men name their penises," Stormy quickly added.

"You did not just say that!" Marcus sounded shocked.

"Do you have a name for yours?" she asked, leaning towards him in her seat and watching to see how long it would take that little line to appear between his brows. It usually happened when he was uncomfortable, agitated or angry. Which was always!

"No!" He shook his head. "Absolut—I mean, no!" He sounded defensive and the little line was starting to form.

"It's okay if you do, Marcus. I once dated a guy who called his Vlad."

"What?"

"Like the Impaler. You know, Vlad the Impaler, because he used to imp—"

"I got it, Stormy. I got it! Trust me, I definitely got it. It's just not something I'm enjoying picturing, thanks."

"Oh, I never met Vlad, if that's what you're thinking," she quickly added. Stormy was really open-minded but having sex with a man who had named his penis "the impaler" and, worse, had actually openly admitted to it, was not her cup of chai tea.

"Can we just stop talking about this . . . *stuff*?" Marcus shuffled in his seat, he looked wildly uncomfortable, and truth be told, Stormy loved it when he was like that.

"Marcus," she leaned in even more, "how is it that you can do what you do in bed, and on the floor for that matter, and let's not leave out the wall, and still be so uncomfortable talking about penises and can barely say the word 'sex' out loud?"

This time Marcus swung around and looked at her. "That's not true. I just don't think it's something you should talk about out loud with people. It's not very gentlemanly, is it?"

"Are you a gentleman, Marcus?" Stormy asked, feeling very amused by this.

"Yes. I like to think of myself as one, especially in relationships," he said.

"So, you open the car door and pull out the seat for your dates, then?" Stormy was curious about this. There had been nothing gentlemanly about him earlier, that's for sure.

"Yes, I would," he said.

"Well, I think that's rather chauvinist actually, Marcus," Stormy said. "You're assuming the woman *wants* a man to pull out her chair. As if she isn't capable of doing it on her own, what with her inferior little lady muscles. Maybe she doesn't even want to sit on the chair, ever thought about that? Maybe she'd like to sit on the floor?"

There was a pause, and she could see he looked thoughtful. "I've never thought about it like that," he finally said. "Don't worry, I'll never pull your chair out or hold the door open for you."

"Good!" Stormy quickly replied. "I would hate for you to think I wasn't capable of my own door opening."

"Trust me. No one would ever think that about you, Stormy." Marcus took his eyes off the road and faced her, looking deep into her eyes. And the second he did, that feeling was back. The little zip. The fizz deep inside and—

"Stop!" Stormy suddenly shouted, getting totally distracted as something caught her eye. "Giraffes! Look!" There were several giraffes standing just off the road behind a fence.

"We must be driving past the game reserve," Marcus said as he slowed the car down and pulled onto the side of the road.

"Can I take a super quickie look?" she pleaded. "Two minutes." Stormy crossed her heart with her hand. "Cross my heart, hope to die, stick a pin in my eye."

"I haven't heard that since I was about six," Marcus said chuckling. "Two minutes," he reiterated, shooting her a look.

"Two minutes. I promise." She threw her hands in the air. "Goddess, forbid we run late for anything," she mocked as she opened the door and stepped out of the car into the scorching heat. The tiny fan in the car had been providing more cool than she had initially imagined, and the difference between the inside and the outside of the car was huge. She walked towards the fence, hearing Marcus behind her.

Stormy marveled at the giraffes. They were majestic animals, so strangely disproportionate and yet at the same time perfectly designed. "I wish I'd brought my camera," she sighed longingly. She had an old camera that still shot on film. A friend of hers developed the pictures for her, since everyone was digital these days.

"You have a camera?" Marcus seemed shocked at the idea as he came and stood next to her.

Stormy rolled her eyes at Marcus and he returned the look with a bemused shake of his head. "I'm not *that* behind the times," she countered. "I know you probably think I'm from prehistoric times because I don't have a Facebook."

At that, Marcus laughed out loud. "I would never expect

Stormy-Rain to have a Facebook account. That would be pushing it." He took a step closer to her and started digging in his pocket. "Here." He took out his phone and handed it to her. Stormy took it in her hands and held it like she was holding something contagious.

"I had one of these e-phones for about one week once. I still don't know how to use them, though," she mumbled, eyeing the thing suspiciously.

"It's an iPhone, but close enough," he said, smiling.

Marcus moved in closer, and Stormy felt his shoulder touch hers as he stood next to her and held the phone out in front of them for the tutorial. Stormy took a slight—and unnecessary—step closer to Marcus. She liked the feel of his shoulder next to hers.

"See, this is the camera. Hold it up, press this," he demonstrated by turning it on her, "and there. We have a photo."

"And how do I see it?" Stormy asked, staring at the shiny contraption with no buttons—that had always mystified her. She knew she was harping on this but, buttons. You needed buttons, people.

"Like this." Marcus showed her how to find the phone's photo album and her picture popped up. "And you can scroll through them by doing this," he said as he moved his finger across the screen and the next picture popped up.

Stormy felt like someone had poked her in the ribs. The screen was suddenly filled with the most beautiful woman she'd ever seen. She was the kind of woman who could literally stop traffic, with her long red locks and pouty lips. She had that whole 1950s bombshell thing going on—curvy and elegant. She was wearing a skintight red dress, showing off perhaps the biggest breasts that had ever grown on a woman's chest. Her waist was tiny, her hips rounded and her shapely legs were so damn *long*. She was looking into the camera seductively, there was no two ways about it. She had her hand up and her finger was beckoning the photographer closer. Her eyes were screaming bedroom words—dirty words. Filthy words. The photographer was Marcus, and this was one of those pictures that shouted "have sex with me *now*."

"Uh . . . wh-who's that?" Stormy stuttered a little. She hadn't meant to.

"Um . . ." Marcus sounded tentative, as if he hadn't meant for her to see the picture. And why would he? It was clearly a photograph taken seconds before hot sex, with a very hot woman. "Emma. My ex," he explained.

"She's very beautiful," Stormy managed, but barely. She was too busy picturing this woman on top of him, her ridiculous boobs bobbing up and down. (Those things could probably take someone's eye out if she wasn't careful, possibly even a ceiling fan!)

"I guess she is," Marcus muttered, and quickly flicked back to the photo of Stormy.

"So . . . how long have you been broken up?" Stormy couldn't quite believe she actually cared so much and was venturing down this line of questioning.

"A month."

"So recently." She didn't like the way those words had sounded. They came out fast and desperate, sounding like someone who might be jealous. Which she was not! *Obviously*.

## Marcus

Marcus was finding this conversation very awkward, especially given the nature of the photo—there was no misinterpreting it. No mistaking that look Emma had in her eye. He remembered exactly what had happened the second he put the phone down and walked towards her . . . At the time, he'd considered her to be one of the sexiest women he'd ever met, not to mention the best in bed (by far); but now, all that had *very* unexpectedly changed.

"The break-up was inevitable," Marcus explained, trying to smooth things over. For some desperate reason, he didn't want Stormy to think he was pining for someone else. "I'm totally over her, if that's what you're worried about."

Stormy turned to face him. "Why would I be worried if you were over her?" She sounded indignant.

"Uh . . ." Marcus was grappling for a reason. "Just in case you think I was, um . . ." He sighed, giving up. "I don't know why I said that."

"I mean, it's not like that matters to me," Stormy responded, shrugging. "It's not like I care if you're thinking about her big breasts."

"What? No. I'm not thinking about her breasts," Marcus said.

"I wouldn't blame you if you were," she replied. "I'll probably think about her breasts myself."

"You'd think about her—" Marcus could barely finish that sentence. Suddenly he was imagining Stormy thinking about breasts.

"Oh no! No!" she quickly said. "That's not what I mean." She flapped her arms in front of him. "I did *say* that, but I didn't *mean* it. Not like that anyway. I'm not into women or anything, except for that one time when I was nineteen and I went out with that girl for about a week, but we just kissed, once. I mainly liked her hair."

"Uh . . . Uh . . ." Marcus's mind was filled with all sorts of images now. Images he wasn't sure he was ever going to forget. "I think we should put an end to this conversation. Right now."

"Why?" she asked, looking genuinely confused. Marcus blushed and Stormy suddenly gasped.

"Oh my Goddess, you were thinking about me kissing a girl, weren't you?" she asked, a massive smile breaking out across her face.

"No," he quickly denied it. But he could see she wasn't buying it.

"It's okay if you were." She smiled sweetly and started rocking from side to side. "In fact, it's kind of hot."

Marcus threw his hands in the air. "Right. This conversation is officially over now."

"Fine," Stormy said, a playful smile lighting up her face. "But I don't know why you're getting so worked up about all this, I mean, it's not like you and I are a—"

"No. I didn't say that," Marcus cut her off.

"This thing going on between us isn't even a thing," Stormy added.

"It's not even going on anymore," Marcus said.

"Exacto-mundo!" Stormy exclaimed. "It's like, we had sex twice, *no big deal really*, and now we're just road trip buddies," she offered.

"Exactly."

"Exactly."

"So true." Stormy's eyes drifted over Marcus, from top to bottom, and his skin tingled under the intensity of her gaze.

"True," he whispered back.

"Yes. So, so totally true," she said, getting all breathy.

"Totally . . ."

"Yup."

"Indeed."

"Yup."

But the way they were looking at each other, and the way their words were getting softer and slower and breathier, told a different story. And then, silence as they stood there staring at each other. Marcus cleared his throat, breaking the strange spell that had fallen over them.

"We should probably get back on the road." He tapped his watch and started walking back to the car.

"Wait," Stormy called after him. "What's that thing that Lilly is always doing with her phone . . . where she holds the phone and takes a photo of herself . . . a selfie?"

"You want to take a selfie?" he asked.

"Yes, with the giraffes in the background!"

"Uh . . . sure." Marcus walked back over to her and held the phone up. They moved closer together and as he pressed the button, Stormy smiled and put her head on his shoulder.

The giraffes behind them made a sudden noise, and Stormy turned to investigate further. Marcus looked at his phone and flicked through the pictures.

*Fuck*, she was beautiful. That thought still surprised him, even though he'd thought it several times today already.

He zoomed in on her face and stared at her features. A naughty pixie. That's what she reminded him of. Or a colorful character from a Manga comic book.

He flicked to the picture of Emma again and looked at her—looked at the woman that ninety percent of the men in the world would find hot. Suddenly she did nothing for him anymore.

# CHAPTER TWENTY-ONE

## DUCKS OF A FEATHER

~

Stormy

*S*tormy didn't like what she'd just seen.

The way Marcus had been staring at the picture of Emma after they'd taken their selfie together, when he thought she'd been looking at the giraffes. He'd been gaping. Open-mouthed even. He'd been lying to her. He was longing to paw her again—it was obvious. They were back in the car and driving again, and Stormy was desperate to know the truth . . .

"So, shame . . . A break-up, hey?" Ambiguous. Pointed in the right direction, yet discreet and friendly sounding. Or not, judging by the look that had just swished across Marcus's face.

"Huh?"

"Your ex, hey. A month ago, huh? Harsh. Hectic. I mean, shame. Sorry." That had sounded a bit too staccato for her liking.

Maybe she wasn't doing such a great job of hiding her feelings after all.

"Not really. It wasn't working, for me anyway," Marcus said, eyeing Stormy suspiciously. She had a feeling he was starting to see where the conversation was going, and she noticed a tiny smile on his face.

"Why the sudden interest?" he asked. "I thought we'd spoken about all that?"

"No reason. None. Just, you know, thinking out loud, per se, et cetera, and so forth," she replied in what she hoped was a vague, innocent tone.

"About what?"

"Nothing really! Just thought I would offer condolences."

"She's not dead," Marcus smirked.

"No, but you look like you miss her." Marcus slowed the car down and turned to look at Stormy properly.

"Why do you say that?" he asked, sounding genuinely surprised.

"Just the way you were looking at her picture on your phone. You looked sad, like you love her but can't have her, in that whole parting-is-such-sweet-sorrow-Romeo-and-Juliet-drinking-poison kind of way. That's all."

## Marcus

Marcus found himself in an interesting predicament. A part of him wanted to tell Stormy that he'd been looking at a picture of *her*, but how could he admit to that?

"You must have misinterpreted the look," he said.

"No, I didn't. I don't misinterpret looks," she insisted. "I've acted, remember. I know looks, Marcus. I can *see* looks."

"You were far away, standing by the fence," he countered.

"I can read people like a page, Marcus."

"Like a book."

"Stop changing the subject. I can *see* it." She was getting increasingly agitated, and for some reason, the thought that Stormy was jealous of Emma sent a little thrill up his spine.

"See what?"

"You're longing for her."

"I swear to you, I'm not."

Stormy scoffed loudly. "Okay, fine. Pick a card." She pulled a pack of small Tarot cards out of her handbag. They looked old, worn and grubby—she obviously took them everywhere. "The cards never lie," she said imperiously. "They will uncover the truth."

"That's ridiculous, Stormy."

"Are you afraid to reveal your true feelings?"

"What true feelings? There are no true feelings to—"

She cut him off. "Then just pick a card, Marcus."

"Fine." Marcus sighed loudly. This was absolutely ridiculous, of course, but he didn't have much of a choice—she had practically shoved them up his nose while he was trying to drive. They had a strange smell, too—like something old and dusty. He almost sneezed.

"Wait, don't choose one yet," she quickly said and began digging in her bag again. Marcus watched her out of the corner of his eye. She pulled out a pair of the oldest-looking glasses he'd ever seen.

"Oh fudge!" she half mumbled to herself, as she held the pair of glasses up and one of its arms fell off. He could see that it had been previously sellotaped. *Were those really her reading glasses?* One of the lenses was cracked and they looked like those glasses that women in the eighties had worn, back when their hair was big and their eye shadow was very blue.

"No worries," she said, again, as if talking to herself. She dug in her bag some more and this time emerged with a piece of gum. She put it in her mouth and started chewing.

"No!" Marcus immediately said when he saw where this was going. "You are not, not, thinking of sticking your glasses back together with gum?"

"It's only temporary." She seemed so unperturbed by this, he couldn't believe it.

He watched in utter jaw-dropping horror as she pulled some gum out of her mouth, rolled it into a tiny piece and then went about gluing her glasses back together.

"Oh my God!" Marcus finally managed. "I can't . . . I mean, you didn't . . . you . . ." He was stumbling, but what he really wanted to say was, "What the fuck, Stormy?"

"What?" She looked so nonchalant about the whole thing, as if she'd glued other things together with unhygienic, germ-ridden gum all the time. "It's just gum."

"From your mouth," he added.

"Just choose a card and stop getting your knickers in such a mess." She shoved the cards back under his nose.

"Fine." He pulled a card out and handed it over to her.

She immediately gasped. "The Star. I knew it."

"Please . . . what does that even mean? It doesn't prove

anything," Marcus said dismissively, thinking how truly stupid this whole exercise was. He was shocked that he was even participating in it.

"Um . . ." She swiveled her head dramatically and looked at him knowingly. Her glasses were terrible. Too huge for her face, a hideous tortoiseshell color and completely skew. *But fuck*, she looked adorable in them.

"The Star," she smacked her hand on the dashboard, as if trying to add some dramatic emphasis, "the Star signifies hope, expectation, promises and opportunities not fulfilled, desires disappointed," she rattled off.

"You're making that up." There was no way it meant that. That was way too convenient.

"Why don't you check it on the World Wide Web you're so fond of, if you don't believe me."

Marcus looked over at her, torn between exasperation and the desire to laugh. Who the hell said "World Wide Web" anymore? That was *so* Stormy.

He pulled the car over to the side of the road and whipped his phone out. The reception was painfully slow, but he eventually found what he was looking for and started reading the meaning of the card out loud.

"Oh . . . Hope, expectation, promises and opportunities not fulfilled, desires disappointed . . . I see."

Stormy crossed her arms and looked at him triumphantly.

Marcus had no idea how it had happened, that he'd pulled out the card that proved everything Stormy had been trying to say—it was obviously not true at all, but he knew Stormy believed in that crap and he didn't want her thinking that he was longing for his ex.

"Maybe I wasn't looking at her picture," he said, cringing at the coyness in his own voice.

"Oh . . ." She sounded shocked. "So, you have pictures of *other* women on that phone then, too?"

"No, just one other woman."

He looked at Stormy pointedly, and her eyes came up to meet his. Something flashed between them. Something that pulsed with charge and made him want to reach over and, and . . . God knows what!

"You were looking at me?" Stormy asked shyly, not taking her eyes off him. The gum clearly wasn't really doing its job and the arm was falling off so her glasses looked ever more skew on her face.

"I was, actually," he admitted.

"Why?" She sounded genuinely astounded.

"I told you. I think you're beautiful."

## Stormy

This was the second time he'd said it and she was still in shock.

Marcus?

Mr. Legal Law Guy, with his starched collars, fat credit cards and shiny leather shoes. He had a big fancy car, no doubt, like one of those Lambochinos or BNWs. He probably had a color-coded closet—*all beige*—and personal grooming habits that took longer than hers—he probably waxed off his chest hair, for Shiva's sake. He was everything she didn't like in a man, *and more*.

So why was her heart thumping and her breath quickening? Why was her face growing hot, her palms getting moist and a little girly smile curling the corners of her mouth?

"Thanks . . ." she said, finally breaking the silence. She lowered her head, feeling bashful, and a few strands of hair fell in front of her face. "You're quite handsome yourself . . ." She put on a jokey tone. "Even though you're not my type at all!" She looked up at him and smiled playfully.

"Of course not!" Marcus's tone was also playful.

"I usually go for guys who wear hand-me-down knitted jerseys that their grannies made."

"And tie-dyed cotton pants?" Marcus offered.

"Definitely tie dye. I also prefer them to have bells on, if that's at all possible," she smirked.

Marcus laughed at this.

"It's also preferable if they do weird street magic, or something like that."

"Or are a busking, vegan graffiti artist?" Marcus added with a smile and Stormy laughed.

"Well, now that you mention it . . ."

"Wait? You've dated an actual busking, vegan graffiti artist? Such people exist?" Marcus turned and looked at her.

"Well, he was vegan and a graffiti artist, I'm not sure if he busked." Stormy laughed at this, but Marcus didn't. Suddenly he wasn't looking as amused as he had been a few moments ago.

## Marcus

"What?" she asked, clearly sensing the change in his mood.

"Why do you date guys like that, Stormy?" Marcus asked seriously.

She shrugged. "I don't know. Ducks of a feather, I guess."

"Birds," Marcus corrected with a grin. "Well, I think you're selling yourself short. You can do much better than guys who can't provide for you and who name their genitals."

"Providing is not everything. There's more to relationships than that," she replied.

"But don't you want the whole package one day? Husband, kids, house, a comfortable life?"

Stormy shook her head immediately. "No ways. I'm not the settling down type of gal. That's not my thing. At all."

Marcus met her gaze. "So you don't want kids one day?"

"No, no, no! I'd make a terrible mother," she quickly said. "I'm not into marriage and the suburbs. That's probably your thing, though?"

"I guess," Marcus said casually, trying to downplay how badly it was that he did want those things.

"I'm super surprised you're not already married with a pretty, stay-at-home wife slash mom and two kids and a Labrador and garden gnomes," Stormy said.

"I guess you could say I'm struggling to find Mrs. Right," he confessed.

"Why?" Stormy sounded genuinely surprised. "Those types of woman would be mad not to go out with you . . . even though you can be really irritating and stubborn sometimes."

"Uh, thanks. I think." He wasn't sure if that was meant as a compliment or an insult. Maybe it was a little bit of both.

"Nah," Stormy put her legs up on the dashboard again, "no kids and marriage for me. Definitely not. I'm quite happy the way I am."

Marcus looked at her out of the corner of his eye . . .

*Why didn't he believe that?*

# CHAPTER TWENTY-TWO

## HASHTAG BLESSED, HASHTAG GRATITUDE

~

Stormy

*S*tormy was lying. She'd always wanted kids. Especially a little girl—she could imagine picking wild flowers with her, making brightly colored dresses, plaiting her hair and tying it up with luminous ribbons. They could skip and play with dolls and when she was older, she would teach her all about what life was really about, hold her hand when her heart was broken for the first time, and get giddy with excitement when they chose a pink wedding dress together.

Actually, now that she thought about it, a boy would be good too—a muddy, naughty little boy she could catch frogs, build tree houses and play pirates with. A boy who would grow up to be a gentleman, and respect women and be the best dad possible to her grandchildren.

She'd thought about this a lot.

But the truth was, she would never dare to have kids. She was terrified of turning out just like her mom—or her dad, for that matter. They were both equally terrible. She didn't have a single example of good parenting in her life. Even her foster mom had been a total cow. She'd constantly accused Stormy of trying to seduce her fifty-year-old husband, when in fact it had been the other way around. He had a thing for young, pretty blonde girls who looked "innocent and ethereal;" those were the words he always used.

Nothing hectic happened, except the odd inappropriate brush past her in the passage; but when it looked like it might turn into more, she went out, dyed her hair bright green and got a nose ring, and he'd never looked at her again. And then the look just kind of stuck. In fact, she'd quite liked it. It had brought a splash of color into her otherwise dark world and it had also served her well over the years, keeping a certain type of person away—normally people like Marcus, actually.

They'd been traveling for hours already and had fallen into a comfortable half silence, half chitter-chatter kind of thing. Marcus was no longer irritating her, which she was somewhat surprised by. She rested her forehead against the window and looked out, feeling strangely content. The landscape was really flat here and seemed to stretch on like that for miles and endless miles. Red sands. Tall brown grasses, and dry, leafless trees with thin gnarled branches dotted the side of the road. It was hard to imagine that life actually existed in a place like this, it seemed so harsh and dry and unforgiving. But beautiful. There was something so beautiful in all its nothingness. But it certainly wasn't the kind of place you wanted to get stuck. The sky was a light, hazy blue color and there wasn't a cloud in it. In the distance, Stormy could see an ominous flock of birds circling, probably waiting for an animal to die so that they could feast. Their massive wings were outstretched, as they glided in slow and steady circles, getting lower and lower to the ground. A long mountain range began to appear on the horizon, like a dark blue smudge; nothing more than that at this point. The heat also made it impossible to make out the shapes of the mountains, as it blurred their outlines in a rippling heat haze.

Stormy closed her eyes happily and thought she might be able to drift off to sleep again.

## Marcus

Marcus yawned and tried to stretch. His massive frame was not meant for a car like this. It was also rather taxing work driving it. It had no power steering, the gears were sticky and hard to change and the suspension was shot; each time he went over a pothole—which was often on this road—the car felt like it was going to fall apart.

But other than that, Marcus was feeling surprisingly good. He was enjoying the comfortable silence that he and Stormy had fallen into, as well as getting to know her better today. Like this, he'd almost forgotten all the things about her that had driven him absolutely crazy. He glanced over at her, she looked sleepy, her eyelids getting heavier and heavier as she looked out the window. Everything seemed to be going okay. They were still cutting it very fine if they were going to make the flight tonight, though, a thought that was making Marcus feel slightly anxious. When the woman behind the counter at the airport had called it a nine-hour drive, what she hadn't taken into consideration was that this car seemed to have a top speed of a mere eighty kilometers an hour. But still, if they pushed on at this speed, they would probably just make the flight, it was past twelve at night anyway. But suddenly, all that changed when Marcus felt the car shudder, this time in the absence of any potholes.

"What's that?" Stormy said, gripping onto the dashboard as the shudder increased.

"Shit!" Marcus cursed. "I don't know." He clutched the steering wheel tightly as the entire vehicle shook and vibrated. This went on for a few moments, until it ended in a dramatic backfiring sound, followed by a loud, long hiss and then a massive puff of white smoke came billowing out of the bonnet. Marcus slammed on the brakes and veered off the road and the car came to a skidding halt.

"Oh no, what's wrong with Sammy?" Stormy looked genuinely concerned for the car's wellbeing. Marcus was more concerned about *their* wellbeing.

"Old piece of junk, that's what's wrong," Marcus muttered.

"Hey," Stormy turned and whacked Marcus on the arm, "you can't speak like that in front of her."

"What? That's ridiculous!" Marcus rubbed his arm. She had quite a punch on her. "I can say what the hell I like."

"You'll hurt her feelings!" Stormy raised herself up onto her knees so that she was at eye level with him and glared.

"A car. Does not. Have feelings!" Marcus said it slowly so that she would understand.

"Negative thoughts and words can be very destructive." She leaned towards him and continued. "It's been proven scientifically. If you shout angrily at water, the water molecules actually become distorted and look ugly." Marcus turned and raised a brow. "I swear. Google it. It's true." Stormy cut off his response, predicting his usual skepticism.

"I will." And he absolutely intended to.

The billowing smoke and hissing sound had gotten even worse. Marcus glanced at the dashboard and saw that the internal dials reflected dramatic overheating.

"Crap! You're kidding me," he exclaimed loudly, banging on the steering wheel in frustration. He quickly glanced down at his watch, *and to think he'd actually thought everything was going fine a few moments ago!*

"This is just what we need," he spat. At this rate, they weren't even going to make it to the wedding, especially since they were clearly in the middle of nowhere. He'd hardly seen a car pass them since the start of their journey, and a tow truck would take hours to reach them. They were completely stuck, by the look of it, and he did not have much faith in Sammy's spontaneous healing abilities. In frustration he hit the steering wheel again.

"Stop hitting Sammy!" Stormy pulled his hands off the steering wheel angrily. Marcus swung around, the full force of his irritation was back—he hated it when things didn't go according to plan, and having a car break down on them was definitely not part of his plan right now.

"Seriously, Stormy! Seriously!" He couldn't believe he'd forgotten how irritating she was. Suddenly, a massive puff of smoke filled the entire car and Stormy and Marcus started coughing. The smoke rushed into his lungs and immediately his head began to feel whoozy. He quickly climbed out. A coughing Stormy was right behind him. He walked round to the back feeling pissed off as hell. He tried to open the bonnet, but it was too hot and the smoke almost choked him again. "What a piece of crap!" he cursed in between coughs.

"I told you. Negative energy. That's why she's broken down."

"No, Stormy, 'Sammy,'" he gestured inverted commas around the name sarcastically, "has broken down because it's an old, piece of crap from last century that probably hasn't had a service in years or hasn't had its oil changed since the turn of the millennium."

Stormy gasped as though she was really, truly shocked that he was saying this in front of the car. "Just give her a few minutes to cool down and she'll be okay again. I know she will."

Suddenly, her upbeat positivity was infuriating. Her whimsical, glass-half-full attitude was rubbing him up the wrong way. "No, she won't be okay, Stormy."

"How do you know?" Stormy placed her hand on her hips defiantly. *Fuck, that irritated him!*

Marcus raised his voice at her. "The engine has completely overheated and that smoke there is not a good sign. I know a thing or two about cars. Sammy is going nowhere anytime soon."

"You don't *know* she won't start again."

"No, Stormy, I do. Trust me."

"Do you have to be so negative? Why don't we look on the bright side?" she berated him.

"What bright side?" Marcus wiped his brow as a bead of sweat trickled down it. God, it was hot out here—it was making him feel quite delirious. "Stormy, we are stuck on the side of an almost-deserted road with no traffic passing by, in the full blazing sun, and we are about to miss my cousin and your stepsister's wedding preparations and maybe even the actual wedding if we don't get going." Marcus wanted her to understand that some situations were just crap, and no amount of looking on the bright rainbow sunshine side of things would change that.

Stormy walked up to Marcus boldly and poked him in the chest with her finger. "That kind of attitude is going to get us nowhere."

"No, having a shit car break down on us is going to get us nowhere."

"You stress way too much, Marcus."

"And *you* stress way too little. Or stress about the wrong things—like cows and cars having feelings and ridiculous crap like that." Marcus was getting really worked up now.

"Your stressing is going to cause your chakras to—"

"If you say 'chakra' once more on this trip, I swear I'm going to, going to—"

"What? You're going to what, Marcus?" Stormy had stepped all the way forward now and was waggling her angry little finger at his. There was a small pause and then she opened her mouth.

"Don't!" Marcus warned.

"Chakra," she said.

"That's it. I'm so over this crap. Do you know how ridiculous you sound most of the time?" He put his hand on his hips, imitating Stormy. "Oooh, this car's chakra is not aligned. Poor car, quick, I need to send it some positive healing vibes through the power of my enlightened, spiritual mind."

Stormy's eyes widened in what looked like horror. The car was hissing and smoking angrily. Marcus was thirsty and hungry and the sun was blazing down on him, his sanity was quickly slipping. Or *had* already slipped. He pranced up to the car like Stormy might do. "You know what Sammy needs," he said, "it needs a shoulder rub." He began doing a fast and furious karate chop on the car's roof as Stormy stared at him in total shock. "How's the pressure, Sammy?" He stopped momentarily and glared at Stormy mockingly.

"You think I'm ridiculous?!" She took an angry step forward. "Let me tell you a little something about you and your stupid big shiny watch and black-hole negativity that was probably even responsible for the plane almost plummeting from the sky!"

"What do you mean negative?" he said mockingly. "I'm not negative, I'm too busy absorbing the happy vibrations of the sunshine and using its rays to grow my organic kale leaves to make smoothies that will detoxify my body before I make my dreamboard . . . hashtag blessed, hashtag gratitude, hashtag . . . *oh wait, I forgot*, you don't hashtag because you're the only person on the planet who isn't on social media."

There was a pause in the conversation and Stormy scowled at him. If looks could kill right now, hers would. "Oh, so you want to go there, do you, Marcus Lewis? You really want to take it there?"

"Yes, I do. Let's take it there, Stormy-Rain!" he answered.

And then suddenly, dramatically, she turned on her heel and marched to the trunk of the car. She emerged moments later with the emergency triangle and a spanner in her other hand. She glared at Marcus for another moment, before putting the triangle around her wrist and then looking down at it.

"Oh, what is my big, logical, law-abiding watch telling me now?" She tried to put on a masculine voice. "Quarter to NO HOPE!" she yelled. "Quarter to we're going to die out here in our piece of shit car, because that's what my big logical watch is telling me. Because logic is reason and reason is what we learned in school and therefore it must be right. *And ooooh*, what is that? A feeling? Quick, call a doctor! I'm having a feeling, make it stop or it might lead to an original thought. Oh no, the world's ending, I might as well start digging my own grave!"

Stormy threw herself on the ground and started poking it furiously with the spanner.

"What the hell are you doing?" Marcus asked, staring down at her.

"Isn't it obvious, Marcus, I'm digging my own grave. Can't have vultures pecking on me, that would be messy, not to mention unhygienic." She was barely digging. It was more a stupid poking of the ground. But it was enough to grate at Marcus's already shattered nerves.

"Great, you do that, while I do a dance to the Gods of car repairs, since that is how cars get repaired, not through silly things like science and mechanics and engineering. Look, I'm taking my shirt off," Marcus took his shirt off, "and now I'm waving it in the air like a lunatic to summon my spiritual ancestors." He waved his shirt in the air while Stormy continued the futile soil poke, only managing to shift a small amount of soil. She stopped what she was doing, glared at him and then sat in the tiny hole she'd dug and started putting soil on her lap.

"Look, I'm burying myself." She continued to put handfuls of soil on her lap. "Here lies Marcus Lewis," she suddenly announced in a loud, official-sounding voice. "He lived a practical life, a germ-free, no-fun life—his favorite color was beige—*doesn't show dirt, you see*—his favorite volume was half, wouldn't want to cause a scene and wake the neighbors, and his favorite hobby was not wasting time on hobbies!"

Marcus was just about to counter her stupid argument when his phone rang. He pulled it out of his pocket and Damien's name flashed across the screen. He answered it, putting it on speaker phone while simultaneously eyeing Stormy.

"Hey, how's the journey going, are you guys almost there?" Damien asked.

"Oh, it's going fantastic! I'm about to defy the limits of logic and science by creating a car powered purely by the invisible flow of positive energy."

"Huh?" Damien sounded confused. "What are you talking about?"

"I'm talking about taking the unicorn by the horns," Marcus said, scowling at Stormy for added effect.

"Are you okay?" Damien sounded tentative.

"Never been better! Best day of my life," he said.

"Cool, glad it's going so well . . . I think." Damien sounded very confused. "Is Stormy there, I'm sure Lilly wants to chat to her?"

"Sure, I'll give her the phone." Marcus tossed the phone over at Stormy.

"Hey, Stormy, is everything okay there? What are you doing?" Lilly asked, sounding somewhat concerned.

"Just lying in my own grave," Stormy replied casually.

"What?" Lilly asked.

"You know how it goes, Lilly, you go to school, then university, get a job, get married, have kids, get divorced and then die," she replied, glaring at Marcus pointedly.

"Uuuh, are you guys okay? Have you been smoking something?"

"OH NO! I don't do drugs. That would be too fun. Too wild and crazy."

"Um . . . Stormy, should we be worried about you?" Lilly asked.

"No! I'm fine. Perfectly beige and fine."

"Okay. So, we'll see you soon, at the wedding, right? You'll get there?" Lilly asked.

"Oh, of course. I would never be late! Because I have a big watch and that just wouldn't be very beige of me!"

"Okaaaay, whatever you say, Stormy. Travel safely, bye . . ." Lilly hung up and Stormy immediately passed the phone back to Marcus. She folded her arms across her body and looked quite out of breath and sweaty from the mini-tantrum she'd just had.

# CHAPTER TWENTY-THREE

## THAT WOULD BE LOGICAL

~

Stormy

*M*arcus took the phone from Stormy and put it back into the pocket of his *beige* shorts. She watched him as he walked off towards the car and then slumped across the bonnet with a long sigh, as if he'd just given up. Stormy also slumped back down into her shallow grave. She was dripping with sweat and the sun was roasting her fair skin—not to mention those fumes had made her feel a little dizzy.

She tried to catch her breath and when she finally did, turned her attention to the sky above her. It was blue, a pale watery blue. A single solitary cloud floated across it. Slowly, languidly. She watched the cloud as it drifted aimlessly above her—almost becoming hypnotized by its slow movements. And then, suddenly, she sat up. Her eyes widened, her jaw dropped open in shock and she stared at it. The cloud looked like a giant finger pointing at her. She blinked quickly to make sure it was still there. It was.

A giant finger. Pointing down at her from the heavens as if she was in trouble. As if she'd just been caught doing something wrong. Caught. Convicted. *Guilty!*

She sat up even more and shielded her eyes with her hands so she could look at it better . . . *maybe she was imagining it?*

But she wasn't. The accusatory finger continued to point at her and she shuddered. She carried on watching it, half in shock, half in fear—*was this the finger of Goddess?* Passing judgment on her. Suddenly, she was acutely aware of the overly dramatic fight she'd just had with Marcus. *What the hell had she just done?* What the hell had she been thinking? *Oh, right*, she hadn't been thinking.

The finger seemed to be pointing at something with blatant disapproval. She swallowed hard and looked down at her wrist. The emergency triangle prop was still around it, masquerading as the big shiny watch she'd just mocked. Her cheeks began to heat up, not from the sun, but from thinking about her ridiculous outburst. And it was as if the finger was pointing this all out to her. She wanted to tell Marcus what she was seeing, but quickly stopped herself. He would mock her and tell her that a cloud couldn't look like a finger. It was only a group of watery atoms, or whatever clouds were made of.

Marcus stirred and she looked over at him. He was still spread out on the bonnet of the car. He pushed himself onto his elbows first, and then into a full sitting position and stared up at the sky. He held his hand up to shield his face from the sun.

"Hey," he mumbled, "is it my imagination, or does that cloud look like a giant finger?"

Marcus squinted into the light and then it looked like something was dawning on him. "Wait, is it . . . pointing at us?" he asked.

"I think it is," she replied, watching Marcus swiveling his head from side to side, as if he was trying to get a look at it from all angles.

"I feel like I'm in trouble." He finally turned to look at her.

"I was thinking the same thing." A tiny smile spread her lips.

Marcus smiled back at her and his eyes slowly drifted down to the ground. "You know," he said softly with a hint of amusement in his voice, "a grave is meant to be six feet deep." His smile grew.

"How are your ovaries, by the way?" Stormy asked with a smile.

"My what?"

"Well, that dance you were doing was more reminiscent of a Mayan dance of fertility than a dance to summon your ancestors," she said.

"Really?" Marcus's smile grew even more.

"Yup!" Stormy replied.

"Thanks for letting me know, Stormy," Marcus said.

"It's my pleasure, Marcus," she replied.

Marcus pushed himself away from the bonnet of the car and started a slow walk towards her. The sun was bright and when he was finally in front of her, his body cast a much-needed shadow across her, blocking out the sun's now-burning rays. He extended his hand for her. She looked at it for a few moments, not sure if she should take it.

Tentatively, she reached out and laid her hand in his. He closed his fingers around hers tightly and tugged her gently. In one swift, fluid movement, he managed to pull her up onto her feet. They stood there, face to face, observing each other in total silence for a few moments. Finally, his eyes left hers and drifted down to her dress. She followed his gaze and was confronted by a once white dress which was now a shade of muddy red. A few frantic-looking ants were scampering around on it and she quickly wiped them off with her hand.

"I know, I know," she said, flicking the last ant off. "You're dying to grab your antibacterial wipes and disinfect me."

Marcus shrugged. "Nah. Red kind of works better with your hair color."

"Well, I guess that's what I get for lying in my own sandy grave." She smiled and so did Marcus.

"Oooh." Stormy winced loudly and pointed at a crack that was now running the entire length of Marcus's shiny watch face. "It's cracked!"

Marcus looked at it. She was surprised to see how unperturbed he seemed to be. "That's what I get for trying to give a car a massage, I guess." Marcus suddenly swatted Stormy's shoulder and she flinched. "Sorry. Ant," he said.

"Thanks." They stood looking at each other again and fell into yet another strange silence. Their smiles started off small and grew steadily as they both started shaking their heads.

"What the hell, *the hell*, did we just do?" Stormy threw her hands in the air.

"Let's just put that down to dehydration, heat stroke and temporary poisoning by car fumes, why don't we?" Marcus said.

Stormy chuckled. "That would be logical."

"And beige," he added.

And that was it. They both burst out laughing.

The total ridiculousness of what they'd both just done caught up with them and all they could do was laugh. When their laughter had finally tapered off, Stormy looked around. They were still stuck on the side of the road. "So now what?"

"Well," Marcus picked up the spanner that Stormy had been using to dig her own dramatic grave, "I think I'll give Sammy a bit of a look and see if I can't get her started and get us back onto the road again."

# CHAPTER TWENTY-FOUR

## ROSES ARE SOMETIMES RED AND SOMETIMES NOT

~

Stormy

The sun was so hot that Stormy decided she needed to build something that would shade her. She looked around and found two similarly sized sticks. She took her newly purchased sarong and slammed two corners of it into the car's doors. Then she pushed the sticks into the ground a little way away from the car and tied the other corners of the sarong to them. And ta-da, a tent. Stormy sat under her makeshift tent, intrigued as she watched Marcus open the bonnet and peer inside as if he knew what he was doing. She wasn't going to say anything just yet, but she would be willing to bet (if she believed in betting or had any money to do so) that he knew nothing about cars.

"Do you really know what you're looking for?" she finally asked, after he climbed under the car and emerged covered in grease and sand.

Marcus nodded confidently and rubbed his hands together. "I'm pretty sure I can figure out how to fix her." He said it with so much confidence that she wanted to believe it, but when he went back to the engine and continued doing the same thing he'd been doing to it for the past ten minutes, with a slight look of confusion on his face that he couldn't hide, she wasn't so sure.

After about an hour of watching Marcus fiddling with the car, she was bored. And she also had to rehearse Lilly and Damien's wedding gift, so she got her guitar out of the back seat and sat back down in the sand on the side of the road. She'd written them a wedding song as a gift, which she intended to play at the reception. She started strumming on her guitar. She'd never been a great guitar player, and she knew she didn't exactly have the voice of a nightingale either, but she'd never let things like that hold her back when it came to doing and trying things she wanted to.

## Marcus

Marcus immediately looked up from what he was doing when he heard it. It was ridiculous. Her playing wasn't terrible, per se, but the guitar sounded old and off-key. Some of the strings had snapped, which gave it a tinny sound. And the lyrics!

*Roses are sometimes red and sometimes not, And violets are definitely purple or a darker shade of blue, And Lilly and Damien, I just want to say that I love you. Both. Not just one, but two-oooh-oooh. But still not as much as you love each other, ooooohhhh . . .*

Was that the verse? She started strumming even more enthusiastically as she began belting out the chorus. The jangling bangles seemed to add some percussion to the thing, perhaps that was what they were for. He leaned against the car and watched. He was completely intrigued by her, now. She seemed lost in the moment. As if she was completely separate from everything around her. She existed in her own strange world, and nothing seemed to faze her or get her down. *Dance like no one is watching*—an expression he'd heard many times before, always thought was silly, and had never fully understood, until now. She was sitting under the shade of her home-made tent, and something about the way she'd gone about making it had completely impressed him. She wasn't like other women who would probably be panicking at this point. Instead, she seemed to be one of the most resourceful people he'd met in a while.

When she was finished singing her song, he clapped.

"That was great," he said.

"Really?" Stormy looked up at him, genuinely surprised. The sun was getting lower in the sky, and the color of the light around them had begun to turn to orange. A shaft of warm orange light hit the side of her face and did something incredible to her green eyes.

"Yes. What's it for?" he asked.

"It's Damien and Lilly's wedding present." Stormy grinned up at him. "Do you really like it?"

Marcus nodded. "They'll love it." Because he knew they would. He'd bought them an expensive weekend away at a luxury resort, and she'd written them a song.

"So how's Sammy looking?" she asked, putting her guitar down and stretching out her legs. She looked like one of those traveling hippies from the sixties—all she needed was to be pulling a peace sign and the picture would be complete. Marcus wiped his greasy hands on his once-beige shirt, and although he hated being wrong, he had to admit defeat.

"Okay, so I don't *really* know what's going on with Sammy." He looked down at his watch and couldn't quite believe how late it was, not to mention how cracked it was. The day was almost over and they would be stuck on the side of the road in the middle of nowhere if they didn't hurry up and get going again.

He dug his phone out of his pocket and started scrolling for the number he was looking for. He would just call the hotel and they could organize someone to come and fetch them. Why hadn't he thought of this earlier? Mind you, his brain hadn't exactly been its usual analytical, solution-finding self lately. Marcus found the hotel's number—unfortunately, even if they left now to fetch them, they'd probably only be here in four hours. So, there would still be a long wait ahead for them. But as soon as Marcus dialed, the "No service" icon popped up.

"You're kidding," he groaned, feeling more amused than irritated. Of course this would be happening now.

"What?" Stormy asked.

"No cell reception here all of a sudden."

"But we chatted to Damien and Lilly," Stormy said.

"I know. I don't get it." He held his phone up in the air and started walking up and down.

He tried to dial again, and stared at the phone, willing the reception to come back. But it didn't. He then walked in the opposite direction, swinging the phone above his head. He jogged up a small hill nearby and when that didn't work either, he jogged back down to Stormy. "Where's your phone?"

"The battery's dead."

Marcus looked up, the sun was starting to set, and unless they got cell phone reception, they would be spending the night in the car and then walking tomorrow morning until either they got reception, or someone drove past.

He let out a long, loud sigh. He wasn't even angry or irritated anymore. He was more amused. It was unbelievable just how many things seemed to be conspiring to keep them from getting to the wedding.

"Looks like we might be stuck here for the night," Marcus said, flopping down onto the ground next to Stormy.

## Stormy

The sun was starting to set and Stormy was feeling hungry. "So do you have anything else to eat, other than those genetically modified bars of synthetic nutrients?"

"You mean the protein bars?" Marcus was sitting next to her on the ground and she felt his shoulder bump hers playfully.

"Yes. Those things," she said, bumping his shoulder back.

"I actually have a confession to make about the protein bar."

"What?" Stormy turned and looked at him.

"You were right."

"About what?" She was genuinely confused by his statement.

"As much as I hate to admit this, because I am hardly, ever, ever, ever wrong, as you know." He smiled at her.

"Of course not. How could Marcus Lewis ever be wrong?" she teased playfully.

"I think it was actually the protein bar that made me sick earlier today."

"What?" Stormy jumped up onto her feet and looked down at him. "Are you really admitting that you were wrong and I was right?" The light was turning red and the effect it was having on the lines of his face was artistic—like he was some great beautiful oil painting.

"Just this time," he said. "And just about *those* protein bars specifically. There was obviously something wrong with them. My usual ones are fine."

"I doubt that." She was skeptical. "I don't believe in protein bars, Marcus."

"And why not?" Marcus had a playful quality to his voice now. It was strange, since having their ridiculous outburst, something between them seemed to have changed. Everything felt so much more relaxed and easy. As if they'd just needed to blow off some steam—much like Sammy.

"Protein bars are not meant to be eaten under normal circumstances. They're the kind of thing we should only eat when the world has gone post-apocalyptic and all our food crops have been destroyed—possibly by an invading alien species, or by a giant solar flare. So, do you have anything else on you we can eat?"

Marcus burst out laughing "No, Stormy-Rain, I don't have anything else. As surprising as this might sound to you, I just don't carry organic alfalfa seeds with me."

"Aha." She jumped happily. Finally, something she could correct *him* on! "They're *sprouts*, not seeds." Stormy pointed at Marcus, feeling elated, and did a little happy jig as she sang, "*Marcus doesn't know everything, Marcus doesn't know everything!*"

Marcus smiled at her. "Fine. I'll admit my knowledge of vegan cuisine is limited."

He got up, walked over to the car and grabbed another packet from inside. But when Stormy saw what was coming out of it, she let out another sigh. She pointed at the offensive object in his hand. "Diet Coke? Do I have to tell you about the evils of artificial sweetener too, Marcus? Do you know what that stuff can do to you?"

"Enlighten me. Please." Marcus had a smile on his face.

"Well . . ." Stormy took in a deep breath, before she launched into it. "They can cause migraines, nausea, joint pains, inflammation, diabetes and even *impoten*—" Stormy broke off in the middle of her sentence.

"Well . . ." Marcus sounded slightly defensive. "It's not like I have that prob—"

"Oh no, you don't." Her smile spread. "You certainly don't."

"Uh . . . thanks." Marcus sounded coy. "I'll take that as a compliment."

"You should." Stormy looked up at him, his cheeks seemed to have gone slightly redder.

"Hey!" she said, suddenly working something out. "We didn't have sex!"

"When?" Marcus asked.

"When we were fighting earlier. Usually we would have had sex, this time we didn't."

"Instead we just lost our minds and acted like total idiots," he said. "Maybe it would have been preferable to have sex, instead of dancing, digging our own graves and causing our friends to possibly consider us certifiable."

"You think we should have rather had sex?" Stormy asked, feeling her temperature rising slightly at the mere thought of it.

"No . . . that's not what I'm saying," Marcus said and then looked at her.

Their eyes locked. They stared at each other. That familiar thing was building. And building and building and . . .

"Oh fuck it!" Marcus said suddenly, grabbing Stormy around the waist and pushing her back into the car door.

# CHAPTER TWENTY-FIVE

## WRESTLE A MAN-EATING LION

Marcus

Stormy and Marcus lay on the bonnet of the small car looking up at the sky, watching the sun go down. The rich rust color of the sand that surrounded them deepened further in the fading light of the setting sun. The world looked like it was bathed in a bright-red glow. They continued to watch in total silence as the sun finally disappeared and the first tiny star pierced the dark-blue sky.

"Ooops," Stormy said at last. It was the first word either of them had spoken since the whole thing had happened.

"Ooops," Marcus repeated, admitting some kind of defeat to himself.

"Pretty sunset," Stormy said innocently.

"Very," Marcus said. "Nothing quite like an African sunset, is there?" He thought about all the sunsets he'd seen over the years. It was true though. He'd traveled a lot, but there was nothing that compared to a sunset, or a sunrise for that matter, in Africa. There was something about the sun here, it seemed different in some way. More raw, more real, more beautiful, *just more.*

"We had sex again," Stormy said.

"I know," Marcus replied matter-of-factly and they fell into another mutual silence.

"The stars are really beautiful, Damien would love it here," Stormy said after more and more diamond-colored pinpricks had started popping up all over the now deep-grey sky.

"He would," Marcus acknowledged, although he was happy Damien wasn't here, or else they might have to hear the names of every constellation.

"You know we're naked, right?" Stormy said.

"I know." Marcus sighed. It was a long, slow sigh. A sigh of total and utter resignation. He gave up. Officially. He just couldn't fight this thing between them any longer, no matter how hard he tried. There was a certain quiet relief that followed.

The last faint shaft of light disappeared and they were surrounded by total darkness. And as if timed, as if it had been waiting for this exact moment, the world around them came alive with a cacophony of the strangest noises. Unrecognizable noises. Noises Marcus didn't particularly like. He sat up for the first time and took stock of their situation.

"It's getting noisy out here, I think we should get into the car now." He stood, peeling his sweaty back off the bonnet of the small car. *How had they even managed to have sex like that?* Well, it might have had something to do with the fact that Stormy was very, very bendy; she'd managed to bend her legs all the way back so that her toes were somewhere on the roof of the car.

"Scared you might have to wrestle a man-eating lion?" Stormy also stood up.

"Something like that," Marcus said, trying not to stare, but she was standing in front of him completely naked. He'd seen her naked on several occasions already, but he wasn't sure he would ever quite get used to it. And each time she was naked, he also seemed to discover another tattoo. This time he was looking at the one on the side of her ribcage; a little paper plane that had left a trail of tiny stars behind it.

He forcefully pried his eyes from her body and turned his attention to locating their clothes. He was surprised to find Stormy's panties hanging from the side mirror. He handed her the clothes and they both got dressed in silence, stealing quick glances at each other as they did. Something on the ground glinted and Marcus picked up the condom wrapper—thank God he'd taken some from the roadside dive. He'd had a suspicion that he might need that, and he had.

Marcus opened the door for Stormy. "Climb in."

"I thought we said you would never hold the car door open for me," she said with a smile, but walked up to the car and climbed in anyway.

"We also said we'd never have sex with each other again." He closed the door and walked around to the other side of the car, climbing in himself.

"We seem to say a lot of things that we don't mean." Stormy pulled her knees up to her chest and wrapped her arms around them, getting herself comfortable in the seat.

"We do," Marcus admitted.

"Why do you think that is?"

Marcus shrugged. "You know what, Stormy-Rain, I have no fucking clue!" He threw his hands in the air, hitting them on the roof of the car as he momentarily forgot about the lack of space. "Since meeting you, I have no idea what the hell is going on. You seem to have some strange effect on me and I keep landing up doing things that I can't even believe I'm doing, to be honest."

"Me too," Stormy said, her stomach rumbling at the same time. "I'm starved."

"Here." He passed her a small pack of peanuts that he'd taken from the plane, since protein bars were clearly off the menu. He took one too and ripped the bag open, tossing all the peanuts into his mouth at once. But Stormy didn't. She took the peanuts between her fingers, nibbled around the edges of some slowly, then at one stage even built a small peanut tower on the back of her hand and tried to get it as high as possible before it all tumbled and she tried to catch the falling peanuts with her mouth. He couldn't help thinking about how a few minutes ago her mouth had been all over his body in the most amazing way. He could still feel the burn of her lips on his stomach, the ache of her tongue on his nipples. He cleared his throat quickly, trying to think about something else.

"So, what are we going to do in here?" Marcus asked, as she finally, *finally* finished the last of her peanuts by throwing them in the air and catching them in her mouth.

"We could get to know each other some more," she said, now tearing open the empty peanut packet and folding the corners of it. "In a friend zone sense," she corrected quickly, flattening the packet against one of her knees.

Marcus nodded. "Okay, so tell me, how did you happen upon your name? I've been wondering about that since I met you." He could see, even in the dim light of the inside of the car, that her expression suddenly changed, and she looked more solemn than he'd seen her look before. She seemed sad, even.

"Well . . ." she started slowly and tentatively, while seeming to plait the pieces of plastic together. "Apparently, the story goes that my mother actually gave birth to me in a storm."

"Apparently?" Marcus asked, confused. Surely everyone knew the story of how they came into the world?

"I don't really know my mother—I've only met her once. So I don't know what's true and what's not," she explained. Marcus watched as she started to do that hair-twirling thing again.

"What happened to her?" he asked, treading lightly. He could see this was a sensitive issue.

"Um . . . she left me to run off with this cult. People of the Moonbeam, or something."

"What?" Marcus couldn't believe this. It was up there with one of the most bizarre things he'd ever heard.

"It's true," she said quietly. "My life is literally stranger than nonfiction," she said emphatically and Marcus didn't think this was the time to correct her obvious mix-up. "Apparently, though, after she gave birth to me and held me in her arms, the rains cleared and she saw a rainbow."

Marcus felt a sense of pity welling up inside him, and he couldn't help but reach over and touch her face gently, reassuringly. She reached up and took his hand in hers and held it tightly.

# CHAPTER TWENTY-SIX

## CHANNELING THE POSITIVE RAYS OF THE SUNLIGHT

Stormy

*S*tormy had often pictured the moment when she was born, and tried to imagine the perfect bliss her mother must have felt, holding her tiny baby girl in her arms as Mother Nature rewarded her labors with a riot of colors emblazoned across the sky . . . But somehow, her mother had still been able to walk away, leaving Stormy with nothing more than the image of a rainbow to remind her of her mother. And every time she dressed in the colors of the rainbow, she somehow felt connected to her, even though, in reality, she knew she wasn't. No matter how old she was, or how many years had passed, the thought still saddened her, somewhere in her very core.

It was as if the pain had been incorporated into her DNA. That acute sense of rejection. It's unnatural for a mother to give her child away, and Stormy had often wondered if there had been something wrong with her . . . But she couldn't let her mind go down this path again. It was a path that led her to the unhappy place, where Bambi's mother was six feet under and there were no pots of shiny gold.

"And you?" she asked. "I bet you had these perfect parents. I bet your mom wears strings of pearls and was on the PTA and went to all your rugby games and made you these awesome school lunches, and when your dad was around you went camping and did boy stuff—"

"Actually," Marcus cut her off, pulling his hand away. "Not at all like that. Well, not for any length of time anyway." He looked really solemn and Stormy remembered something.

"Sorry, you don't have to tell me, I know you don't like to talk about personal things," she said reassuringly.

"It's okay, like I said, I seem to be doing and saying lots of things I don't usually do," Marcus said, and then paused for a while as if he was building up the courage to tell her something big. Stormy waited for him.

"We were a pretty normal family before my dad died. But when he did, it changed my mom, for the worst." He sounded sad, and Stormy felt her heart breaking for him.

"What happened?" she asked.

"It's kind of hard to explain," he said. "I'm not sure I understand it myself."

There was another pause in the conversation, and Stormy watched as Marcus fiddled with his fingers. "My dad died quite suddenly. I was twelve when it happened. He woke up one morning with pins and needles in his fingers, and that night he was dead. A stroke."

"Oh, Goddess," Stormy gasped and placed a hand on Marcus's shoulder. "I'm so sorry, that's awful." She felt a knot forming at the back of her throat. She could never talk about things like this without feeling what the other person was feeling. Sometimes it was a curse, she felt too much and struggled to hide it. Once, her neighbor's cat had died and she'd been in tears for an entire week—she'd only ever seen the cat in the corridor.

"After that, my mom sort of went . . ." Marcus paused again. "It started when she wouldn't throw any of my dad's things out, and then it grew. Soon she wouldn't throw anything out, and then she started buying things that my dad would have liked. Sets of golf clubs, suits, she would even buy his favorite groceries. He wasn't there to eat them, though."

"She must have really loved him," Stormy said.

"But loving him became unhealthy. After a few years, you couldn't walk in the house. The floor was completely covered. Everything was covered. I used to lock my bedroom door so she couldn't get in. It was the only room in the house that was . . . safe."

Stormy nodded, listening to Marcus's story. It was all making so much sense to her now. She could see why Marcus was the way he was. In control. Neat. Clean.

"I tried to pretend it wasn't going on, so I never told anyone. I would go to school and smile and get good marks and play sports and win and keep myself neat and clean, even though at one point I had to start showering outside with the hosepipe because the shower became a storeroom."

"That's terrible." Stormy was so touched that Marcus was opening up to her like this and then a thought hit her and she suddenly gasped. "I teased you about being such a neat freak and the hygiene police, I'm so sorry." She felt overwhelmed with guilt. "I'm so sorry, that was so mean of me. I was so judgmental!" She threw her arms around Marcus and pulled him into an embrace. She buried her head in his neck and wanted to hold onto him and cry.

"It's fine," Marcus said, wrapping his arms around her and pulling her closer. "You didn't know."

"Exactly," she whispered into his neck, "so I should never have teased you about it."

"Well, I teased you too, so we're even." He pulled away from the hug and looked her in the eye.

"You did tease me, didn't you?" Stormy agreed, smiling at him. "And like you, I also have very good reasons for being the way I am." She reached out and ran her hand down the side of his face.

"You have very pretty skin," she said, feeling the texture of it under her fingertips. "It's very smooth."

Marcus burst out laughing. "Thanks. I think."

"It's a compliment."

"So, what are your reasons for being the way you are?" he asked.

"Mmmmm." She smiled at him. "Why am I so irritatingly optimistic and always channeling the positive rays of the sunlight?"

"Oh, God, did I say that?" Marcus grimaced at her.

"Something like that."

"Sorry." He shook his head. "Sorry."

Stormy looked at him. His eyes were soft and he seemed genuinely interested in hearing what she had to say. "I had to be that way. Everything was so dark around me growing up. If I didn't bring some color and cheer into my own life, who would?" She twirled her hair in her fingers again. "When I was six, I used to lie under my bed and draw pictures of rainbows over and over again. I used to imagine sliding down them, and finding my mother, a pot of gold and a leprechaun even." She shrugged. "You probably think that's stupid. That it makes me mad, or something."

"No, I don't." Marcus sat up in his seat and reached across to her. He took her hair from between her fingers and she stopped twirling it. "I think that makes you very Stormy-Rain." He smiled at her.

## Marcus

Marcus had liked their conversation. Under normal circumstances he hated sharing his feelings, but it had been worth it, because he'd gained a better understanding of Stormy, not to mention a whole new respect for her as well. She was, without a doubt, the strongest woman he'd ever met. She didn't wear a tailored suit, have a high-powered career and earn six figures—what some might consider strong—her strength was subtler than that. It took a little bit of looking to find, but when you did find it, it was undeniable. After their serious conversation Marcus began shuffling in his seat, trying to get comfortable, but space was very limited and his shoulders were starting to feel stiff from sitting for so many hours. He rubbed his neck and moved it from side to side a few times, only to regret it instantly when he saw the look on Stormy's face.

"Neck giving you issues, huh? Shoulders feeling a big tight, *mmmm*? Head hurt?" Her tone was playfully sarcastic and Marcus knew immediately what she was referring too.

"Are you going to say that word again?" he asked.

Stormy looked at him innocently and smiled. "What word? I have no idea what you're talking about."

"This has nothing to do with chakras, I assure you. It's purely a logistical problem. The space is just cramped."

"Mmmmm," Stormy mumbled conspiratorially. "Well, we'll soon find out." She leaned forward and started rummaging through her handbag, pulling out handfuls of colored stones.

"What are you doing?"

"Remember, I owe you for the sarong, and now is as good a time as any." Marcus stared at the stones in absolute horror.

"What *exactly* are you going to do with those?"

But she ignored his question. "I need you to lie in the back seat," she instructed him.

"There's no space."

"Space is what you make of it, Marcus," Stormy said, shooting him a very meaningful look. She indicated for him to climb into the back and Marcus started trying to squeeze himself through the tiny gap in the seats and make his way into the back. His frame was so big and the car was so small, that the slightest movement inside seemed to make it shake a little.

"I thought you'd forgotten about this," Marcus said, settling onto the back seat.

"Oh, I never forget when I make a promise with someone. And I know what you're thinking, by the way," she said, trying hard to glare at him in a serious way, but the twinkle in her eyes was too playful and cute. "But I don't care if you think it's stupid and it doesn't work, because a deal is a deal, so lie down and close your bloody eyes!"

"Do I really have to close them?" he asked. Truthfully, he wanted to watch her.

"Fine, keep them open then," she sighed.

Marcus lay down on his back, bending his knees to try and fit. Stormy positioned herself between the front seats and started making some swooshing movements with her arms.

"What are you doing?" Marcus was sure she was making this up as she went along.

"I am making the Cho-Ku-Rei symbol on your third eye," Stormy explained, repeating the movement a few times.

"Third eye?" Marcus asked sarcastically. "Now I have body parts I didn't ever know existed?"

"Shut up, Marcus, you're ruining the healing vibe here." Stormy stopped her swooshing and started running her hands up and down his body, a few inches above him. "I'm just scanning your body to check for imbalances." Marcus chuckled loudly and Stormy's eyes flew open again, shooting him a death stare.

"Okay, okay," he said, resigning himself to it. "Scan away."

Stormy continued her slow scan of his body, until finally, after what felt like ages, she spoke again. "Just as I suspected," she said as she opened her eyes and looked at him, a hint of triumph in her expression. "Your throat chakra is in need of special help, although your others are also pretty out of whack."

"Whack? How scientific." Marcus smiled to himself. He'd humor her, especially because she looked so damn fucking cute leaning there and swooshing her arms around.

"Relax. Breathe deeply," she said as she placed a stone on him. "Now, I want you to imagine this red color penetrating into your lower abdomen." Marcus chuckled. "Excuse me," she said, a slight edge to her voice. "Now I'm going to put this rose quartz on your heart chakra, and I want you to think of the color pink washing over you as you breathe in deeply." Stormy started doing some more strange hand gestures, as if she was swatting imaginary smoke away from him.

"And now," she said, laying down a stone on his throat, "we come to the main event." The stone felt cold against his skin. "I'm putting a blue kyanite crystal here. This is going to help get the flow moving better through this chakra and that will help with those neck and shoulder pains you've been having. It will also help you articulate your feelings better."

She went quiet, and he had to admit, lying there with his eyes now closed, listening to her gentle breathing, feeling the cold pressure of the stone and the slight warmth from her hand that seemed to be just millimeters away from his skin . . . it was quite relaxing. *Was this really working?* But then suddenly it stopped being relaxing—"Hey, what are you doing?" he yelped as he felt her hand put something down way, way too low on his body.

"I'm placing a stone on your root chakra."

"Is that what you call it these days?" Marcus squirmed as the palms of her hands settled by his pelvis and swooshed around, causing some unwelcome friction. He caught her hands in his.

"Marcus! I have touched your penis before, in case you don't remember," she said with a naughty tone in her voice. "In fact, I've done more than touch it!"

"Oh my God, Stormy, the stuff that comes out of your mouth, I still . . . I still . . . I just don't know what to say to that." Marcus shook his head, still holding her hand in his. "That's enough heal-ing for tonight, though, I think." He quickly sat up, still holding her hands tightly. "Thanks for that, Stormy. I actually do feel a little bit more relaxed."

"Really?" Her face brightened up and she looked completely thrilled. Marcus thought that he could quite easily let her do anything she wanted to him, if he could be graced with that same bright smile at the end of it.

"Really." He nodded at her and her smile intensified.

"See. I told you," she said in a sweet, singsong voice.

"Yes, you did." Their eyes met and Marcus realized he was still holding both her hands, and as if on cue, they both intertwined their fingers in each other's. They continued the intense eye contact, the tension and feelings between them growing. Marcus wasn't sure if he could stop himself from leaning forward and kissing her—this time he didn't want anything else from her—he only wanted to kiss her.

Stormy leaned forward a bit, and that was his cue. He lifted his body up, moving towards her in the still, calm silence of the car. With their eyes still locked, they continued their slow, deliberate lean but the moment was suddenly broken by the sound of stones crashing down onto the floor of the car and bouncing around. They both jumped back at the deafening clatter.

# CHAPTER TWENTY-SEVEN

## SEXY. DIRTY. NAUGHTY AND SO DAMN CUTE

~

Stormy

$\mathscr{S}$tormy took the stones crashing all over the show as a sign to keep her lips to herself. Marcus had obviously heeded the warning too, as he was shifting away from her in the back seat and clearing his (now unblocked) throat uncomfortably.

Stormy stashed the stones away in her handbag and stared out of the window at the inky black sky, her heart rate slowly returning to normal. After a few moments of silence, she suddenly felt nature calling. "I need a wee," she announced to Marcus as her hand reached over to open the car door.

"Hey. You can't go outside in the dark!" Marcus sounded adamant and he pulled her hand away from the door quite forcefully.

"Well, unfortunately Sammy doesn't have a built-in toilet, so unless you want me to—"

"Okay, no need to get graphic, I'll come with you." Marcus let her hand go and she opened the car door. "I'll also . . ." He stopped himself. Stormy knew this kind of conversation would make him feel awkward.

"Kinky. I didn't know you were into that," Stormy said playfully, hoping to rile him. She loved watching him squirm. It was so damn cute. "It's so *Fifty Shades of* . . ." Stormy paused for a moment. "Of *whatever-that-color-is*."

"*Grey*. And I'm into all kinds of things you don't know about, Stormy." Marcus smiled and teased back.

"Ooohhh." She was delighted he was playing along. "If you tell me yours, I'll tell you mine."

"Your what?"

"All my deepest, darkest sexual fantasies." She gave him a little wink and his body stiffened up—but it wasn't from tension this time.

"Okay. Tell me." He stood in front of her now, arms folded. Waiting.

Stormy had to think about it for a while, running them all over in her mind. And her conclusion was quite surprising. "Well, actually, now that I think about it, we've kind of already done them all."

"Oh?" Marcus tried to hide it, but he was smiling. Sexy. Dirty. Naughty and so damn cute.

"Except of course," she suddenly remembered one, "I've always wanted to have sex while floating in the Dead Sea."

He burst out laughing. "I don't think I can help you out with that one."

"Pity." She shrugged playfully. "It would be fun."

"And probably highly illegal too, since it is a public beach area."

"Illegal? That hasn't stopped you in the past . . . the elevator."
She found herself biting the inside of her mouth just thinking
about it.

"And you remember how that ended, don't you?" His smile
had grown now.

"True!" She gave Marcus another playful smile and then
walked off. She hadn't realized that the car had been acting as
such a successful sound barrier between them and the outside
world. The night was alive with strange, loud and sometimes
frightening sounds.

"Hey. Not too far," Marcus warned. It was pitch black outside,
apart from the millions of stars that were splashed like silver
glitter across the night sky. It was beautiful. Stormy loved things
that sparkled and twinkled—kind of like Marcus's eyes right
now, as they seemed to reflect the pinpricks of light in the
night sky.

Stormy started squatting as gracefully as she could. It was so
unfair, she'd often thought, how men had such an easy time of
this, peeing standing up, whereas women always had to get into
that precarious squat position that required both strong leg muscles and expert coordination. There was something rather flawed
with the whole design—sexist, even. Clearly a man had been
behind this design, possibly the same one who'd designed bras
and made sure that woman menstruated once a month!

"Hey." Marcus turned and covered his eyes immediately.
"What are you doing?"

"You said not to go too far . . ." She was amused once again by
Marcus's reaction.

"I didn't mean you should go right . . . right *there*." With his eyes still closed, he waved his finger around in Stormy's general vicinity.

"Well, don't look if you think it's such a big deal."

Marcus turned around, looking highly uncomfortable. Something about the whole thing put an amused smile on Stormy's face—the way he was now sighing and pretending to look at the stars and then at the ground again.

"Can I get you a tissue, or—" He stopped short. "Oh, I guess we don't have any."

What a gentleman, Stormy thought. "It's okay. I'll drip dry!"

"What!" Marcus half-shouted the word. "Did you really just have to say that, Stormy? Was it truly necessary to say that out loud, I mean . . . *drip dry?*"

"That is so sexist and wrong. You guys all do the three-shake jiggle—"

"Whoa!" Marcus threw his hands up. "Stop talking about my . . ."

"Penis!" Stormy added quickly with a giggle as she watched Marcus's momentarily unblocked chakras start blocking again.

"I'm just saying, it's okay for men to do a little jiggle, what about us poor women? You have it easy, just standing up and whipping it out—"

Marcus cut her off again. "You're still talking about it."

Stormy smiled to herself. She liked winding him up, and it was so easy. She'd figured out exactly what his buttons were—unlike his phone, he had some rather cute buttons that she liked to push. She got up and straightened herself out. "Your turn."

"I'll wait until you climb into the car," he said, finally turning around with a kind of frazzled look on his face.

"Stage fright?" Stormy teased.

"No. It's just that—unlike you—I know what's appropriate and what isn't," he said indignantly.

"Well, who says what's appropriate and what's not?" Stormy had always been fascinated by most people's punitive self-imposed boundaries. Their rules and regulations.

"Societal norms and the law usually dictate that kind of thing," he answered quickly.

"Lucky I don't believe in the legal system, then," Stormy said.

Marcus shook his head. "Maybe you've forgotten, but I'm a lawyer. And if we didn't have laws, we might be running around like savages doing whatever we wanted to." He looked slightly put out and Stormy felt bad again—she hadn't meant to attack his belief system. She knew all too well how that felt.

And he *did* make a good point—humans were just animals, after all. Maybe they did need a few rules. "You're right. I'm wrong," she admitted gracefully.

## Marcus

Marcus launched into his defense. "If the world just did . . ." But he paused. Had he actually heard correctly? "Did you say I was right?"

"Fully," Stormy said with a smile. "You're totally right. I mean, if we didn't have rules like that, I might have knocked you over the head ages ago, dragged you into a cave and had my way with you. *Well*, not that you need to be knocked and dragged . . ." She gave Marcus a big wink before striding back to the car and climbing in.

Marcus stared after her. He had never met anyone like her. Someone who said what they thought all the time, almost to a fault. A woman who seemed so comfortable and confident in her own sexuality. God, she was more comfortable than him when it came to that. She seemed to look at people and the world in such a unique way, and he was finding himself very attracted to it. Attracted to the way in which her brain seemed to work.

After taking care of his business Marcus climbed back into the car, pulled out two antibacterial hand wipes and passed one across to Stormy, while cleaning his own hands.

"What else do you have in that little bag of yours?" Stormy asked, looking over at it.

Marcus dug in his bag and started pulling things out: shaving cream; a face cloth; a razor; waterless hand soap; more antibacterial wipes.

He ran the back of his hand over his face. "I hate not shaving," he muttered quietly.

"You'll look good with stubble though," she said.

He shook his head as if that was the last thing in the world he wanted. "I hate stubble, it's so, so . . ." He paused.

"Messy?" Stormy offered gently. A few hours ago she might have teased him about this, but he could see she wasn't going to. And he appreciated it.

# CHAPTER TWENTY-EIGHT

## A POTENTIALLY DEADLY WEAPON

Stormy

*S*tormy wasn't going to tease him about his need for a clean, smooth face. He'd offered her a glimpse of his inner self, something she knew was hard for him. And she would treasure that. She always felt honored when people opened up to her. It was the ultimate gift that one person could give to another. To tell someone their truth. Unedited.

"I figured you more as an electric razor type of guy," she said, looking down at the items he'd taken out.

"You get a closer shave the good old-fashioned way," he replied.

Stormy took the razor and shaving cream from him. "Let me."

Marcus's eyes widened. "You can't shave me." He looked panicked.

"Of course I can," Stormy said, and without asking, climbed onto Marcus's lap, straddling him.

He jumped in his seat. "What are you doing?"

"Well, you don't want me to cut you, do you?"

"I don't want you to shave me, full stop," he said, his voice quivering slightly. She got it. Marcus was a control freak. This was hard for him.

"Besides, how will you do it, in a car?" he asked, looking around.

Stormy reached for the wipes and the facecloth that he had. She poured a little water onto the facecloth and laid it on the seat next to her. As well as a few of his wipes.

"Easily," she said, starting to shake the tin of shaving cream in her hand.

"Wait!" He put his hand up, blocking her. "I've never let . . . I . . . no one has ever . . . I . . ." he stuttered.

"Shhhh." Stormy gently placed a finger over his lips and stopped him. "Do you trust me?" she asked, looking straight into his eyes. His pupils dilated.

"I don't know," he said breathily. "Should I?"

"That's for you to decide," Stormy said, sitting back on his lap and giving him a moment to make his mind up. She wasn't going to force herself on him.

Marcus stared at her. He looked like he was sizing her up, taking her all in and considering everything—like Marcus would. That was so Marcus.

He finally spoke: "I'm not sure why the hell I am saying this, but yes, I trust you."

"Good." Stormy smiled and started shaking the can again. She was just about to start coating his face with the foam when he stopped her once more.

"Wait, you have done this before, haven't you?"

"No. But I'm sure I know what I'm doing."

## Marcus

Stormy looked like she was concentrating hard. And when she did, the tip of her tongue shot out of her mouth and traced her lips. And soon, he stopped thinking about what she was doing—rubbing a potentially deadly weapon over his skin—and became transfixed by her darting tongue. He was overwhelmed with a desire to kiss her, to put her tongue to good use, but he didn't.

She was really taking her time, running the razor very slowly and precisely over his skin, and then cleaning it on one of the wipes perfectly. He wondered how many times she'd bothered to clean something so perfectly, and suddenly felt touched that she was doing it like this, probably for his benefit alone.

He started to relax more and more as the shave went on. And the more comfortable he got, the more aware he was that she was straddling his lap, her face mere centimeters from him, her skirt bunched up and her almost-naked body pressing into him, in just the right spot. And every time she leaned to the right, to wipe the razor off, the slight friction caused a very pleasant feeling to rise in him.

"Finished," she finally announced. She then took the water-soaked facecloth, and with such gentle care, wiped his face clean. She took her hands and dragged her fingertips down the side of his cheeks, smiling to herself as if she was satisfied. "Smooth."

Marcus felt a shiver run through his body as her warm hands

cradled his face and she looked him straight in the eye. Her green eyes, he'd recently come to decide, were the most beautiful eyes he'd ever seen. And the feeling he got when she looked at him with them was something he'd never really felt before. The feeling was hard to explain, it seemed to be a combination of a million different emotions all rolled into one.

"I'm going to kiss you now, Marcus," Stormy suddenly declared, leaning towards him. Her statement caught him off guard and he pulled back as she leaned in. *Wasn't this meant to be his line?* The guy was supposed to be the one saying these things, the one that was in control.

"Close your eyes," she commanded. Marcus wasn't used to being told what to do, but he liked it coming from her.

Stormy continued to lean, until he could feel and smell her breath on his face. She stopped as her lips were about to touch his. The tips of their noses were touching and she'd moved her entire body forward so that it was pressing into his.

"Keep your eyes closed," she whispered against his mouth.

"Okay," he managed breathily, deciding that right now, he would do whatever she asked of him.

# CHAPTER TWENTY-NINE

## JUST A KISS

~

Marcus

*H*er lips were so soft. They connected gently with his, and at first, he could barely feel them. His hands had been at his sides, but now he gently placed them on her waist. It was so small that his hands almost touched in the middle by her belly button. As she dragged her lips over his, his excitement kicked up a notch. He squeezed his hands a little tighter, and gently pulled her body even closer to his, pressing her down into him.

Finally, after what felt like hours of delicious, yet torturous teasing, she parted his lips with hers. She was in total control of this entire thing, and although it was hard to resist, hard not to take over, he let her continue. The tip of her tongue worked its way between his lips and then, softly, rubbed against his. The electric shock sensation that shot through him made him momentarily startle. Once the shock of the initial feeling had subsided, though, they settled into a soft, steady rhythm of slowly massaging each other's tongues. But Stormy settled into another rhythm too. Each time her tongue swept over his, she would move on his lap. She would slowly grind into him and arch her body forward. Marcus didn't know how much more of this he could take. He didn't know how much longer this could just stay a kiss. And just as he was thinking that, she opened her mouth even more, and buried herself deeply into his.

He tilted his head to the side, making sure he got all of her. The rhythm built. Faster, harder. She gripped the side of his face with more pressure now and he wrapped his arms around her back and tangled his fingers into her hair and the base of her neck. She moaned into his mouth when he did this, which excited him even more. She began to make small circles on his lap, swaying and grinding back and forth, from side to side. Wiggling and writhing on him as the kiss deepened further. Marcus was hard as a rock now, and Stormy gave a chuckle of pleasure as she ground into him even harder.

*Fuck, he could come like this.* And by the look of it, so could she. And then suddenly, she stopped all movement. She didn't move her mouth though, instead she kept it there, still cradling Marcus's face in her hands. Marcus followed her lead and slowed all his movements to a total stop. The tension building like this, when they were dead still, was insane. Their breathing increased to an almost pant. Holding onto each other, not moving and yet feeling the intense flow of sexual energy rolling through them. They weren't having sex. They were barely even touching each other, and yet it was more intense than anything he'd ever experienced.

Stormy finally, slowly, pulled her lips away from his and sat back on his lap. He opened his eyes, his lids felt heavy, and he looked up at her. She was smiling down at him; her green eyes were hooded, her pupils dilated and her cheeks flushed a bright pink.

"What was that for?" Marcus finally asked, the words getting stuck in his throat as they came out.

"I just wanted to," she said, finally letting go of his face. He felt such an acute loss at this small movement that it surprised him. "Besides, we haven't really kissed each other, properly anyway."

Marcus thought about this. It was true. Their kissing up until this point could barely be described as such. It had all been so frantic and messy and had never been the main focus of the event.

"How about we break with tradition and leave it as that . . . *just a kiss*." She smiled at Marcus sweetly and he found himself nodding at this, even though his body wanted so much more.

"I'm tired," she said, looking around the car.

"So, how should we do this, then?" Marcus asked, trying to figure out the best way for them both to get comfortable in the car.

"Whatever works best," she said, dazzling him with yet another Stormy smile. That specific brand of smile that only she had—cute, friendly, open and sexy. A smile that suddenly made everything in the car look a little brighter.

"Why don't you take the back seat?" Marcus offered.

"Always the gentleman," Stormy responded, climbing off his lap and then through the gap between the two front seats. She sat down and looked at him. She patted the seat next to her. "Join me?" Another dazzling smile.

Marcus didn't have to think twice about it. He climbed through the gap and into the back seat with the grace of an elephant—this car really wasn't big enough for them. At all.

They maneuvered around a bit until they found a comfortable position together. It felt so good to be this close to her, and he wasn't even feeling anything sexual right now. In fact, quite the contrary.

Marcus heard Stormy sigh. "Goodnight, Marcus."

He smiled to himself; he liked the sound of that. "Goodnight, Stormy-Rain."

# CHAPTER THIRTY

## AIR-MOUSE

~

Marcus

Marcus woke up before Stormy did. It was already ten o'clock and he couldn't believe he'd slept that long. Perhaps it had something to do with the fact that he'd just had the best sleep of his entire life. Possibly because Stormy had landed up sleeping with her head on his shoulder and her arm on his chest.

Marcus took out his phone and switched it back on, doubting that the reception would have somehow (miraculously) returned overnight. He was wrong—the screen showed that full signal had returned. Strange—he'd been fully expecting to climb another hill, or maybe Kilimanjaro today, just to find reception.

Suddenly, a familiar sound overhead made Marcus look up. And then, he was hit by an idea that he couldn't believe he hadn't had earlier. It was so clear. So logical.

Most of the luxury game reserves around here had helicopters for game-viewing purposes. And according to the road signs, and his trusty iPhone Google Maps app, they were currently surrounded by five reserves—which meant luxury lodges with helicopters.

He looked up at the skies and wondered just how many helicopters were close. It was only a matter of phoning some of the surrounding lodges, hoping they weren't all busy, and waving his credit card around. Simple. Easy. Much quicker than a car.

He'd need to call the airline and book another flight to Prague though, since they'd missed theirs last night. Maybe they didn't need to rush it either. They still had time to get to the wedding. Maybe they could spend the night in Mombasa and only catch a flight out tomorrow? He looked over at sleeping Stormy. Was it selfish of him to want to spend another night with her, alone? Before the chaos of friends and family at the wedding. They probably wouldn't even see each other once the wedding got into full swing.

Besides, he was really looking forward to Mombasa, with its white sandy beaches and tropical waters and air-conditioned rooms with ablution facilities. Now all he had to do was convince Stormy that a helicopter was a good idea.

That might be problematic.

## Stormy

Stormy had been watching Marcus pacing up and down on the phone for the past ten minutes. She couldn't hear him talking, but he'd called at least four or five different numbers, and from the look on his face, whatever plan he'd concocted was working. He looked so authoritative and confident. He looked like a man on a mission. She bit her bottom lip, trying to suppress the feelings that were welling up inside her. She couldn't help it; God, he looked yummy, being all manly like that. Perhaps those feelings were somehow intensified this morning because of how they'd slept the night before. She'd landed up with her head on his chest—not by accident, mind you. They'd also ended up holding hands—again, not by accident.

She'd never liked manly men who made plans and took charge and watched *The Big Game* on big TVs from their big couches. The kind of men who knew how to barbecue a cow and swigged back beer while they talked about their golf handicaps and shrewd investments.

But Marcus . . . He looked good doing it.

So, *so* good.

And not only that—she was suddenly overcome with a strange feeling of safety. This was a particularly unfamiliar feeling for her. She'd never felt totally safe before, physically or emotionally. Her father had never really instilled that kind of reassurance in her. He'd once dropped her off at his cocaine dealer while he went to draw money from the ATM downstairs. Not to mention how she'd felt around her foster dad, or her other foster family, who hadn't noticed she was missing for three whole days when she ran away. In fact, the only time she'd ever felt remotely safe was holding onto Lilly in bed with the duvet pulled over their heads while they sang pop songs together, trying to drown out the sounds of their mad parents fighting.

Yet now, even though she was stranded on the side of the road in the middle of nowhere, she felt safer than she'd felt in years. Marcus was the kind of guy who just instilled that in you. He was one of those natural provider-and-protector types. Not that she would ever trust a man to protect her. Not that she *needed* protecting, either; she made her way in the world perfectly well without a man looking out for her and providing for her.

But for some strange reason, with Marcus looking out for her right now, organizing and planning and pacing on that phone, it felt good. She decided to momentarily bask in the feeling. *Only momentarily*, though. It was not a feeling she should get used to.

But just when she'd built him up to being some magical knight in shining armor, he dropped the bombshell . . .

"NO, no, no, no, no." She felt sick. "Absolutely NOT. No, no, no."

"But it'll be the quickest, easiest way out of here," Marcus pleaded.

"Well, you can go on your own, then. I'll walk."

Marcus shot her that look again, the one that always came with a raised eyebrow and that line. "You'll dehydrate if you walk."

"I'd rather dehydrate on my own two feet than plummet to my death from a flying soup can with spinning things on its roof, thanks." Marcus laughed. His reaction couldn't have been more terribly timed, though, because it only served to rile Stormy even further. "How does it even fly? At least you can kind of understand an airplane—it has wings. Those blades just go round and round and *what* . . . it just lifts into the sky like that? It's unnatural," she huffed.

"The blades work by pushing air down, thus lifting the helicopter up," Marcus explained patiently.

Like that was supposed to make her feel better. "And I suppose you learned that on the Google?" she scoffed, her voice dripping with disdain.

"No, it's a scientific fact."

"Oh, a *fact*—like the 'fact' we evolved from monkeys?"

The look that came over Marcus's face was one of pure confusion. "We didn't?"

"NO! Extraterrestrial visitors genetically modified our DNA, obviously."

And then he was laughing again. Stormy couldn't believe how inappropriate he was being, laughing at a time like this. And not just ordinary laughing, either. Noooo, his shoulders were shaking and he was holding his stomach. He was in hysterics.

"Aliens?" Marcus gasped in between his annoying laughter. "I should have guessed."

"Yes, a very highly evolved, peace loving, spiritual, friendly race of aliens who—" His laughter stopped and he smiled at her queerly, which made her stop talking immediately. "What?"

"Oh Stormy, you're something else."

"No, I'm not." Though he seemed to say it indulgently—fondly, even.

"I mean it in a *good* way. You're unique. You're . . . lovely." He smiled again.


## Marcus


*Lovely!*

It had shot out of his mouth before he could even think about whether or not it was appropriate to even say. But it was how he felt. He'd woken up this morning and when he'd looked at her, she somehow seemed different from the day before. Everything about her seemed lovelier. Even her truly annoying habits; sweeping, dramatic statements, botched-up fake-news-style versions of reality, her mixed idioms, her made-up words. In fact, today, none of those seemed to annoy him at all.

But he couldn't let himself get distracted right now—he had a plan that needed to be implemented.

"Look, the helicopter will be on its way soon," Marcus said brusquely, looking at the time on his phone. "I've sent them our coordinates and they are on their way."

Suddenly she was twirling her hair again. Terror flashed across her face . . . and he wanted more than anything to make it go away.

"What about Sammy? We can't just leave her alone," Stormy said, pouting adorably.

"I've called the car rental company and told them where she is. They'll come out and tow her as soon as possible. She'll be fine on her own for a few hours." He couldn't believe he was actually calling the car "she" and trying to reassure Stormy of her wellbeing.

And then the tears welled up in her eyes again and Marcus thought he might actually die from the knot that was forming and twisting in his stomach. The first time he'd seen her cry was at the airport. He'd thought it ridiculous that someone—a grown woman, no less—could cry over flying. It had seemed childish and stupid and it had irritated him beyond belief; but now, the tears glistening in those startling emerald eyes evoked the totally opposite feeling in him.

To see her like that stirred such a strong urge to hold her and make everything right. He wanted to wave a magic wand and make her smile again. He knew how corny that sounded the minute he thought it, but it was true.

"I promise, it'll be fine." He was tempted to walk up to her and put a hand on her shoulder and kiss her tears away.

"That's what you said with the plane." The first tear dislodged itself from her eye and rolled down her cheek. *No*, he couldn't take it a second longer. He walked up to her and gently wiped the tear from her cheek. She looked up at him with those big green eyes, made even more brilliant by the wetness.

"I promise you. Cross my heart and hope to die, it's going to be fine. I promise."

Another small tear escaped and he wiped it away again. Her skin was so soft; her cheeks were flushed a pale pink and on closer inspection, she had a tiny spray of freckles on her nose that he'd never noticed before. It must have been from sitting in the sun the day before. He wanted to trace his finger across them. Play join-the-dots.

"Stick a pin in your eye?" she asked with the tiniest of smiles.

"I'll stick whatever you want me to stick in my eye."

Stormy managed a slightly bigger smile. "Whatever?"

"Within reason." He smiled back at her.

"Fine," Stormy said, finally conceding to the whole thing. She nodded and her shoulders seemed to drop a little as she sighed and looked like she was relaxing again. The sound of distant chopper blades suddenly thrummed through the air; they both turned and looked up at the same time, but the helicopter could be heard long before it could be seen.

"Do you know what's in Mombasa, Stormy?" Marcus asked, trying to distract her. His hand was on her shoulder now, which was unnecessary because he had finished with the tear-wiping, but somehow it had just gotten stuck there. She shook her head, looking up at him curiously. "Well, it's tropical. White beaches, warm blue waters, palm trees . . . and air-conditioning and icy cold beverages."

"It's hard to imagine something tropical, standing out here in all this dryness."

Marcus nodded. "I know. But look . . ." He pointed down the road. "It's a mere forty minutes away, as opposed to four hours by car and who knows how many more for someone to find us, or a car to give us a lift, or a tow truck." Stormy nodded slightly.

The helicopter suddenly came into view and was lining itself up to land on the other side of the road.

"Only forty minutes?" He could see Stormy tensing up again as she watched the helicopter approach with trepidation.

"Only forty," Marcus assured her in the most comforting tone he could muster.

"Okay. Fine," she said confidently, even though he could see the hair twirled around her finger getting tighter and tighter.

Marcus pulled the bags out of the car and put the car keys in the glove compartment. He watched as Stormy walked over and rubbed the bonnet fondly. She leaned in and said a few whispered words. By now, he knew her well enough to know what she was saying—no doubt wishing Sammy would feel better, or have a safe journey home, and thanking her. He smiled to himself.

Marcus led the way as they crossed the road to the helicopter. The blades were slowing down now, but it was still windy, and the dust was being whipped up into a frenzy.

"Damn!" He turned to see that Stormy had now frozen in sheer terror. She pointed a finger at the helicopter as if it were a demon.

"It's so . . . it's like a beetle!" she screeched.

Marcus wished he could have blindfolded her so she hadn't seen how small the helicopter really was. It was *very* small. And he had to admit, looking at the thing, that it didn't inspire that much confidence in him, either. He had been hoping for *Airwolf*; this was more like Air-Mouse. But he knew he couldn't let Stormy see his creeping nerves.

"I promise, it's going to be fine." This time it was slightly harder to keep up the authenticity of that reassuring tone.

Stormy shut her eyes tightly and stuck out her hand trustingly. "I can't look. I just can't look."

Marcus pushed the bags into the back; they took up more than half of the seat, leaving only a tiny place for both of them to sit. He quickly glanced at the seat next to the pilot and noted that it, too, was full. This meant that Stormy would need to sit on his lap.

He took her by the hand and pulled her towards the chopper. He then climbed in first and hoisted her up, slipping her onto his lap. Stormy's eyes suddenly opened when she realized where she was sitting.

"Sorry, only one seat. I'm afraid my lap will have to do." He hoped he hadn't said that with a smile. Or in a way that betrayed his innermost thoughts at that moment.

# CHAPTER THIRTY-ONE

## MAYBE, JUST KINDA MAYBE

~~

Stormy

*S*he would deny it if ever asked, especially by Marcus.

Totally, absolutely, utterly, positively, definitely, categorically and any other words in the English dictionary that ended in "ly" *deny it!* She would deny it loudly and proudly and repeatedly— and again using any other words that ended in "ly." She would shout it from the rooftops and the balconies and any other high things that people stand on that allowed them to see other people below, or whatever! Deny, deny, and deny some more, because for the last forty minutes, it had felt like she had been having sex in the back of a helicopter with Marcus.

But, like she said—D E N Y.

Because it hadn't really happened.

Because everything that had happened had been perfectly normal.

Because it was all necessary and perfectly, innocently explainable.

*Okay*, so maybe it hadn't been *entirely* necessary for her to press her back into him like that. But it *could* have been necessary, because that's what people do when they sit on other people's laps to stabilize themselves, don't they? Maybe, just kinda maybe, it hadn't been *entirely* necessary to grip his upper thighs with her hands and squeeze, dig her nails in, but she had needed to anchor herself when the helicopter had gotten a bit wobbly. His thighs were the closest things to grab onto, and they had seemed like a sensible choice at the time—so firm and muscular. You have to hold onto something, right?

Possibly, she hadn't needed to tilt her neck back just enough that her face was only centimeters from his and she could feel his hot breath on the side of her cheek . . . possibly. *Okay*, okay, and perhaps, just a tiny bit, maybe it wasn't *soooo* necessary to slide backwards and forwards on his lap those few times while readjusting her position. But the bags had tilted and pushed her a little and she had needed to get comfortable—that was totally, legitimately necessary. But maybe it had not been *entirely* necessary to have the readjusting take the form of a kind of slow bump-and-grind lap dance. And when she'd felt something beneath her start growing, maybe she shouldn't have let out that tiny moan while opening her legs just a little wider, so that he fit quite perfectly between her thighs, and then closed them again, gripping and tightening around him. Perhaps she'd taken that one a bit far . . .

And some might say it was also unnecessary to accidentally move her hands just that tiny bit higher on his thighs when the luggage had slipped again and bumped her, giving her yet another reason to readjust. But it *could* have all been necessary. None of it was blatantly inappropriate. None of it was totally unnecessary in a way that would indicate she was one of those perverts who got off on dry humping unsuspecting victims. Although, she didn't really need to turn sideways on his lap so that she was now looking him directly in the eye, maybe that had not been necessary? Especially when she'd leaned forward in a way that made it easy for Marcus to look down the front of her dress . . .

But whatever the necessity factor of the whole thing had been, she had just experienced the most erotic, sexually charged, mind-blowingly, amazingly sexy moment of her entire life in the back of the helicopter. Let's not forget the pilot, because they hadn't been alone in there. If they *had* been . . .

## Marcus

Marcus would vehemently deny it to anyone who asked. He had not just taken full advantage of an otherwise innocent situation to the point that it'd felt like he had been having sex with Stormy for the past forty minutes. Having the most exciting, naughty kind of sex that any two people could possibly have. Like in the back of a car at a drive-in, knowing full well they could get caught at any moment. That's how it had felt. But *no—let's be clear about this—no* advantage had been taken. None. He had done nothing inappropriate.

Maybe it hadn't been *totally* appropriate to wrap his arms so tightly around her, but she needed to be held in place, otherwise she might have wobbled around during the flight. He was only doing that for her own protection, really. Any gentleman would have done the same thing in his position. But maybe it wasn't *entirely* appropriate that his hands had sort of slipped a little so that they were more on her upper thighs, *very* upper thighs and he'd accidentally bumped the palm of his hand against her.

And perhaps when he'd moved his hands again, it shouldn't have happened so slowly that they had taken their time tracing their way down her body, over her dress and across her small, petite curves. *Okay*, and maybe it was just a *little* inappropriate that he had moved her hair out the way and let his fingers trace the back of her neck ever so slowly as he did so. But her hair had been in his face. It was basically blowing in his eye; any man would have needed to move it. But maybe someone might have perceived it as inappropriate when he leaned so close to her exposed neck that his face came into contact with it. That he had inhaled her scent and his lips had touched her hair and when he had moved, they had kind of grazed the entire length of her sweet-smelling, slender neck.

And someone out there might also say that it had been unnecessary to sort of . . . well, *okay*, he had kind of pressed himself into her a bit—but only because she had started wiggling on his lap. He couldn't help it. He was a man, after all. It was a perfectly natural response to a woman—a very, very, *very* attractive woman—sliding up and down on his lap.

And then there was that moment when he'd accidentally grazed her breast while . . . *well*, there had actually been no good reason to do it. But she had leaned forward and her dress had gaped and he hadn't wanted the pilot to see so he'd held it closed. But he hadn't needed to let his fingertips move slowly over the tip of her nipple, which was pressing against the fabric of her dress.

Finally, the helicopter landed safely—and they both disembarked. Marcus had to wait a few moments for the swelling in his pants to subside before he was fit for polite society. When he didn't climb off immediately, Stormy had glanced at him, her gaze immediately falling to his lap.

"Ooops," she said, a naughty smile lighting up her face.

# CHAPTER THIRTY-TWO

## Un-Sex

Stormy

*S*tormy felt like she needed to throw a bucket of cold water over her head. The weird thing that had just happened between them in the helicopter. What the hell was that, anyway? Some strange no-sex sex? Had they just invented some new kind of thing? *Un-sex?*

Her hormones were zinging and her body was physically aching for him. The kiss last night and now the helicopter were the longest form of foreplay she'd ever engaged in, and now she was desperate for the main event—something she was quite sure was going to be happening. There was no way the two of them could deny it any longer, something was happening between them, and it was so out of their control.

She looked around for the first time. They had landed near the beach. The most beautiful beach in the entire world.

The place was magical, unlike anything she'd ever seen or experienced before. When she was growing up, family holidays away weren't exactly her dad's (and whichever wife he was currently on) thing. Her foster families had never really taken her anywhere, either. And then of course there was her very limited, stretched-like-old-stale-chewing-gum financial situation, which put a huge damper on things like eating food and travel. Her current financial situation was pretty dire. She hadn't told anyone about it, except she had let it slip accidentally on a call with Jane the other day, that she was officially homeless.

She had nowhere to live when she got back to South Africa. Her landlord, the kindest, most patient man the world had ever created, had finally asked her to leave, after months and months of her being unable to pay the rent. She couldn't even afford a roof over her head, let alone holidays away. But this didn't panic her as much as it might have panicked someone else; she always made a plan. It was how she'd grown up—how she'd been forced to grow up. She'd had to fend for herself from a very early age. But, somehow, everything always seemed to work out. The universe provides what you need, when you need it—especially when the landlord had declared he'd always wanted a pet tortoise and taken Elvis in. She'd miss him, but she knew he was in good hands; besides his flat had a patch of lawn outside, so it was better for him anyway. If it meant spending a few nights at the women's shelter at the nearby church, so be it. If it meant busking with her guitar for a little while to make extra money, that was also okay. She always landed on her feet again; it was just who she was.

Of course, Lilly and Damien always offered her accommodation when she needed it. Damien even said he would build a little studio apartment on top of their garage for her. But she couldn't accept charity, and she didn't have anything to barter with them. Lilly had said that the pleasure of her company was more than enough, but Stormy didn't want to be in the way. Relationships are hard enough without your stepsister living on your roof.

She quickly pushed all those thoughts out of her mind; no use in dwelling on the what if, when, what and how. She was right here, right now, and she was going to enjoy it. Although they were only going to be in Mombasa for a little while, she was determined to do absolutely everything she could to take in the experience. Starting with that sea.

It was perfectly crystal clear at its most shallow. From the clearness, it radiated out and turned into a pale, powdery blue, which almost looked like it would be soft to the touch. The color reminded her of the beautiful blue calcite crystal—that swirly, pale, almost cotton-candy blue. She smiled to herself and turned around to see where Marcus had got to, but when she did and saw his expression, her stomach seemed to involuntarily jump up and down a few times. He had a smile plastered across his face, maybe the biggest smile she'd seen so far, and he was just looking at her. Staring, almost. His pupils looked big, black and dilated, even in the bright light. He was also more casual than she'd seen him before: relaxed with his hands in pockets, his hair all messy and tousled from the wind, and leaning against a palm tree. He looked great. Amazing. Perfect.

The look on his face, though! That look in his eye—the glint, the shine and the depth. She smiled back at him, and they held each other's gazes for the longest time.

She was the one who eventually broke eye contact and turned her attention back to the sea in front of her. She walked down onto the beach and took off her sandals. The warm white sand squished between her toes and she wiggled them, savoring the sensation. She loved the feel of sand beneath her feet, just like she loved the feel of mud between her toes, or rain on her bare skin. The sand was fine, soft and snowy in color. The contrast between the white of the beach and the blue of the sea was breathtaking. Huge palm trees dotted the shore, casting long shadows over the sand, giving it a beautiful, mottled appearance. The scene in front of her was like an exquisite patchwork quilt, bits and pieces of different colors, shapes and textures all blended together to form something wondrous and unique.

"Beautiful," Marcus said, suddenly standing right behind her.

"It is," Stormy replied, turning to face him. He was so close. He reached out and touched her cheek, letting his fingers linger—the touching wasn't sexual at all. Not like it had been a few moments ago in the helicopter. His eyes seemed to trace the surfaces and features of her face; he ran his gaze from her eyes to her lips and then to her nose. His look was so intense that it actually made her nose tickle; she rubbed it self-consciously, and he smiled at her. The wind picked up and strands of her hair blew across her face. He took a strand between his fingers and looked at it.

"Pink," he said, twirling it around his finger. "I like it." He let go of that strand and took up another—a blue one this time— between his fingers. He took a step closer and tucked it behind her ear with such gentle care that it made her feel melty inside. The feel of his fingertips on her ear made her shiver. Stormy was still wearing the colorful scarf that Marcus had bought her at the market, and the wind suddenly picked it up and took it away. It flew for a few meters before landing on the sand.

Marcus immediately moved to get it. He picked it up and dusted it off before walking back up to her and gently putting it around the back of her neck, using it to pull her even closer. Their faces were almost touching.

"It matches your hair," he said, gently knotting it at her throat.

There was something so potent between them, it was impossible, *impossible* to deny. With each encounter, the need to be with him grew tenfold. He was like an addictive drug: the more she had, the more she wanted. More, more, more.

And then he did something that almost knocked her off her feet. He pulled her closer and planted a kiss on her forehead. Just like that, without any reason. A soft, gentle kiss that felt so caring it almost brought tears to her eyes.

"Come, let's go check into our hotel," he said, smiling down at her before turning and walking away. Stormy watched him for a moment, and as if sensing her gaze, he turned his head and dazzled her with yet another smile. A smile that seemed to reach right inside her.

# CHAPTER THIRTY-THREE

## IT REMINDS ME OF
## CHINESE NEW YEAR

~

Marcus

*T*here was something so pure and innocent about her. The way she laughed out loud and played with the sand. The way she looked at things like she was looking at it all for the first time ever. It was such an endearing quality; it was the quality that he liked most about her.

The problem was, Marcus was starting to like *everything* about her. She was a perfect balance of sweet and naughty. The thing that had happened in the helicopter . . . there were almost no words to describe it. To describe how erotic and raw it had been, yet intimate as well, in some strange way, even though there had been a complete stranger only a few feet away. She'd responded to the closeness of his body as he'd responded to hers; she'd craved that intimacy as much as he had.

Her smile seemed to light up the world around her. Her hair

made everything bright and colorful. She was like a rainbow after a storm.

She was all of those things and more. On top of all that, the thing that most people probably overlooked was her intelligence—albeit an unusual one. Her fiery personality, her sense of self-sufficiency. She didn't rely on others for anything, and she gave Marcus a run for his money. She was passionate about what she did and what she believed in. Okay, so maybe he didn't believe in the power of Tarot cards and ancient aliens, but he admired her conviction. And kindness. Maybe the kindest person he'd ever met. Even kind to inanimate objects.

It killed him to think of the life that she'd lived. No family to support her and care for her—not unlike him in a way, of course, but he'd never wanted for money and material things. He'd never needed to barter for goods because he had no money, or take dangerous taxis around town or worse, walk. He hated that she had to do those things. Because she deserved it all. She deserved everything that life had on offer.

He couldn't say how it had happened—*it was total madness and completely illogical and against everything he wanted or believed in or planned for*—but he wanted her. He wanted her in other ways; not to fuck her against a wall and on a car. It was bigger than that. But, she also didn't tick any of his boxes, she filled almost none of his requirements on his Excel spreadsheet. Despite all this, he couldn't take his eyes off her now as they walked to their rooms.

The hotel he'd booked was one of the best in Mombasa—naturally. It sat atop a jagged, rocky cliff face looking out over the clear, azure blue waters of Nyali Beach. Parts of the hotel looked like they had actually been carved into the ancient-looking rock face, giving the illusion that the hotel disappeared into its environment. They walked up a series of steep rocky stairs, winding their way through the lush, colorful gardens, where palms, tropical flowering plants and bougainvillea combined and intertwined to form a thick blanket of foliage that was draped everywhere. Suddenly a flash of bright red caught Marcus's eye and he turned, coming face to face with one of the hotel staff.

"*Jambo*," a woman greeted them cheerfully.

"Jambo? What does that mean?" Stormy asked sweetly.

"It's a Kenyan greeting." She smiled at the two of them. "Are you checking in?"

Marcus nodded. "The name's Lewis."

"Of course." The woman motioned for them to follow her to the reception area, where they were handed their room keys. Marcus looked at the numbers on the keys and his heart had almost fallen out of his chest when he noticed that their rooms were right next door to each other. He was so tempted to slip the receptionist some money and whisper, "*pretend you only have one room left*" . . . but he didn't. Instead, he and Stormy walked in silence once more as she led them to their respective rooms.

He was so reluctant to say goodbye to her when they both slipped their keys into their locks. His mind was drawing a blank as he scrambled to think of something to say to make her stay. To make her *not* close that door behind her . . .

"Do you want to go for a swim soon?" Stormy asked and Marcus's heart sang out. He opened his mouth to reply when she quickly corrected herself. "Oh . . . never mind, I don't have a bathing suit." Marcus was about to say they could go buy her one, but she had already come up with another plan. "Should we go for a walk on the beach? I'm dying to see more of this place."

"I'd love to." The words tumbled out of his mouth.

"Meet me on the beach in half an hour," she said, and disappeared into her room.

As Marcus walked into his room, he regretted even more not offering the receptionist a bribe in exchange for a little white lie. Because he wanted Stormy in this room. In that four-poster bed and in that huge bath. Marcus suddenly felt like a sixteen-year-old boy again, getting ready to go to the dance with the hottest chick at school. He had a shower, washed his hair and brushed his teeth—twice. He rummaged through his bag, feeling almost womanlike in his sudden indecision over what to wear. He'd never obsessed about what to wear so much.

After trying on several things, he opted for a casual pair of shorts and a shirt—they were actually beige, he smiled at that. He then stood in front of the mirror and obsessed some more with his hair, brushing it and gelling it into various styles. None of them seemed to be good enough, so he eventually just ruffled it up and left it. He then practically emptied a bottle of cologne on himself, and immediately regretted it. This was a casual walk on the beach, not a date. Too much cologne, what would that say? So he jumped back into the shower, washed it off and was much more sparing the next time he put it on.

He was about five minutes early when he got to the beach. He had been so eager to see her that he had almost sprinted down. But he felt like he was going to go mad waiting for her, as he paced up and down the little stretch and practiced several cool and casual poses against the palm tree.

And then she came . . . *and almost took his breath away.*

She was wearing a plain white T-shirt (no bra, he noted immediately with a pleasurable little shudder) and some blue shorts. She had tied the scarf around her head and her hair was up in a big, messy bun. Tufts of color were jutting out at different angles, reminding him of fireworks. It was utterly ridiculous and just about the cutest thing he'd ever seen.

"What's so funny?" she asked when she reached him, obviously noting his massive smile.

"Just your hair. It reminds me of Chinese New Year."

"Oh, my Goddess." She gasped. "That's exactly what I was going for!"

Marcus could see she was being serious. He burst out laughing. "Do you realize that you are officially the silliest person I have ever met, Stormy-Rain?" And he couldn't fight it—he placed his hands on her shoulders.

She smiled at him and shrugged.

Deciding to stop even trying to fight it, he added, "You look really beautiful."

She smiled at him and blushed prettily.

"Thanks. I feel a bit weird in these clothes. They were a bit boring, hence the headscarf vibe."

Marcus shook his head. "Trust me. You could never look boring."

Stormy looked down and ran her hands over her shirt. "Thanks again for buying me these clothes, I really appreciate it."

"It's a pleasure."

"I just hope the airline finds my bag, or I'll be wearing these for the rest of my life." Stormy brushed off the comment with a small, dismissive laugh, but something about her statement didn't sit quite right with him.

"What do you mean?"

"Oh, that was all the clothing I had." She sounded so causal as she delivered this news.

"What?" Marcus was shocked. "In that bag? All the clothing you own?"

Stormy nodded. "I don't really have much."

"Why did you put it all in that one bag, though?"

"Oh, because I'm kind of moving when I get back home," she replied flippantly, flicking some sand up with her toes. They had both started walking down the beach now, so close that their shoulders were almost touching.

"Where are you moving to?" Marcus's heart skipped a beat as he suddenly worried she was moving to another city. But when he turned and looked at her, she just shrugged.

"Not sure, really."

"How can you not know where you're moving to?" He was totally confused; this seemed a little haphazard and vague, even for Stormy.

"Oh, I've been evicted, so I'm not sure where to go next! Maybe someone will loan me their couch for a night or two, and then I guess I'll just see where the wind takes me."

Marcus felt like he'd been kicked in the stomach. "You have nowhere to live?"

She shook her head and Marcus's mind shifted into overdrive. Technically, he knew this wasn't his problem; it wasn't like they were dating. But there was no way he could let her be homeless. *No way*. And he certainly wasn't okay with her sleeping on people's couches and God knows where else. He was overwhelmed with the desire to swoop in and rescue her but he knew she would hate him thinking that way. He got the feeling she wasn't good at asking for help, or accepting it, even when she needed it. But he had to figure something out. She deserved more.

"So, how exactly do you make money? What are the things you actually do?" Marcus was wondering if there was some kind of sly way of paying for a year's worth of Tarot card readings or aura clearings, or whatever other thing she had on offer.

She walked ahead of Marcus now and turned to face him, walking backwards down the beach. She'd picked up a palm frond and was trailing it in the sand, making a pattern as she went.

"Well, I do some card readings and Reiki and crystal massages. Not a lot, though. Um . . ." She swooshed the palm frond playfully, as if she wasn't at all bothered by the fact she was going to be homeless. "Then sometimes I paint pictures and sell them . . . Lilly usually buys them, though." Stormy rolled her eyes playfully. "I wrote and directed and acted in a play last year, but theatre never makes money, although it did get a really good review which was cool. Sometimes I play guitar at the old age home, but that's just volunteering. Sometimes they give me things, though. One of the old ladies there, Margaret, always bakes me biscuits, but I've never had the heart to tell her that she's putting in salt, not sugar. And then . . . I don't know, whatever."

"Is there something you *want* to do, though? Like some sort of job or career? Or studying, even? It seems like you have a lot of different interests." Her previously carefree attitude seemed to wane a bit and Marcus noticed a certain sadness in her expression. It broke his heart.

"I don't know." Stormy shrugged. "I like helping and healing people. Um . . . I like theatre, especially acting, although I love directing, too. I've always wanted to teach drama to kids, or music even—perhaps musical theatre. I like painting too, maybe I could learn more about art therapy. Drawing helped me so much as a child, maybe I could use it to help other kids too. Maybe I could learn more about crystal healing and Reiki, most of the stuff I do is self-taught, it would be nice to really learn about it. Officially." She shrugged again. For someone who didn't know what she wanted to do, it sounded like she had a very long list of options. "But I kind of had to drop out of school so . . ." Her voice trailed off and she fiddled with the palm frond distractedly.

"Why did you drop out of school?" he asked, sensing the sadness in her voice that she wasn't doing a particularly good job of hiding.

She stopped walking and turned to look at the sea. "There was this thing with one of my foster dads. I ran away from them and then kind of had nowhere to go for a while."

Marcus's blood suddenly started to boil. "What *thing*?" he asked through a tightly clenched jaw. He wasn't sure what he would do if she told him a story about someone taking advantage of her in that way.

She was avoiding his gaze now. "He was just a bit of a pervert and I got him to back off, but after a while I just couldn't bring myself to stay there anymore."

*Fuck.* He was trying not to show it, but he wasn't coping

with this conversation. The more he learned about Stormy, the more he admired her, but he also felt deeply saddened. She had not had an easy life, not at all. The same thought kept coming back to him, over and over again: she deserved more. *She deserves so much more.*

"How many foster families did you live with?"

She shrugged again. More sadness. "Two." She hesitated. "Unless you count those other weirdos I stayed with for exactly three days before running away. So three, I guess." Stormy finally looked up and met his eyes again. She must have sensed his thoughts, because she gave him a playful smack on his arm and suddenly smiled.

"But it wasn't all bad! When my dad married Lilly's mom, those were the happiest few months of my life. We were like a real family for a while. And also when I lived with Lilly and her dad much later on once he won custody of her, that was pretty cool, too. I even inherited some big brothers."

Marcus suddenly felt ashamed for complaining about his childhood. His father had died, and his mother had become very distant, but he'd always had a roof over his head, food on the table—well, it was too messy to eat on—but it was food none the less. His father had had a life policy that had allowed him to go to the best university in the country, and after that, there had even been a little left over to help him buy his first place. It had all set him up quite comfortably in life and given him an advantage.

"Come, let's feel the water!" she suggested brightly, turning and running towards the water's edge. But he knew now that just below that smile of hers was a part of her that was in pain. A part of her that clearly had regrets and unfulfilled wishes. She may act like she was okay with everything and enjoyed the so-called freedom of her life, but Marcus was now positive that there was a part of her that probably longed for some kind of stability and normality in her life—no matter how much she tried to deny it.

# CHAPTER THIRTY-FOUR

## YOU ONLY LIVE ONCE
## IN THIS LIFE

~

**Stormy**

*S*tormy had never felt such a warm sea before. It was the temperature of a heated pool, and on closer inspection, was completely see-through. She waded in until the water had crept up to her knees.

"Come in," she called to Marcus, who was still standing on the beach, watching her. He had a queer look on his face; she hoped it had nothing to do with what she'd just told him. She'd encountered a lot of judgment over the years, for not finishing school or not having a home or money, and she wondered what Marcus thought of her right now. She usually didn't care what people thought—she could always brush it off easily, like water off a seal's back—but the idea of dropping in Marcus's estimation was a thought she didn't like at all.

But Marcus was smiling at her, and she sensed no judgment

in his look. He started running towards her and she felt her stomach do cartwheels. As he waded in, a small wave broke at his ankles and splashed his shorts. He bent down and tried to wipe the excess water off. Stormy thought it was adorable—they were in the sea, for heaven's sake. Seas contain water. Water splashes.

Stormy waded in further until the water was at her thighs. She desperately wanted to jump in and swim.

"Hey, don't go too far," Marcus called to her, sounding a little panicked.

"What could happen?" Stormy smiled at him.

"I don't know. Sharks. Rip tides. Stinging jellyfish," he replied worriedly.

She raised a brow at him. "As if!" And with that, she jumped into the water with a splash. The water was warm and crystal clear. As she swam, the white sand was whipped up and floated around her like little flecks of silvery white glitter. In the distance, she could see a few colorful fish making a quick escape—no doubt from her. She popped up to find Marcus staring after her in what seemed to be absolute horror.

"Oh, stop being such a baby!" Stormy splashed the water as hard as she could and some of it splattered across his top. "Come on in. You only live once in this life."

## Marcus

Marcus was not sure submerging himself in the ocean was the best idea right now. If there were a wet T-shirt contest happening,

Stormy would win hands down. He glanced around to see if anyone was looking—a thought he didn't much like. Not that they were his, per se. But still . . .

"Come on, is someone a scaredy puppy?" Stormy teased him.

Marcus laughed. "Cat. Scaredy *cat*, Stormy. You know you mix up every idiom?"

She shrugged carelessly. "Dog, cat, parrot, tortoise, they're all pets," she said playfully, with a little glint in her eye.

*Oh hell, why not?* He jumped in and swam up to her. The water was warm and still, perfect for swimming. Marcus and Stormy's eyes met and he felt that familiar feeling again—that unique mix of emotions. There was downright lust, *obviously*, but much, much more than that, too. He smiled at her, this strange little creature bobbing up and down in the water with strands of pink hair sticking to her face and neck.

"Don't cry over spilled . . . ?" Marcus looked at her questioningly and she quickly caught on.

"Don't cry over spilled milk! Ha, even I know that one!" She looked smug and triumphant.

"Okay, let me think of another . . . Ah, a bird in the hand . . . ?"

He knew he'd caught her out on this one. The cute, coy smile that broke out across her face told him so.

"Um . . . a bird in the hand doesn't beat around the bush?"

Marcus laughed, so hard this time that he created little ripples in the water around him. He couldn't remember laughing this much with anyone before.

"Hey, don't tease me!" Stormy protested with a smile and splashed him with water again.

"You are *so* going to regret that!" He swung his arm and made the biggest splash he could. The water flew through the air and smacked Stormy on the face.

"That's it!" Stormy threw herself towards Marcus, trying to push him under the water, but failing miserably.

"Are you seriously trying to dunk me?" he teased her, deeply amused—tiny Stormy had launched herself at him with such wild enthusiasm. She'd pushed with all her might, but he still remained unmoved. "You know I could dunk you with my little finger if I wanted to," he threatened her playfully. Stormy laughed and then wrapped her arms around him. Marcus was determined to make the most of this moment; he certainly didn't need any more encouragement from her. He reciprocated by pulling her closer until they were eye to eye. They simply stayed there, looking at each other, until Stormy reached up and touched his nose gently.

"I like your nose," she said softly.

Her statement made him smile again. Of all the things in the world she could like, of course she would pick a nose. "Why?"

"It has personality," Stormy explained, running her finger down the bridge. He didn't think anyone had ever done that to him before. It was so strange and sweet and intimate all at the same time. And it surprised him how damn turned on he was by it.

"Personality?"

She nodded. "It says strong and powerful, intelligent and friendly."

"Um . . ." Marcus took her finger away and held it in his hand. "I also like your nose," he said, intertwining his fingers with hers. She didn't resist; in fact, her eyes seemed to drift down to his mouth and back to his eyes. "And I really, *really* like your eyes."

Stormy's eyes seemed to light up even more at this. "Thanks. I bet you say that to all the girls," she teased.

Even though Marcus knew this was just friendly, flirty banter, he wanted to make it clear to her that he didn't. He *didn't* say that to all the girls, "I actually don't, Stormy. In fact—"

But suddenly she was looking over his shoulder, distracted. "Camels!" she gasped, clearly delighted. She let go of Marcus and started wading quickly through the water towards the beach. Marcus turned to see about five huge camels, draped in red and gold fabrics, standing on the sand nearby. A few had sat down in the shade of the palm trees. It was quite an odd sight to see camels on the beach, and Marcus was intrigued. He followed her out quickly.

In typical enthusiastic Stormy fashion, she was already talking to the man standing next to the camels, but Marcus couldn't help notice the look on the old man's face . . . "Stormy!" he called after her urgently. "Come here quickly, please."

Stormy obeyed and came skipping up to him. "What?"

Marcus's eyes drifted down to her wet, see-through T-shirt. He hated the fact that someone else had just seen that. And knowing Stormy as he did, she was totally oblivious to it, and even if it were pointed out to her, she probably wouldn't mind.

Marcus pulled his shirt off over his head and wrapped it around her, tying it at the back with a knot.

"There. Better."

She leaned in and gave him a small kiss on the cheek, before turning and running back to the camels. Marcus followed closely behind and as he passed the old man, he flashed him a warning look. He hoped it conveyed his sentiments accurately: *look at her like that again, and I'll punch you.* A coy look flashed across the old man's face and he held his hands up in surrender.

"Hey, don't go too close. Those things bite," Marcus warned Stormy, leaning forward and pulling her hand away when he noticed that she was about to touch one.

"I just wanted to pat the big guy," Stormy protested, reaching out again. Marcus grabbed her hand once more.

"You don't pat camels!"

"Actually," the old man stepped forward, looking skyward as he spoke, "you can touch, and you can also ride. You want a ride?"

Stormy turned, her eyes lit up with excitement. "Yes!"

"Absolutely not!" Marcus was *not* riding a camel. Dangerous. Smelly. Diseases. Flies.

But then Stormy looked to him and said, "Please," her eyes all wide and pleading, a small smile playing at her lips. "That's what camels are for, in fact, did you know that people have been riding them since 930 BC. They were one of the first animals to be domesticated by man, so I guess you could say that camels are also man's best friend."

"Uh . . ." Marcus had not expected that. And she was looking at him so sweetly right now that all his resistance crumbled. He couldn't say no. If she smiled at him like that, there was probably nothing in the world he wouldn't give her.

# CHAPTER THIRTY-FIVE

## SANDY, MANDY AND BRANDY

~

Marcus

*Y*es, the camel ride was uncomfortable. The large creature didn't walk—it kind of swayed and lurched and bashed about on large, clumsy legs. Yes, it was smelly. It smelt like a Labrador that had gone for a swim in the dam and then rolled in duck shit. Yes, there were flies buzzing incessantly about its head, and every now and then, a long, sticky string of drool would come running out of its mouth and splatter on the sand below.

So, it should have been the most unpleasant twenty minutes of Marcus's life. But it wasn't—it might have actually been the best. Sitting on the back of the camel, with Stormy perched in front of him, he got to wrap his arms around her and hold onto her. He got to rest his head on her shoulder, in the crook of her neck, and feel her soft skin against the side of his face. Every now and then, she would turn around and look at him, laughing and smiling like this was the best thing she'd ever done in her entire life.

When the ride was over, they both disembarked and began walking back up the beach to their hotel.

"That was amazing," Stormy finally said as they arrived back at their rooms.

"It was," he agreed.

"Such gentle animals. Great energy! I really felt a connection to him." And he knew she was being totally serious.

Marcus fiddled with the keys in his hand, once again wracking his brain for something to say to her, so that this wouldn't be the end. "Um . . . we should have dinner later," he suggested, almost jumping for joy when that thought entered his scrambled brain.

"I'm starved," Stormy said, rubbing her stomach.

"So . . . Shall we meet outside in an hour? I have to wash the camel off me." He'd caught a whiff of himself a minute ago and had almost passed out. Stormy smiled at him and nodded and then started turning the key in the door.

But Marcus couldn't let her go right now, not like this. He suddenly grabbed her hand, stopping the motion of the key in the door, and pulled her towards him.

"What are you . . ." Stormy giggled sweetly.

"I'm going to kiss you now," he said, taking her face between his hands. "If that's okay with you?" he asked, not really waiting for the answer and going in for a kiss anyway.

But this kiss was nothing like the slow, gentle one of last night, it picked up exactly where the helicopter ride had ended. Marcus pushed Stormy up against her door and held her in place with the weight of his body as he kissed her hard and hungrily. The moment his lips touched hers, it was as if everything changed. Up until this moment he'd been living in monotones, and now everything was full color. Bright, explosive, dazzling color and he didn't know if he would ever be able to go back to beige again. His world had been flipped upside down and pulled inside out by her . . .

She lifted her leg and he grabbed it behind her knee and wrapped it around him. He held onto the back of her thigh, gripped it, kneaded it. And then he pushed his hand higher, until it slipped into her shorts. She wiggled to give him better access, and he took full advantage of the invitation. He gripped her ass with one hand, grinding himself into her as he squeezed it and pulled her forward. And then . . . he let go, let his finger trace a line down her cheek, trace a line under it, until it came to where it wanted to be. He slipped it under her panties, twisting them around his finger and pulling. And then another finger, seeking her out, needing to be inside her, needing to make her come and scream and . . .

The sound of someone's throat clearing made them both stop.

"Oh, my Goddess," Stormy gasped and then giggled and then without a moment's hesitation, flung her door open, threw herself inside and slammed it behind her.

Marcus turned slowly as one of the staff quickly stifled a grin, averted her eyes and went walking off quickly in the opposite direction. Marcus quickly darted into his room too.


## Stormy


Stormy threw herself face first onto the bed. Her heart was racing. Her stomach was churning and her legs were shaking. She felt mad and drunk and hot and cold all at the same time. Her face flushed bright red at the thought of him. *Of him*.

She buried her face in her hands and kicked her legs a few more times against the bed. She felt like she was going to physically burst all of a sudden. The way he'd kissed her at the door had been so unexpected and had felt so damn wrong and right all at the same time.

She lay sprawled out on the bed, looking up at the ceiling with the biggest smile on her face. And then there was that moment when he'd been all macho and protective by taking off his shirt and wrapping it around her . . . She felt the red heat burning in her cheeks again. The way he had held her on the camel and smiled at her. The way he'd held her hand in the sea . . .

She kicked her legs a few more times. This is what madness must look and feel like, she thought. Because right now, she felt like she might actually be able to float, to fly, to skip meters off the ground. To run through a field of flowers without her feet touching the ground, to slide down a rainbow and land on soft pink cotton candy. To dance with wild abandon and scream at the top of her lungs.

But then a thought quickly yanked her back to reality. Before she got carried away on a fantasy here, she needed to think about a few things. *Marcus things.* There were obviously a few major issues to take into consideration. Marcus was unlike any guy she'd ever been with before. He was a real man. An adult with a mortgage and bills, who went to work in a suit and tie and probably hosted dinner parties for his business partners and their wives with three sets of knives and forks next to the plate. He was a proper adult. A grown-up.

And she was not. She was none of those things. She'd never fit in there with all his legal work colleagues and their pearl necklace, pastel-cardigan-wearing wives who probably had names like Sandy, Mandy and Brandy. She would just land up saying the wrong thing and totally embarrass Marcus.

And this was only issue number one. Issue number two was even greater: she just didn't do long-term relationships, and Marcus was the kind of guy who did.

She knew all too well that relationships did not work; they all ended badly. In ugly, bitter hatred and contempt. Loathing, disgust and resentment so terrible you could feel it. Four (sort-of) stepmothers, a few too many foster homes and a couple of court cases involving her dad and some or other disgruntled ex, not to mention the screaming, throwing of empty Jack Daniel's bottles and even the odd punch, was all the proof she needed. Relationships *did not work*.

Lilly had once confronted her on the issue and asked Stormy if she thought that she and Damien would get divorced and end up hating each other one day. She hadn't been able to answer that properly, because a part of her believed in "The One" and *real*, chocolatey-box love. But she believed in it for other people, not for her.

Her giddy feelings disappeared and she was filled with sudden anxiety. Stormy was usually a *go-by-her-gut* kind of girl—she always listened to her inner voice. But right now, it was speaking ancient Greek.

She reached for her pack of tattered Tarot cards and started spreading them on the bed. The cards never lied. She scratched for her glasses again, the gum had not held and they were officially missing an arm.

She took a deep breath and asked, "What should I do about Marcus?"

She reached out and turned one over.

Death.

The Death card stared her in the face and she inhaled sharply. Most people didn't realize that this card had nothing to do with death, but it was still the most powerful card in the whole pack, and she knew what it meant. And suddenly, it was striking a very deep chord in her . . .

*Death: When the Death card appears, big changes are heading your way. Usually this change refers to something in your lifestyle: an old attitude or perspective is no longer useful and you have to let go of it. Often what you need to "let go of" is some sort of self-limiting belief or attitude. Sometimes you cannot see how your attitudes are hurting you, and when that is true, the Death card is your wake-up call. Even though one door may have closed, another is opening . . .*

*But will you have the courage to step through it?*

# CHAPTER THIRTY-SIX

## EXTENSION 179

～

Marcus

*M*arcus was flipping through the hotel brochure in his room, after he'd had his shower and changed. He looked at his watch, he had some time to kill before they met and he was desperately trying to pass the time in anticipation of seeing her. But it was hard to think or concentrate on anything else but her, and that kiss . . .

And then something in the brochure caught his attention. A full page spread. A photo of a couple sitting on the beach. It was night-time, the stars were out, the moon was full. They were sitting on a picnic blanket, sipping from glasses of champagne and watching the silver, still sea in front of them.

He glanced to the bottom of the page. *To arrange a special dinner, dial extension 179.*

Marcus looked at the page and then looked at the phone in his room. He looked at the page again, *was this too much?* What would this say to Stormy if he arranged it for them? He was second guessing himself. But he also knew she would love it.

He jumped at the phone and dialed quickly before changing his mind. It rang several times, and he was just about to hang up and give up, when someone finally answered.

"*Jambo*," the voice on the other end of the call said.

"Hello, this is Mr. Lewis, I was calling to see if I can arrange one of your special dinners for tonight?" he asked.

"Calling for special?" the voice on the other end answered back. Her accent was very thick and her English was very broken.

"Dinner," Marcus said slowly. "Calling for the special dinner."

"Aaah, dinner at eight o'clock," the voice said back.

"No." Marcus tried again. "In your brochure I saw a picture of your special dinner on the beach."

"Aaah, yes, beach is close," the voice said. Marcus was growing frustrated and decided he would try this one more time and then give up if she didn't get it.

"In your brochure, there is a photo of dinner on the beach, on a blanket, under the moon—"

"Honeymoon!" She cut him off excitedly, as if she'd finally gotten it.

"No. No, not honeymoon." He was getting exasperated.

"Special honeymoon picnic," she said. At the word "picnic" Marcus wanted to jump out of his skin with excitement that they were almost on the same page.

"Yes! Special picnic!" he quickly replied. "Not honeymoon, though. Just special picnic!" he reiterated.

"You want?" the voice asked.

"Yes. Please. Is that possible?"

"Yes. Want room too?" The voice asked.

"I am in room eighteen." Marcus was speaking very slowly.

"Room?" she asked again.

"Yes, room." He paused. "Eighteen. Lewis."

"Yes. Mr. Lewis."

"That's me."

"Okay." The voice suddenly sounded very confident and happy. "I make."

"You'll sort it out?" he asked, not quite sure they had fully understood each other, but somewhat hopeful that at least enough had been understood that he and Stormy could have a nice picnic on the beach together.

"I make!" The voice sounded so confident now and hung up. Marcus felt good about this.

Finally, it was time to leave the room and meet Stormy outside. He couldn't wait to see her, and more than that, couldn't wait for her to see their special picnic on the beach. He walked out of his room and she was standing in front of his door waiting. He almost did a double take when he saw what she was wearing. She was wearing the same outfit that he'd seen her in at the airport when they'd met. The long dress with the canary yellow sunflowers, and added to this now, she'd clearly taken some bougainvillea and had made herself a floral crown that sat on top of her head. Her long colorful hair was down and it was wavy from the humidity.

He felt his jaw slacken. Two days ago, he'd considered this to be the most hideous, atrocious outfit that he'd ever seen. But tonight, it looked completely different on her. Perhaps it wasn't actually the outfit that looked different. Perhaps she looked different. Perhaps he was seeing her differently. Over the last few days he'd gotten to know the woman underneath the outfit, and now he could see all of her.

"You look beautiful," he said walking up to her.

"Here." Stormy produced something from behind her back and handed it to Marcus. It was a small piece of bougainvillea.

"What must I do with this?" he asked.

Stormy took a step forward and took it from him. Then, very carefully, she undid the top button of his shirt, and slipped the flower through the buttonhole. She stood back and looked at him for a moment and then smiled. Marcus was sure that if he looked in the mirror, he probably wouldn't like having a flower sticking out of his shirt, but he was willing to overlook it because she was smiling at him like that.

"Shall we?" Marcus said, extending an arm for her. She happily looped her arm through his and they walked off together.

# CHAPTER THIRTY-SEVEN

## SOMETHING MAGICAL

Stormy

*H*er stomach had done a flip when he'd walked out the room, and it was flipping even more now that she was walking arm-in-arm with him. They wound their way past all the rooms, across the lawns until the beachfront restaurant was in front of them. It was perched high up on the hill. The view from there was probably spectacular.

Marcus immediately broke away from her and walked up to the receptionist.

"Hello," he said in that cool, calm authoritative voice that was really starting to grow on her. "I have a reservation for Mr. Lewis."

"Aaah." The receptionist jumped into action and smiled at them. "Oh, the special picnic," she said. "Come with me, please." She walked off and Marcus and Stormy followed close behind her.

"What's going on?" Stormy asked Marcus excitedly.

"You'll see," he said with a smile. They followed the reception-ist down a long series of steps that wound down the hill towards the beach. It was flanked on all sides by massive palm trees and what seemed like a wall of thick, tropical plants. Stormy ran her hand across each one they passed. She loved trees.

The air was hot and sticky and humid and smelt sweet and salty all at the same time. Stormy didn't think she had smelt any-thing that made her feel so happy and alive in a long time. There was something magical about this place; about the way the breeze rustled the palm leaves, the way there was a constant background chatter of insects and birds, that created a white noise that under-pinned everything. And there was something even more magical about sharing it with Marcus.

They finally reached the beach and the woman stepped aside. "Here we go."

Butterflies swarmed her stomach the second she saw what was waiting for her and Marcus. Marcus even let out a gasp.

The most elaborate picnic had been set up for the two of them on the beach. A large picnic blanket was sprawled out across the soft-looking sand and around that, a large heart-shaped perime-ter had been made from the sand. Tea light candles had been placed along the heart-shaped ridge. Bougainvillea and the sweetest-smelling magnolia had also been placed around it. The candles flickered in the slight sea breeze, causing an orange glow to ripple across the snow-white sands. A path of bright-pink pet-als had been laid out for them all the way up to the heart-enclosed picnic blanket. Stormy hadn't ever seen anything more beautiful in her life. This was something straight out of the pages of a fairy-tale book. It was something that she herself wouldn't even have been able to conjure up in her wildest imagination.

Stormy swung around to Marcus and threw her arms around him.

## Marcus

Marcus had just been on the verge of telling the receptionist that there had obviously been some kind of big mistake. A massive misunderstanding. He'd wanted the toned-down version of the beach picnic, not the version that made it look like he was bringing Stormy here to propose to her! God, this was so over the top. And embarrassing. He wondered what Stormy was thinking. She was certainly standing there staring at it all in silence for long enough. And then she turned. He was waiting for her to launch into an awkward speech about how she wasn't sure they were at the hearts and candles phase of their non-relationship yet, when she threw her arms around him and hugged him.

"Did you do all of this for me?" she asked. Her entire face was lit up by her massive smile. Her eyes dazzled in this light and looking into them like this, he imagined that he could get very lost in there. His head started nodding before he even knew it was, which caused her smile to grow even more.

And then a tear. A small tear gathered in the corner of one of her eyes and his heart felt like it was being ripped out of his chest. "No one's ever done anything so nice for me before," she said quietly. The tear escaped her eye and slowly trailed down her cheek. He reached out with his thumb and gently swept it away.

"It's a pleasure," he said softly, the mood between them shifting as she wrapped her arms around his neck and looked at him with the sweetest smile. A smile that had somehow gotten inside him. Wormed its way in. And now, he wanted to make her smile like that constantly. And if she did, it could be the smile that made him break all of his rules.

It dawned on him. Came crashing, rushing, falling, tumbling in . . . *this was becoming something*. Something that he could really care about.

"Shall we?" He gestured for them to sit, as much as he wanted to stay there with her arms around him indefinitely.

She let go of his neck and they sat. A bottle of champagne was chilling in an ice bucket and he reached for it and the two glasses that were next to it; if there was ever a perfect champagne moment, this was it.

"Oh, I don't drink." She held her hand up when Marcus began wiggling the cork out of the bottle.

"Really?" He hadn't thought to ask this question, he'd just assumed that everyone drank.

She shook her head. "I have a long family history of addiction, it's better not to tempt fate," she said quietly.

"Fate?" he asked.

"Well, addiction can be genetic. So, I've got a fifty-fifty chance of going there one day. And I'd rather not. I would hate to end up like either of my parents."

"You could never end up like your parents." Marcus felt compelled to tell her that as quickly as he could.

"You don't know that," she said.

"No. No, I do." He put the champagne bottle back into the ice cooler. "You are far too nice, and kind and considerate to ever,

ever become like them." He stared her straight in the eye, trying to convey to her how seriously he believed this.

"I hope not. It's my worst nightmare." She looked distant. As if she were disappearing into her head, going off on a thought tangent, and he wanted to reel her back.

"Hey, hey," he reached out and put his hand on her knee, "you will never be like that woman who gave you away, or that father that let you go to foster homes. Ever."

Stormy slipped her hand over his and gripped it. He never wanted her to let go.

# CHAPTER THIRTY-EIGHT

## MAKE A WISH!

Stormy

The basket contained a fresh-fruit platter which Stormy headed straight for. She couldn't quite believe that she was here. The setting was so otherworldly and surreal that she thought she might need to pinch herself. Only she didn't need to. *This was very real.* The just-right breeze tickling her skin, the soft sound of water as the tiny waves broke on the shore, the subtle light that drenched everything in a silvery glow that made it look like someone had thrown glitter down onto the world around them. And then there was Marcus . . .

In this light his eyes looked less brown and more golden caramel. His features were soft, the breeze was making his hair move around gently, giving it a slight messy, relaxed look. Even his signature beige shirt looked good. In fact, everything about him looked good, and yet nothing about his look had changed from the first moment she'd seen him, only her perception of him had. Her perception of Marcus was completely different now and it made him look nothing like the too-shiny-shoed, concrete-stiff, uptight man he'd appeared to be at the airport. Sure, he was still those things. Antibacterial wipes and everything in the right place, but now she saw it in a completely different light. Marcus was, without a doubt, the most surprisingly sweet and kind man she'd ever met—despite his gruff exterior.

She looked up at the sky. The moon was so pretty like this, a small, curved silver sliver suspended in the black sky. The huge arm of the Milky Way cut the sky in half and, to her, it looked like a rock had been broken in two, exposing a burst of bright crystals inside. This moment could not be more perfect, but as she thought that something caught her eye.

"Shooting star! Shooting star! Shooting star!" Stormy pointed, as the tiny dot of light shot across the sky. "Make a wish! Make a wish!" she said excitedly to Marcus.

"Where?" He sat up straighter and looked into the night sky.

"There, there." She pointed frantically, as the star totally disappeared from sight.

"I didn't see it," Marcus said.

"Make a wish anyway." She turned and smiled at him.

"What should I wish about?" he asked.

"Anything. But you can't tell me what it is, otherwise it doesn't come true," she quickly pointed out.

Marcus gave a small chuckle. "Okay."

"And you have to close your eyes too," Stormy quickly added.

"Okay." He started closing his eyes.

"And then when you're done, you need to toss a handful of sand over your shoulder."

Marcus chuckled again. "I think you're mixing them up."

"What up?"

"It's tossing a pinch of salt over your shoulder. And isn't that to ward off bad luck?"

Stormy felt genuinely confused for a moment or two and then shook her head. "Well, that's what I do." She closed her eyes tightly and thought about what wish she wanted to come true right now. When she was younger, she'd always made the same wish over and over again: she'd wished for a family. A normal one. Now, at this age, her wishes tended to vary, depending on her current mood. Right now, she was torn between two: one was for Damien and Lilly, wishing them a long life of happiness and ever-afters; and the other was for her. She carefully considered it, and then decided that the wish had better go to Damien and Lilly, since it was their wedding.

She grabbed a handful of sand and threw it over her shoulder to conclude the wish—to make sure that it really did come true. When she opened her eyes, Marcus was staring at her.

## Marcus

"What?" Stormy finally fluttered her eyes open and looked at Marcus. He knew he was staring, but damn, he couldn't help it. He was entranced by her. The fact that someone had gotten to her age and still placed so much importance on things like making a wish the right way, and then, without a second thought to who might be watching or what they would think, went about executing it. It was amazing.

"I hope your wish comes true," he said.

"Thanks. It was for Damien and Lilly, though," she said, lowering herself into a lying position on the blanket. Marcus did the same and lowered himself onto the blanket too.

"You gave your wish away?"

She nodded, settled onto the blanket and spread out on her back. Marcus followed her lead.

"You should take my wish then for yourself," Marcus said without really thinking about it.

"What?" she exclaimed. "Didn't you use yours?"

Marcus raised himself up onto his elbows and turned to face her. "No. Have it. It's only right that you use a wish on yourself, since you saw the star." She looked at him seriously for a few moments, as if he'd just proposed something incredibly serious to her.

"Are you sure?" she asked earnestly.

Marcus had to bite his tongue to keep himself from smiling. "Yes," he said, with a sense of immense gravity.

She nodded slowly and solemnly. "Are you sure you don't want it?"

Marcus tensed his jaw, still trying to fight off the smile.

"No. I have everything I could ever want," he said. "You can have it."

"Really?" Her eyes brightened like a kid on Christmas morning. "Thanks." She fluttered her eyes closed again, as if she was making the wish.

He couldn't quite believe that he'd just had *that* conversation with someone. The Marcus of a few days ago would have found it to be the most puerile, pointless conversation of his entire adult life, and yet, he knew how much these kinds of things meant to her. Stormy needed to believe in magical things like wishes and the power of positive thoughts, and because of that, these things were now strangely important to him.

The night sky was beautiful. And he and Stormy were admiring the massive Milky Way that stretched across it when the receptionist from earlier appeared. Marcus looked up at her, she was dangling something over them and Marcus began to sit up.

"Your room key," she said, dropping the key into his hand. Marcus looked down at it; a normal, simple silver key, attached to a huge heart-shaped key ring.

"The honeymoon suite that you asked for." She smiled sweetly at the two of them and this time Marcus knew he needed to protest.

"Wait, I think there's been a bit of a misunderstanding." He started handing the key back the woman. "We already have rooms, I didn't ask for this."

"You don't want the honeymoon suite?" She looked surprised and terribly confused.

"He's just joking!" Suddenly Stormy jumped up and snatched the key away from Marcus before he was able to hand it back. She gave him a smile and then turned back to the woman. "Where is it, exactly?"

The woman pointed down the beach and Marcus and Stormy looked. In the distance, nestled against the lush green bush, right on the beach, a literal stone's throw away from the water, there was a small free-standing suite.

"Oooohhhh, see that, *honey*?" Stormy looked at Marcus, a devilish twinkle glinting in her eyes. The woman smiled at them both and then walked away, leaving Stormy clutching the key.

"Honey?" Marcus asked, feeling amused. "I'm sure you could come up with something better than that. Something less beige."

Stormy burst out laughing. "You're right. That was the beigest nickname ever."

Marcus sat back and folded his arms, in anticipation of the barrage of strange names that was about to be thrown his way.

"But I like it," she said, surprising him.

Stormy climbed to her feet, dangling the key above Marcus's head. "So, want to go see our room?" she asked.

"Uh . . . you sure?" Marcus asked, fully aware of the implications in that statement. That they would spend the night together in a honeymoon suite.

"Marcus the gentleman," she teased playfully, swinging the key from side to side now.

"The gentlemen who'll never open a door for you though, don't forget that!"

"You better not." She held her hand out for him. "Come!" she said in an authoritative, manly-sounding voice and Marcus laughed again.

"Do you really think you can lift me off the ground?" He raised an eyebrow at her.

"I have muscles you don't even know about, Marcus. I could take you down if necessary." She crooked her fingers, indicating for him to take her hand.

He shook his head. "You could take me down?"

"If necessary. So don't underestimate me." Her outstretched hand turned into a waggling finger now.

"Oh, trust me, I would never underestimate you. Ever." He

took her hand in his. "Having said that, though, I still don't think you can pull me off the ground."

"We'll see." She grabbed his hand with both of hers and began pulling as hard as she could, leaning back, trying to use what body weight she had to get him to his feet. It wasn't working. He didn't budge.

When it looked like she'd given up, he gave her tiny hand a tug and she came flying down towards him with a shriek. He caught her under her arms and then in one swift motion stood up, picking her up with him and finally coming to rest with her draped over his arms.

"Are you going to carry me all the way there?"

"That was the idea," he said, feeling confident he could do it.

"You can't do it. I'll get too heavy."

Marcus laughed again. "Do you have any idea how light you are? Besides, I've carried you before."

"Mmmm, I don't know. You're walking on sand this time."

"Ye of little faith." Marcus started walking with her and she giggled, kicking her legs as they went. The first few meters were easy, the second few meters, still easy. But it was the last few meters that now had him completely out of breath and feeling like he couldn't go on. She'd been right. The sand made this feel a hundred times worse than it really was.

"Told you." She jumped from his arms. "I would hate for you to be tired out before we got to our room." She winked and then ran ahead of him.

# CHAPTER THIRTY-NINE

## KENNY G WAS IN THE HOUSE

Marcus

*T*hey walked into the room and it was obvious that the staff had really gone to great efforts for them. There was another bottle of complimentary champagne in an ice bucket, more lit candles and even more flowers. An enormous four-poster bed dominated the middle, surrounded by thin, wispy white net curtains that were blowing in the fresh breeze rushing in. Through the open doors at the other end, Marcus could see a deck and Jacuzzi that overlooked the sea. The room practically screamed romance. You could almost hear the slow, sultry sound of a saxophone. Kenny G was in the house tonight!

Stormy hadn't said a word to him since walking in, instead she'd made a beeline for the open doors and was now standing on the deck looking out across the sea. The faint silvery light of the moon was making her skin even paler. The colorful strands of her hair moved gently in the breeze and in this light she was more beautiful than ever.

A knock on the door pulled Marcus's attention. He walked over and opened it and received a delivery of fresh towels. When he turned around again, Stormy was no longer standing on the deck. It took him a moment to realize where she'd gone. And when he did, his heart began to gallop. Her clothes lay in a pile on the deck and she was in the Jacuzzi. She had her back to him, still looking out over the beach. And that was it . . . no explicit invitation necessary. He strode out onto the deck and started taking off his shoes. Stormy turned and looked at him with eyes that confirmed everything he was thinking, and her expression urged him to carry on taking his clothes off . . .

## Stormy

Stormy watched as Marcus kicked his shoes across the deck. He suddenly looked very determined. He picked up his pace and frantically pulled his shirt off, tossing it aside so exuberantly that it actually fell off the deck and into some bushes below. He momentarily looked in its direction, but obviously decided to leave it as he started tugging at his shorts, almost losing his balance as he struggled out of them. He would make a terrible stripper! But he was so cute.

Maybe cute wasn't the right word, actually, because there was absolutely nothing cute about him right now. He was all hard and muscly and chiseled and breathtakingly beautiful in a way that she'd never thought could be beautiful. Basically, he was everything that she never knew she liked in a guy all rolled into one.

Finally, he stood there in nothing but his underwear, and looked at her almost as if to ask a question. She knew exactly what he was asking.

"Well . . ." She couldn't hide the feelings in her voice, the whispery huskiness of it was a dead giveaway. "I took mine off . . ." She let the implications hang in the air before Marcus jumped into action and went to work on that last little bit of fabric that separated them.

Stormy couldn't tear her eyes away as Marcus climbed out of the final item of clothing and into the hot, bubbling water.

As soon as he was in, he made his way over to her. She was expecting a kiss, but he didn't. Instead, he stopped a few inches from her face and simply stared . . .

## Marcus

Awe.

That was the only word Marcus could think of, just inches away from a totally naked Stormy under the moonlight. He knew what was about to happen—there was absolutely no doubt any longer—so he decided to savor the moment and take it all in. Take *her* all in. She looked up and smiled at him, that unique Stormy smile that made him feel positively stupid.

They'd already had sex a few times, but this felt nothing like those other times: this felt like a first between them. Marcus reached out and cupped her face, pulling her closer until her naked body was pressed against his. The air around them was warm and so was the water, but she shivered.

"You're so beautiful . . ." Marcus slipped one arm around her and rested his hand in the small of her back. He let his fingers run up and down the length of her spine as he stared into her eyes, trying to convey everything that he was feeling. Finally, he leaned in and brushed his lips against hers—gently, softly, slowly. He licked his lips; she tasted sweet and salty. He felt her body go slightly limp in his arms as she let out a long sigh—it was the sexiest sound he'd ever heard. He looked down at her as she closed her eyes and parted her lips for him. He couldn't hold back anymore.

"Fuck, Stormy," he breathed. He took her under the arms and lifted her until they were both at eye level. The sudden move made her open her eyes momentarily and look at him. She was so light that he held her up against him with one arm while the other came up and grabbed the hair at the base of her neck. His next kiss was deep and full of need and desire.

Marcus pulled away from her abruptly. She looked at him, a little shocked, as if she'd said the wrong thing.

He scanned the features of her face. Her large green eyes, her tiny nose and pink wet lips. He wanted to make sure he remembered this moment.

"Not here," he said. "Let's do this properly. The good old-fashioned way."

# CHAPTER FORTY

## FATE HAD SET THE STAGE

~

### Marcus

*M*arcus knew that tonight wasn't the night for sex in a Jacuzzi, against the floor, a wall or bent over a bed. It was the night for so much more than that.

Because it was the perfect night, as if Fate had set the stage just for them.

He picked Stormy up out of the warm water and lifted her into his arms, climbing out of the Jacuzzi. Stormy wrapped her arms around his neck as he effortlessly carried her inside. The warm glow of the flickering candles lit the room, and Stormy changed with the light. The orange glow made her look like she was coated in gold and her eyes turned an even darker green.

Marcus placed her gently on the bed and sat beside her for a while, gazing at her in silence, and while doing so locating another tattoo that was hidden just under her right breast. A tiny pink flower. He ran his fingertips over the tattoo, and her wet skin pebbled.

Marcus took her hand in his and looked at it intently, running his fingers through hers until he brought it up to rest on the side of his face. He needed to feel her soft touch. He looked at her, completely naked and sitting on the edge of the bed, looking utterly ethereal as the candlelight flickered against her luminescent skin. "*You're beautiful.*"

Stormy smiled and shifted closer to him. Marcus's hands traced their way down her body and rested on her tiny waist.

And then a thought came to him. He walked over to the freshly delivered towels and picked one up.

## Stormy

She felt the soft material of the towel across her stomach. There was something so erotic and intimate about this gesture. He was drying her, carefully, gently. She closed her eyes so she could focus on the feelings rushing through her body.

The towel moved up from her stomach and then suddenly, she felt it on her breasts. Her body arched, an involuntary reaction to the soft, fluffiness connecting with the highly sensitive skin on her breasts. The towel moved up to her neck now, collarbones, and then down each of her arms and even her hands and fingers. Her fingertips tingled as he dried each one carefully. She would never have imagined that having someone dry her hands would be such an erotic moment.

When he'd finished with her hands, the anticipation of where the towel would go next made her stomach tighten. Her eyes still closed, she waited. Her heart rate increased and her breathing became faster and shallow. Waiting, waiting, waiting . . . And he was taking his time.

And then the wait was over. She felt the towel on her feet, and then it moved up to her ankles, her calves and by the time it had reached her knees, she was holding her breath in the spine-tingling, almost painful anticipation of where it was headed. Where its final destination would inevitably be. Her lower thighs and then creeping, creeping, creeping . . .

With his free hand he gently started pushing her legs apart. She gasped and then giggled. Her ran the towel up her inner thighs and the sensation was almost too much to bear. It was too intense. Too painfully delicious. She wiggled her hips and opened her legs even more. It was a loud and clear invitation, and Marcus didn't hesitate. This time her entire body shook from the sensation of the towel coming into contact with her. He spent a little longer drying her there: she wasn't complaining.

Once he'd completed her front, he put his hands on her waist and flipped her onto her stomach. The abrupt movement caught her off-guard and she dug her nails into the bed as it bounced slightly. She was completely under his spell right now. He would've been able to do anything to her. And she would let him.

He started at her ankles again and moved all the way up to her bum. Brushing past it though, he ran it up her back, then pushing her hair out of the way, dried the back of her neck. She saw the towel land on the bed in front of her, he'd tossed it there and she wondered what was next. And then, she felt the red-hot touch of his fingertips tracing down her back and soon, they were on her bottom. Her skin tightened, all her senses sprang to life. And then, he slipped both his hands around her waist once more and pulled her upwards into a sitting position. She was on her knees now, her back pressed into his chest and he was right behind her. He pushed her hair out the way and planted kisses on her neck.

But she wanted to face him. To look into his eyes. So she turned. He was also on his knees.

She wanted him so badly, and the feeling was clearly mutual, his dilated pupils told her so. The golden caramel was gone now, instead she was being looked at with dark, demanding eyes. It thrilled her.

"Stormy," his voice trembled, "do what you want with me." She realized what he was saying to her. He was relinquishing control to her this time. All the other times they'd been together, for the most part, he'd taken most of the control—not that she'd been an inactive participant, at all. Now he was handing that over to her. The control freak was giving the reins to someone else . . . *her*.

She took his face between her hands and kissed him, slow, sensual and deep. She relished the feel of his hot tongue, his wet lips, his warm breath on her as it escaped from his mouth in tiny whimpers. She stopped kissing him. "Lie down." She moved out the way for Marcus to lie down on the bed. Which he did. He lay there looking up at her, waiting for her to do whatever she wanted with him. She slowly crawled over him, feeling like some kind of empowered sexual Goddess. She stopped when she reached his lap, then straddled him. She leaned forward, placed her hands on his shoulders and lifted herself up, pausing for a moment to look deeply into his eyes. And she slowly lowered herself onto him.

A moan escaped his lips as she did this and his hands

immediately came up to her hips and gripped her tightly in place. He clearly didn't want her to go anywhere, and she had no intention of leaving. This was exactly where she wanted to be right now.

She rolled her hips slowly and Marcus gripped her even harder. Again and again, she soon got into a slow, steady rhythm as she moved her hips back and forward and then in small, slow circles. Their eyes were open, looking at each other. Looking into each other.

"I adore you," Marcus said softly.

"You do?" she asked, pausing all movement for a moment.

Marcus smiled. "I'd be mad not to."

# CHAPTER FORTY-ONE
## POWERFUL AS A DRUG

Marcus

*H*e wasn't sure he knew what do with all the sensations that were surging through his body. She was intoxicating, powerful as a drug. Their movements picked up pace together, she leaned forward, bringing her face up to his, and he wrapped his arms around her, making sure she didn't move. He wanted to look into her eyes. Their bodies felt like one, moving and rocking together in perfect unison, their breathing was also in time. They were both building towards something together, at the same steady pace.

His breathing started getting faster and more frantic, as she began to let out breathy whimpers, which started to build to moans, which seemed to be getting longer and longer. But she was still controlling the speed and pace of everything, and because of this, because of this letting go of control, the feeling that was building in his body was so strong and intense. Like nothing he'd ever experienced before.

They were getting so close now, she began moving quicker on his lap, grinding harder. They looked into each other's eyes and they sped towards the finish line together. He could see the exact moment that she tipped over, her emerald eyes clouded over with a faraway look and her pupils dilated. She looked so vulnerable and beautiful in that moment. He'd let her take control, he'd let his guard down and dropped his defenses; this was the most intimate moment of his life. And it was all it took for him to feel his entire body explode.

Every single muscle in his body tensed. He closed his eyes and could swear he saw stars. And when it was over, he knew what to do this time, not like the other times.

He pulled her into his arms and held her as tightly as he could.

# CHAPTER FORTY-TWO

## IT WASN'T *JUST* SEX!

❧

Marcus

*M*arcus woke up to an empty bed and, for a split second, thought that the previous night might have actually been a dream, that is, until he saw the strand of bright-pink hair on the pillow next to him. He smiled. A small note had been left for him. Her writing was almost illegible it was so large, bold and curly. And instead of dots on top of her i's she'd used hearts—even her writing reflected her personality.

*Hi, gone to my room to brush my teeth! Woke up with strawberry seeds in them . . . EEEEuuuwww! Anyhoo, see you soon. Probably in ten minutes, depending on when you wake up. I might already be back when you wake up, but then I guess you wouldn't be reading this note and I would be telling you this in person because I'd be in the room.*

*XX Stormy*

Marcus smiled at the note. It was so Stormy! He climbed out of the bed, he also didn't have his toothbrush with him, it had been an impromptu sleepover. He was pulling his clothes back on when his phone rang.

But when he saw the name on the screen, a sudden wave of embarrassment washed over him when he remembered how ridiculously he'd acted on the phone yesterday.

"Damien." He answered the phone in his best "normal" voice.

"Marcus," Damien replied, imitating Marcus's overly serious voice.

"About yesterday . . ." Marcus started tentatively.

"I'm sure there is a very good reason that my most straight-laced cousin was acting like a lunatic," Damien said quickly.

There was a pause—Marcus wasn't really sure what to say.

"So, what was the reason, cuz?" Damien asked.

Marcus had to think about that for a while, because right now, as things were between them, he wasn't sure why they'd ever really fought in the first place. "We'd just broken down on the side of the road—"

"You what? You guys okay?" Damien interrupted.

"Yes, yes, we're fine. We're in Mombasa, we'll be flying to Prague later today. Everything's back on track. We're totally fine."

"Well, apparently not," Damien said. "Lilly tells me Stormy was digging her own grave, which normally we'd take with a pinch of salt. It's Stormy, after all, but coupled with the fact that you were rambling, Lilly and I've been worried."

"We were just driving each other mad at the time. That's all. She was irritating the hell out of me and driving me insane . . ." Marcus said.

"*Was?*" Damien sounded curious. "She's not *still* driving you mad?"

There was a pause. Marcus felt a swelling in his chest.

"Not at all." His words sounded a bit breathy and dreamy. He hadn't meant them to come out that way and clearly Damien immediately picked up on it.

"Marcus ... ?" he asked slowly and suspiciously. "What's going on?"

"What do you mean?" Marcus asked. He heard that slight defensive tone in his voice and wished he'd been able to hide his feelings better.

"Well, something is clearly wrong if she isn't driving you completely mad still. I knew you guys wouldn't get on. So, you've either left her on the side of the road, in her self-dug grave where the car broke down or, or, or . . ." Damien paused. "No!" he suddenly declared. "You aren't, are you?"

"Aren't what?"

"Is something going on between you guys?" Damien asked. As the words were out of Damien's mouth, he heard Lilly screaming in the background.

"*What's going on between Marcus and Stormy? Have they killed each other?*"

"So?" Damien asked again.

Marcus hesitated. He didn't really want to admit to it. It wasn't exactly very gentlemanly, and besides, he didn't know if he had permission to say anything. He and Stormy hadn't discussed it— God, they hadn't even officially discussed them and labeled what they were yet. *What were they?*

"Marcus," Damien sounded serious now. "You know what Stormy's dating policy is, right?"

"No," Marcus replied.

"You know she dates people for exactly three weeks and then breaks up with them. To the day." He said it so matter-of-factly that Marcus thought that he might actually believe him. However, this did seem a really strange practice, even for Stormy.

"Three weeks?" he asked.

"Yes. She doesn't believe in relationships."

"Well, I kind of know that, but surely she's had one that lasted more than three weeks?"

"No. Never."

"*Most don't even make the three-week mark. She's more of a three-date kind of girl*," he heard Lilly shouting in the background again.

"Really?" Marcus felt a rush of panic.

"*She usually ends it with a break-up song she writes and plays on her guitar too*," Lilly added.

Marcus felt his shoulders stiffen. He only realized then how relaxed he'd really been—until now. "Well, I am not in a relationship with her," he started. "It's not like that. We both know that. It's nothing like that. It's just, just—" He was about to say "just sex," when he realized, well, he already knew, it wasn't *just* sex! Something between them had changed last night. *Everything had changed*. And because of this, he felt the gravity of Damien's words acutely. They fell into the pit of his stomach like a brick.

"She really dates guys for only three weeks and then breaks up with them?" he asked slowly.

"*To the day! Never an hour over three weeks*." It was Lilly's voice again. "*Sorry, hi, Marcus. Yes, I'm listening!*"

"I should probably go now," Marcus suddenly mumbled into the phone. He didn't want to continue this conversation. "We'll see you really soon." He hung up the phone feeling . . . *feeling, what?*

A little heartbroken, to be honest.

# CHAPTER FORTY-THREE

## So, You And Marcus?

⌒

Stormy

"*O*ohhhh, Storm, what's going on?" Lilly almost shouted down the phone the second Stormy had answered it.

"Huh? What are you talking about?" Stormy was still in her room and had climbed under the table to talk to Lilly on the phone which was plugged into the wall charging. But the charging cable was terribly short, thanks to the massive twist of knots it was in.

"You and M—"

The phone delivered that crackle again.

"Hang on!" Stormy screamed and pulled the charger out of the wall. She looked around the room and then climbed onto the bed, pulling the phone's long aerial out. "Say that again!" Stormy shouted.

"You and M—"

The crackle and hiss cut Lilly off again. Stormy looked around the room and wondered if she climbed on top of the cupboard whether it would be okay?

"You an—" Lilly tried again. The crackle was getting worse, and Stormy flung the door of the hotel room open and walked outside.

"Hello?" she shouted down the phone. But there was nothing but static answering her back. She ran up a small embankment of grass and stood at the top of it. "Hello?" she shouted again. Still nothing. Stormy looked around. There was a bent palm tree that looked like it had frozen into position in the middle of strong gale-force winds. *Perfect to climb!* Stormy put the cell phone aerial between her teeth, dangling the phone from her mouth, while quickly and with great agility she shuffled up the palm tree. The tree was so bent that it was almost flat in one part and she could sit on it quite comfortably. She put the phone up to her ear again. "Hello?" she shouted into it.

"I can hear you." Lilly's voice was coming through loud and clear now. "So, you and Marcus?"

Stormy gasped. "How did you know?"

"Marcus sort of told Damien, and I eavesdropped. So what's going on?"

Stormy shrugged. "I don't know. It started with almost having sex in the plane while we thought we were going to die."

"What?" Lilly sounded shocked. "Marcus almost had sex on a plane, with you?"

"And we also almost had sex in an elevator too, until we got kicked out the hotel for public indecency."

"I don't believe this. Marcus! Getting kicked out of a hotel?"

"And then we had sex. And then we tried to stop having sex.

But we had it again. We tried to stop again. But argued and had it. And now we're having it."

There was a lull in the conversation and then Lilly spoke. "You know Marcus doesn't do flings, right?"

"I know," Stormy said. A knot started forming in her stomach.

"He's not one of these guys that's into casual sex. It's a very rare quality," Lilly added.

"I know." The knot tightened.

"He's not the kind of guy that only dates for three weeks, like you do."

The knot tightened even more and moved from her stomach into her chest as well. "I know," she said slowly. She knew where this was going. What Lilly was about to say to her . . . *They were just too different. The things they wanted out of life, were different. Incompatible even.*

"He's the kind of guy who's looking to settle down," she said.

"I know." Stormy's voice became very soft.

"You know he wants kids, right?"

"Yes." Stormy swallowed hard. "I know." She felt her shoulders tightening. The phone started beeping at Stormy and she looked at it. The battery was flashing at her, clearly it hadn't charged for long enough.

"My battery is about to die," Stormy said down the phone.

"Wait! I want to say something," Lilly spoke so quickly.

"What?" Stormy asked just as the phone cut out.

Stormy sat there on the tree for a while. She felt a little shaken up by the call.

*Actually, she felt a lot shaken up by the call.*

She only dated men for three weeks. She had done it her entire life. Never let a single relationship go past the three-week mark, by a minute.

*But what did this mean for her and Marcus though?*

And what did Lilly want to say to her? She raced back to her room to plug the phone back in and hope she had enough airtime to send a "please call me."

## Marcus

She hadn't seen him, but he'd seen her. She'd been running around outside waving her stupid phone in the air. Then climbed up a palm tree, he assumed it was to get better reception. He'd watched her on the phone. She spoke with her entire body. Her arms flapped, she bobbed her head from side to side, and even flapped her legs. He couldn't help smiling to himself as he watched her. His conversation with Damien was niggling at him, but right now, she was so interesting to watch that he momentarily forgot about it. But then her face changed. She stopped swinging her legs. Her smile went. Her shoulders stiffened. He hadn't ever seen her look like that. He took a step forward feeling suddenly very concerned.

Then she jumped off the tree and raced away. *What the hell was going on?* Marcus ran after her, worried that she'd just received some terrible news. She disappeared into her room as Marcus started running across the lawn towards it. He heard a phone ring once. And when he got to the room, she was sitting under a table talking to someone. He hovered in the doorway, unsure of what to do. And then he heard something that made him take a step forward.

# CHAPTER FORTY-FOUR

## Or As They Say, Proshchay

~

Stormy

*S*he'd thought it was Lilly calling back when the phone had rung again, only it wasn't.

"Jane!" she shouted down the phone. The hiss was much softer and she could almost hear her.

"Where are you?" Jane jumped right in.

"In Mombasa. It's *ahmazzzzing* here," she said, happy to hear Jane's voice. She was the logical one of the group—*well, usually*, she'd run off to Greece in search of her biological father a little while ago but had found love instead. Which had initially surprised everyone, it was so not Jane. But it turned out to be perfect . . . *Fate had sent Jane her soulmate.*

Despite their many obvious differences, they had something very fundamentally deep in common. Being adopted, given away by her mother, Jane could definitely understand Stormy's situation too. Something they'd talked about over the years, which had definitely brought them closer together.

"Are you going to make it to the wedding on time? I heard about what happened. I'm glad you're okay," Jane said.

"We'll be there. Don't worry," Stormy assured her.

"Good." She sounded pleased. "So, Dimitri and I were going to wait to speak to you about this in Prague, but I thought I'd rather call you now. I doubt there'll be much time to chat once the wedding starts, and it will give you time to think about it."

"What?" Stormy said. She could feel something big coming. Her six senses were tingling.

"So, I know you don't have anywhere to stay when you get back to Jo'burg."

"True," Stormy confirmed.

"Dimitri and I were thinking that maybe you could come back to Greece with us for a while?"

"What?" Stormy grabbed her chest, so touched by this. "You're kidding? You guys would want me there?"

"Well, not in the house." She said it with a smile, and Stormy was sure it was because the two of them had very loud and wild sex! "Dimitri and I got another place and he was going to rent his out, and I thought about you."

"Jane! Oh my gosh! That is so sweet, you guys are . . . I mean, I don't know what to say."

"You don't have to answer right now. But I've started a small practice and I could do with a receptionist? If you'd want to?"

"Wait! You would let me answer the phone at your fancy dental place?" Stormy cleared her throat. "Hello, Dr. Jane Smith's office. How may I direct your call?"

Jane laughed. "Something like that."

"Wow. That is so . . . I don't know what to say to you guys. That's so . . ." Stormy felt a tear well up in her eye. And it wasn't just because of how touched she was by her friend's kind gesture. She was thinking about Marcus too. Thinking about what Lilly had said. How they were so incompatible. Despite all the current feelings she was having for him right now, if she was totally honest with herself, come three weeks she would probably be breaking up with him. Because that was what she did. *What she had to do!* It was all she knew how to do.

And like Lilly said, Marcus was a settle-down kind of guy. They were getting on so well at the moment, but they were both not in their natural habitats. What would it look like if the two of them continued this back home? Was Marcus going to introduce her to his friends and take her to work dinners. *Goddess, was she going to invite him to meet some of her friends?*

"Greece," Stormy said loudly, trying to decide if it sounded good. "I'm Stormy-Rain from Greece," she said again and Jane gave a small chuckle.

"Think about it," Jane said.

Stormy wasn't usually one to think things through, she usually went with what her gut was saying. She closed her eyes and tried to listen to what was being said. There were a lot of mixed messages being thrown her way, though. Last night with Marcus had been amazing. Like a dream. *But where to from here?* They were like two peas in separate pods. Like cheese and pencils. They marched to different tunes and were on totally different bookshelves. And she would probably, *no, definitely*, break up with him after three weeks, that's if they even made it that far. Just like Lilly had said. And did he even want to pursue something with her? She didn't know. Besides, Greece . . . adventure, travel, new places and new people. She usually jumped at that kind of thing (now that she flew on planes, that is).

She sighed. "Maybe," she said into the phone. "Yes. Possibly. Maybe."

Jane laughed again. "Think about it. I'll see you soon."

"YES! Okay. Yes," she quickly said again.

"Yes, to Greece?" Jane asked.

"Um . . . eighty percent *yes I'll come stay with you in Greece*, ten percent *let me think about it,* fifteen percent *I need to run it by the Tarot cards*."

"That's one hundred and five percent," Jane said.

"You're right, twenty percent *run it past the Tarot cards*," Stormy quickly corrected.

"Uh . . ." Jane paused. "Sure. Chat later."

"Okay, bye. Or as they say, *proshchay*," she said.

"That's Russian, not Greek," Jane pointed out.

Stormy shrugged. "Close enough."

"Mmmm, not really."

"Same continent," Stormy shot back.

"Yes. But very far away from each other."

"It's all Greek to me," Stormy said quickly. "Besides, how do you know how to speak Russian?"

"I don't, but I've overheard some of Val's conversations."

"Why does Val speak Russian?" Stormy asked. Val was one of their best friends.

"She's Russian," Jane said slowly.

"NO!" Stormy gasped. "You're kidding, I didn't know tha—*oh wait*, I did know that." It all came back to her. She did know that. She'd met Val's grandparents when she was younger and had loved them and their crazy accents.

Jane laughed. "Okay, Stormy, see you soon." She hung up.

Stormy looked down at the phone, there were two missed calls from Lilly, she was just about to ring her back when . . .

"You're going to Greece?" Stormy jumped, getting a fright at the voice, and then turned. It was Marcus.

# CHAPTER FORTY-FIVE

## DEAF AS A DORMOUSE

~~

Marcus

"What do you mean you're going to stay in Greece?" he asked. He'd heard the entire conversation.

"Uh . . ." Stormy looked hesitant. She was still sitting cross-legged under the table. "Jane has asked if I want to come stay in Greece for a while."

"For how long?" he asked.

She shrugged. "I don't know. But she offered me a job there."

"I see." Marcus suddenly felt queasy. He walked further into the room and closed the door behind him and proceeded to sit down on a chair. "That's quite a drastic change, isn't it?" he asked.

"I told you I don't have anywhere to stay when I get back to Jo'burg," she said, sounding somewhat defensive now.

"I know," he said, "but Greece? It's so very far away."

Stormy eyed Marcus up and down curiously. "Well, I can't

exactly stay with you, now can I?" She said it with an edge to her voice.

"No. I guess not," Marcus agreed. *Because that would be madness.*

"Where would you like me to live, Marcus?" she asked.

"Honestly, I don't know."

"Well, think about it . . . I don't have a job, or any money. Not a cent. Literally. Not one. And now I don't have clothes either." She paused for a while. "Besides, it's really nice of them to ask me. And it's an adventure and I've always wanted to travel. And Greece I've heard is really pretty."

Marcus ran his hands through his hair. Reality had come crashing down on them. Hard. Like a rock falling from the sky. Smashing him over the head. He stood up, not sure what he was feeling. Anger, sadness, disappointment . . .

"So, this . . . this thing between us . . ." he started tentatively. Slowly. Not sure how to say it, choosing his words correctly. "It's over? We're not going to see where it goes?" he asked, feeling vulnerable. Stormy looked so casual and relaxed down there under the table, and he was starting to think that the things he'd been feeling for her were much stronger than the ones she'd been feeling for him. The thought hit him in the stomach like a hard punch. Suddenly, his throat tightened, his mouth dried and he felt a sharp stab in his solar plexus. *This hurt! A lot.* His question seemed to unsettle her too; suddenly she was looking all over the room and not at him.

"I didn't know you wanted to see where it went," she said quietly.

"Well, I might have. Maybe. No. I don't know. But you clearly don't want to, so . . ." he said quickly, not wanting to put himself and his feelings out there too much, because he was starting to get the distinct impression that they could get very trampled on. "Do you really break up with people after three weeks?" he asked.

Stormy stiffened up. "Yes."

"No one has ever made it past three weeks?"

"No," she confessed.

"And do you think anyone ever will?" He wished he hadn't asked that.

Stormy looked at him with wide eyes. As if she wasn't able to answer the question. Her silence spoke volumes. She didn't need to say it.

"I see," he said. He could feel his once relaxed shoulders tensing again.

"I didn't know you wanted to try . . ." she said, still under the table.

"I didn't say that." An old feeling was returning. *Why was she sitting on the floor under a desk for heaven's sake?* "I never said I *wanted* to try, I just didn't realize that that was totally off the table."

"I'm not even sure I'm going to Greece," she said.

"You're eighty percent sure though," he said, getting more and more frustrated that he was having this kind of conversation with her while she was on the floor. This was a serious conversation. Not a lounge-about-on-the-floor chat.

"That's not a hundred percent though." She started twisting her hair around her finger. Marcus felt irritated by it.

"Eighty is a pretty high percentage," he said.

"But you heard what I said. I still have ten percent *let me think about it,* twenty percent *I need to run it by the Tarot cards*."

Marcus threw his arms in the air. He couldn't help it. "That doesn't even add up to a hundred, Stormy."

"Huh?"

"Eighty plus ten plus twenty does not equal one hundred percent!" He was getting very frustrated. This conversation, or the feeling he was getting from it, was very familiar and it was making the hairs on the back of his neck prickle. It was making all the muscles in his body very tense, especially his jaw and shoulders.

"Gee, maths police," Stormy said ... *still under the fucking table!!!!*

"Why the hell are you sitting under the table anyway, for heaven's sake?" he asked, the words coming out at a volume that took even him by surprise.

Stormy flinched. Her eyes widened. She cocked her head to the side as if she was confused, and then she tried to stand and banged her head.

"Ouch!" She grabbed her head and rolled over dramatically.

Marcus threw his hands in the air again. "That's why you *don't* sit under a table." His tone dripped with sarcasm.

"What?" She crawled out on all fours across the floor and then stood up and glared at him.

"I said, that's why you don't sit on the floor under a table." He glared back at her.

"I heard you, Marcus. I'm not deaf as a dormouse, I'll have you know."

"DoorKNOB. Door fucking knob!" he spat back and it suddenly hit him all at once. A moment of clarity. Like a veil being lifted from in front of his face. *What the hell had he been thinking?* Nothing he'd done in the last few days had been vaguely rational, normal or logical. He hadn't been himself. They had been on a wild, adventurous romantic road trip through Africa, landing up in one of the most beautiful, romantic places in the world. They'd let themselves get carried away and swept up in the excitement of it all. Things had run away from them. Her hands were on her hips again, and this time, he didn't think it was cute.

"You're right. You should go to Greece," he said and started walking towards the door.

"MARCUS!" she screamed at him and he spun around. "I did not say I *was* going to Greece."

"Sssshhh, lower your voice."

Stormy shook her head and then rolled her eyes. "Lilly was right," she said almost under her breath.

"Right about what?"

"Us. That we are too different. For Goddess's sake, the cards said that too!"

"Well, Damien said the same thing about us."

"He did?" she asked, looking hurt all of a sudden.

"We should listen to our friends then," Marcus said.

"We should, right?" Stormy suddenly looked panicked.

"Yes. We should?" he said, although it sounded more like a question. He turned and grabbed the door handle. He was just about to open the door when he stopped and looked back to her.

"I wish you all the best in Greece, Sto—" He cut himself off when he felt and heard his voice start quivering.

"I never said I was definitely going to Greece," she said softly. Defeated.

"Well, you should." He opened the door and walked out, closing it behind him.

# CHAPTER FORTY-SIX

## SURE AS SHIVA

Stormy

Stormy blinked a few times after Marcus walked out of the room and shut the door behind him. The blink was a mixture of several different emotions; there was confusion, anger and *what the honest to Goddess hell had just happened?*

She didn't really know, but she was sure as Shiva going to find out. She started marching towards the door and was just about to fling it open dramatically and then barge into Marcus's room and demand that they continue this conversation so they could work through whatever was going on and get to the bottom of it, when the door opened and almost hit her in the face. She jumped backwards, just as Marcus unexpectedly stepped into the room.

"Marcus! I was just coming to talk to you," she said.

"Me too," he said.

"Okay, you go first." Stormy stood back and folded her arms

expectantly. Feeling relieved that Marcus also wanted to continue this conversation.

"We have to be at the airport in an hour," he said.

"Okay." Stormy nodded and then paused. Waiting for him to say more. Surely he had more to say to her than that?

"And?" she urged.

"And what?" His words were short and clipped.

"Is that all you have to say to me, Marcus?"

"Yes!"

"Are you sure?" She took a step closer to him.

"I'm quite sure, thanks." Marcus took a small step backwards.

"So, aren't we going to talk about what just happened between us?"

"What's there to talk about, Stormy? We're from different worlds. We argue. We irritate each other, bad, unpredictable, unmanageable things happen when we're together. Our friends think it's a bad idea. Your cards and stars and whatever else crap you believe in thinks it's a bad idea, you're eighty percent going to Greece and you break up with people after three weeks. There's nothing really to talk about."

"So, what are you saying, that we're back to *not* liking each other anymore?"

Marcus looked at her thoughtfully for a moment or two before answering, "I think it's definitely easier that way. Don't you think?" He turned and walked out again.

\* \* \*

The drive to the airport was tense. They sat squished in the back of a taxi, shoulders bumping, legs touching and whenever the taxi went over a pothole—which was rather often—their bodies would bump into each other with a thud.

"Sorry," Stormy said on one occasion when she'd had to grab his thigh to stop herself from falling over.

"Fine. Fine." He moved away from her, crossed his legs and cleared his throat in response (all the good work she'd done on his chakras, ruined!).

She wanted to open her mouth and say something, but what? It felt like they were right back at the beginning with each other. Right where they'd started three days ago in the airport, as strangers. It was as if everything that had happened to them these last few days hadn't meant a thing or changed anything. Or maybe it had, but that change had just been temporary. So fleeting that if you blinked, you missed it. Lilly was right, they were too different. The stars had been right too, *not good in relationships.* She tried to console herself with these facts; that her trusty stars, and her stepsister who knew her best in the entire multiverse, must be right. *But then why the hell did this all just feel so terribly, terribly wrong?*

Why did it feel so wrong that she and Marcus were sitting in strained silence, as far away from each other as possible and staring out of opposite windows? Stormy usually trusted the universe. She had total trust in what it provided, and when it provided it. She had total trust in its ability to know what was right for her and to only throw her as much as she could handle. So, she would throw this out there, this Marcus issue, and see what answer came back. If she and Marcus were meant to try, if they were meant to be together, the universe would send them a sign. She was sure of that.

And she didn't have to wait long for the universe to answer back . . .

## Marcus

"What do you mean, we're on different flights?" Marcus was shouting now. "But I called and booked."

The woman behind the counter looked frightened, but Marcus didn't care. "I'm sorry, sir, there was obviously a mistake made."

"Well, if you made the mistake, you better fix it." He slapped his hand down on the counter and the woman flinched. She started pressing the keyboard in front of her frantically and shaking her head as she went.

"I'm so sorry, sir. But the flight is full, we have a Miss S. Masters on one flight and a Mr. M. Lewis on another."

Marcus could feel his anger bubbling up. "And what time does the second flight leave?"

"Four hours after the first flight," she said.

"What's wrong?" Stormy was by his side now, twirling her hair.

"We're not on the same flight. And my flight leaves late. I'll almost not make the wedding." He grabbed the tickets that the woman was handing over to him and read them quickly, to make sure this woman wasn't making a mistake. But she wasn't. Stormy and Marcus were definitely on different flights.

"We're not on the same flight?" Stormy's panicky voice went up an octave.

"No. You fly now, and I'll fly a little later."

"But, what do you . . . but . . . what . . . but . . . Goddess!" Her hair twirling got frantic. "I can't fly by myself," she wailed loudly, too loudly. He looked up, a few people were looking their way.

"Stormy!" Marcus was firm. "You have to. You have no choice." He turned and started walking towards the check-in counter, away from the queue that they had just been in.

"Wait." He felt a tiny hand come up and grab his arm.

He sighed and turned around. "What?" He came face to face with Stormy and it was as if he was transported back in time to the moment that they'd first met. She stood there; pale, stiff, glassy-eyed and terrified. But instead of only feeling the way he'd felt a few days ago, there was something else too. Something that wanted to reach out and pull her into his arms and hug her. Something that wanted to tell her that she would be okay, that he believed in her and that she could do anything. But he couldn't be thinking like that now and he pushed that part away quickly.

"Stormy, you are a grown woman who's afraid of flying!" he said. The words came out sounding harsher than he'd intended them to and he tried to dial it down a notch. "You have to get over it."

Stormy blinked at him a few times. "Get over it?"

"Yes." Marcus handed her the ticket. "You have a wedding to get to and you're going to be late if you don't get going now."

"But I can't—"

"You have to!" Marcus cut her off and pushed the ticket towards her.

Stormy took the ticket from him. He could see she was shaking. She brought the ticket up to her face and looked at it. Squinted. She started digging in her handbag, and out came her hideous glasses once more. The bubble-gummed arm had not held up.

She put them on and they swallowed her entire face up again. She read the ticket, biting her lip at the same time and then running the tip of her tongue over it. Marcus watched. She read it for ages. Over and over again, as if she was trying to psych herself up. And then finally she took her glasses off, dropped them back into her bag and with a cool calm manner, one Marcus had never seen before, she looked up at him.

"Goodbye, Marcus," she said in a calm voice that had such finality to it.

Marcus stood up a little straighter. "Okay. Goodbye, Stormy," he said back to her, and then, for some reason, extended his hand for her.

She took a step forward and slipped her hand into his. "It was nice getting you know you," she said. There was sadness in her tone and his stomach twisted.

"Uh . . . okay." He stumbled. "You too."

They stood there, hand in hand, looking at each other. This was not an ordinary goodbye. This wasn't a *"goodbye, see you in Prague,"* it was a much more final goodbye. A goodbye that signaled that this was the end of their journey together.

"Goodbye, Stormy," he said softly. Sadness welled up inside him.

"Goodbye." She was still holding his hand, and then suddenly, she walked all the way up to him and brought her face up to his. "I'll never forget these last few days. Thank you for everything," she said into his ear, and planted a soft kiss on the side of his face.

"Me too," he whispered back. *God, she smelt good.*

She pulled away from the kiss, turned away from Marcus and started walking away. He stood there in total silence watching her brightly colored hair get further and further away from him until it totally disappeared into the massive crowd and he could no longer see her. She was gone. It was over.

## Stormy

It took all her strength and courage to take that ticket in her hands and walk away from Marcus. Not just because she was flying for the first time by herself, but because she suddenly realized that it was all over. Everything that had happened between them had now officially ended and was being punctuated with a massive full stop.

*The end.* Their crazy, sexy, funny adventure was over now. It was back to reality. A reality that didn't include Marcus. The universe had provided her with the answer. They were booked on separate flights, for Goddess's sake; how much clearer could it be?

Stormy wasn't as terrified of flying this time around as she had been the first time. Perhaps it was due to the fact that she had other things on her mind to distract her. She made it safely onto the plane, found her seat and buckled herself in.

The plane started moving down the runway and Stormy looked out the window at the airport that was quickly moving further and further away from her. She imagined Marcus standing in the airport and she imagined that there was an invisible string connecting them, and that when the plane took off, that string would be severed. The plane began speeding up. It roared down the runway getting faster and faster and faster until . . .

It was in the air and Stormy no longer needed to imagine the string between them. She could actually feel it. She could feel the connection that she and Marcus had shared getting weaker and weaker and finally, *breaking*.

She grabbed her chest as a sharp physical pain exploded inside it. Her throat tightened and she felt the salty sting of tears gathering in her eyes. She looked out the window as the plane turned and glided and saw the airport one last time before it disappeared out of sight, *forever*.

\* \* \*

When Stormy finally landed in Prague, it was with enough time to spare to get ready for the wedding with everyone. But Marcus would be cutting it fine—not that she cared. *Did she?* Why on earth would she care about where he was, if he'd gotten onto the plane, if he was safe, if he would make it here on time and what he would look like in his best-man outfit?

Lilly's brother Adam and his wife were there to fetch her once she landed. Even though they were not related at all, she considered them family. She considered all of Lilly's family to be her family, too. And in turn, they had kind of adopted her as an honorary sister.

"Storm." Adam threw his arms around her. "So glad you made it on time. Can I take your ba—" He looked down, clearly confused that all she had with her was her guitar case, a handbag and a small shopping bag. "Where are your other bags?"

"Um . . . long story."

"Storm." His wife Mel, demon-lawyer-woman and wearer of high, expensive heels, hugged her too. She quickly looked Stormy up and down a few times. "You know we love you . . . but what the hell are you wearing?"

Stormy could tell that the fashion-conscious woman was even more appalled than usual by Stormy's apparel. This was a regular joke they shared—she'd been determined to give Stormy a make-over from the day they'd met.

"Well, I think it's very . . . *creative*," Adam piped up, although his voice gave his real feelings away. Mel put her arm around Stormy's shoulders and they started walking out. "Do I need to sue someone for dressing you like that?" she asked with mock concern.

Despite the rather dark mood that she had been in for the flight, Stormy laughed; she'd missed them all so much. Mel was always trying to sue people—it was her favorite thing in the world. She'd probably sue her own children for messiness, if she had any.

Driving from the airport to the hotel, Stormy was speechless. Prague was the most beautiful city she'd ever seen. She thought it might be the most beautiful place in the entire world. Before coming here, she'd gone to the library (yes, those actually still exist, with real books, that have paper in them) and taken out a book on Prague. There had been pictures in the book, but they did not do it justice.

With a history dating back almost a thousand years, the city looked frozen in time. The oldest buildings in Prague dated back to 900 AD, and it showed. It was a magical, almost fairy-tale city of cobbled streets and a hundred spires. Stormy felt like she was entering another world.

A river wound its way through the city, dotted with ancient

stone bridges. All the buildings that lined the roads were old, covered with ornate decorations and designs. Some were also covered in golden sculptures, and all of them had terracotta-colored roofs. At the very apex of the city stood Prague Castle, an absolute wonder, with its Gothic spires that were built in the ninth century. Stormy remembered reading that it was the largest, oldest castle in the world, full of beautiful art, sculptures and unbelievably high vaulted ceilings. She'd been looking forward to seeing it.

And of course, the hotel was just as spectacular. Damien had spared no expense, and he could certainly afford the very best. It was a beautiful old building, and Stormy felt like she was stepping into some kind of medieval castle. A very luxurious one. It seemed eerie and almost mysterious inside. Despite that, Stormy was receiving good vibrations from it.

The temperature was a chilly six degrees Celsius, which to a South African felt like an Antarctic winter. Still dressed in summery clothes, Stormy froze the second she got out of the car.

Once inside, Stormy braced herself for a moment or two before entering the hive of wedding activity that was no doubt taking place in Lilly's room. She thought about Marcus again, and wondered how long it would be till she saw him. For Goddess's sake! She berated herself for that thought. It felt so wrong to be apart, but . . .

She took a deep breath and reminded herself that this day was all about Damien and Lilly, and pushed Marcus as far out of her brain as possible.

# CHAPTER FORTY-SEVEN

## MEN ARE APRIL
## WHEN THEY WOO

~

Stormy

"Stormy!" Lilly threw herself on Stormy as soon as she walked through the door and put her mouth to her ear. "Thank God you're here, Val has gone mad!" she whispered urgently.

"Val's always been mad," Stormy corrected.

"She's madder than usual."

At that moment, as if on cue, Val walked in from the adjoining bathroom. "Stormy." She pointed imperiously. "Nails. Hair. Make-up . . . Go! Now! Oh, and hello, nice to see you."

And then after a quick hug, Val dragged Stormy towards the pair of women on the other side of the room, who were wielding brushes and hairdryers. One looked at Stormy's hair and pointed, said something in Czech, and then shook her head.

Val looked at her watch. "Yes. Making good time, people. But let's not slow down. Come come, people." She clapped a few times and then tapped on a clipboard that she seemed to be carrying around. "Go, people, go!" She was saying "people" an awful lot.

And then Annie swooped in. "Stormy!" she shouted. "Hi! Yay, you're here. Sorry, no time to talk. I need a steamer, pronto. Dress has a crease. Steamer. Now. Crease." And she darted back and forth a few times for added urgency. Annie was a fashion designer and had made Lilly's first wedding dress, the one that had landed up on the floor in tatters, after they had all been forced to cut it off with a bread knife due to the fact that Lilly's fiancé had left her at the top of the aisle by slipping a note under the door.

"See what I mean?" Lilly whispered to Stormy with a smile. The room was manic with frantic activity, and Stormy made sure to obey Val by sitting down for her manicure. Jane was already there, and when Stormy walked in and sat down, they shared a small smile. No words exchanged. Just a knowing look. Clearly, this was as overwhelming to Jane as it was to her.

And then when things felt like they were just about to settle down into a simmer, Lilly's mom tottered in. The whole room stopped and stared. She was carrying an open bottle of champagne—clearly, she'd started early—which was not unlike her.

"*DAHLINGS!*" she shrieked to the room at large. She always made a loud entrance. It was probably from her decades on the stage—she was a renowned theatre actress of some fame and fortune.

She looked towards Stormy, and let out an exclamation of delight. "Dahling stepdaughter! Kisses," she cried, swishing over and giving her a few of her signature air kisses. Then she looked around and burst out crying, before slumping down in a chair.

Lilly and Stormy looked at each other and rolled their eyes. "What's wrong, Mom?" Lilly asked wearily.

"It's just . . ." she wailed and put her hand on her forehead. "My baby has grown up. My baby Lilly has blossomed into a woman."

Lilly went over and gave her mom a hug and a pat on the back, still smiling resignedly at Stormy. "It's okay, Mom, it's okay."

And then her mom jumped out of her seat and threw her arms wide with dramatic flourish, spilling a few drops of champagne as she shouted, "As Shakespeare says, men are April when they woo, December when they wed. Maids are May when they are maids, but the sky changes when they are wives."

Everyone had stopped what they were doing and were staring, transfixed. Lilly's mom took this as the sign of an appreciative audience and did a bow. "Thank you. Thank you. You've been a great audience."

She turned back to Lilly. "But seriously, dahling, I'm so happy for you." More air kisses were dispensed, and then she turned to Stormy again. "Don't you dare marry. I don't think I could bear both my girls leaving the nest."

Lilly and Stormy hadn't lived in "her nest" for over a decade, but hey. Stormy suppressed a smile and made a non-committal noise as her former stepmother pulled her in for another hug.

"And please change out of that hideous dress. Love you, sweeties." She swung around and looked at Jane and Val. "Love you all." She nodded in the direction of the hair and make-up people. "I don't know you. But I could love you, too."

And then, with one last bow, she was gone.

There was silence in the room for a few seconds; there was

always silence after Ida exited. Val cleared her throat and tapped the clipboard loudly, breaking the stunned hush. "Well, that performance made us lose two minutes, so hurry, we need to make it up."

Things calmed to a simmer once more as all the girls were seated for hair and make-up. The hairdresser put Stormy's hair into a fancy up-do, not something she particularly liked, but hey, this was Lilly's wedding. She would deal with pearly clips and all that hairspray.

But Lilly looked stunning: her lips were painted a delicate shade of pink, her blue eyes popped beneath a subtle bronze eye shadow, and her cheeks were dusted with a hint of rosy hue. A collective sigh rose up as the finishing touch was added—a small vintage tiara, which the hairdresser pinned carefully into her honey blonde hair.

"Oh my God, I think I'm going to cry!" squealed Val.

"Me too!" Jane jumped in.

"I'm already crying," said Stormy, because she was. The make-up artist looked a little pissed as she tsked and dabbed at Stormy's face. Everyone laughed. It was hard to describe the beautiful feeling of that day. Stormy felt surrounded by love. She was practically overflowing with happiness and her heart was swelling, but then . . .

She burst into tears.

"Okay. It's not *that* emotional," Jane said, trying to calm Stormy down with a pat on her shoulder.

The make-up artist grabbed Stormy under the chin and started fanning her face frantically.

"What's wrong?" Lilly moved to sit next to her. Stormy tried to keep it together. But she couldn't.

"You were right about Marcus and I," she wailed. "We're just too different. We could never be together."

"Wait. Did you just say Marcus?" Jane sat up in her chair. "As in, the guy with the perfect hair and shiny shoes who only seems to wear beige?"

Stormy nodded, suddenly wondering if beige, not pink, might actually be her new favorite color.

"What?" Jane's jaw slackened and she almost did a double take with her head, as if this was simply beyond her comprehension.

"Marcus?" Annie's head appeared from around the corner. "What?"

There was a pause as everyone waited for Val to also jump on the "*what, Marcus?*" bandwagon. It took her a while, but finally . . .

"Marcus?" Val finally joined in. "As in the guy that only wears beige?"

Jane rolled her eyes playfully. "Yes, we've established he likes beige."

Stormy started nodding her head. "We had a fight and broke up. Well, it's not like we were together. At all. It wasn't like that. It was just sex, nearly on the plane, and then nearly in the elevator, but then we got kicked out of the hotel, but then we had sex in the other hotel, twice. But then he bought me a scarf and we saw giraffes and I shaved his face in the car and then we kissed and then there was the beach and it was so romantic, the picnic, and then we were in the honeymoon suite—"

"Honeymoon suite?" Annie walked out of the other room and sat down. Even the hair and make-up ladies seemed to have all sat down. Everyone was watching Stormy intently.

"Hang on," Val said again. "Just to be clear, you're talking about Damien's cousin Marcus? Marcus Lewis. That Marcus?"

Stormy nodded.

"But he's *sooooo* not your type. I mean, he has a job and he washes his hair and he eats meat and he's a lawyer, for heaven's sake! How the hell did that happen?"

"I don't know," Stormy wailed, "it just did. Over and over and over and over again." She put her face in her hands, she could feel all her mascara smudging. "But you were right," she looked up at Lilly, "we're just too incompatible and it wouldn't work between us."

"Uhhh . . . I never said that," Lilly said.

"Yes, you did. You pointed out how different we are. He settles down, he wants kids, he doesn't have casual sex, he doesn't only date for three weeks." She started listing the differences that Lilly had pointed out to her on the phone the day before.

"I did say that, but I didn't say I thought you guys shouldn't be together."

"Huh?" Stormy wiped her face, her hands coming away black from the make-up.

"I was going to say, but then the phone cut out and I tried to call you back and you didn't answer—"

"I was on the phone with Jane," Stormy quickly said. "What were you going to say?"

"Well, I was going to say that you guys might actually be great for each other."

"What?" Jane was first with that one. Annie followed and then so did Val.

"Guys," Lilly looked up at all of them, "look at Damien and me. You all said the same thing about us, that we were too different. That it wouldn't work. And now look at us." Everyone kept quiet.

"True." Annie spoke and Stormy couldn't help it, but her eyes drifted down from Annie's face to her chest.

"Goddess, your boobs are HUGE." Stormy was suddenly completely distracted by the things that Annie had on her chest.

Annie cupped her hands over them and gave them a jiggle. "Ten liters of milk in each will do that to you. I sewed in some extra padding in my dress so that if I leaked, it wouldn't show!"

Everyone laughed, the laughter helping to bring Stormy's distress down a notch. And in that moment when she was less emotional, the implications of what Lilly had just said hit.

"You what?" She turned and almost shouted that at Lilly.

Lilly jumped in surprise, clearly not sure what Stormy was saying.

"You didn't say Marcus and I should *not* be together? You didn't say that we would *not* make a good couple? That Marcus and I were just too different? That Marcus and I would never work?"

"Uh, no," Lilly said matter-of-factly. "What I wanted to say was that although you guys are very different, that there's something about the two of you that just makes sense. You could be good for each other."

"But, but . . ." She stumbled. "I thought you meant . . . and that's when I said I might be going to Greece and that's when everything went prune shaped . . ." She face-palmed. She stayed like that for ages, not daring to move.

"You okay?" Jane asked tentatively.

"Yeah, what's happening? I'm a bit lost. Do you *not* like Marcus, or do you like Marcus?" Val asked.

Stormy's head flicked up. "I'd just break up with him in three weeks, wouldn't I?" She looked to Lilly for the answer to this question.

Lilly shrugged. "I don't know, Storm." She reached out and placed a hand on her knee. "But you'll never know if you don't try."

"So, you're saying I should try?"

"Do you want to?" Lilly asked.

And then a knock on the door interrupted them. Annie ran off and opened it. Jess was standing behind it. Everyone looked up and gaped. It was the reaction Jess got everywhere she went. She was just *that* cool. And Stormy was sure that secretly everyone in the world must have a crush on her.

"Yo, guys!" And she also said things like "Yo," which was super-extra cool. Jess greeted the room and walked in looking stupidly hot: short cropped black hair, red lips, perfect almond-shaped eyes and wearing a tailored black suit with bright-red high-heels. The suit's sleeves were rolled up, exposing two full-arm tattoos.

"Damien wanted me to give you this," she said to Lilly, walking over and handing her a note. "Don't worry, it's not like the last note," she added quickly. "Also, I believe we're delaying a bit until Marcus arrives."

"*Mmmmm.*" A collective mumble wafted through the room at his name and everyone looked at Stormy, who just face-palmed again.

Jess looked around, slightly confused. "Yeah, okay." She smiled. "I'm going back to the other room." She blew everyone a kiss and walked out.

"So hot," Val said as she watched Jess stride out.

"Hot," Jane echoed.

"So Ruby-Rose," Annie added.

"Totally," said Lilly, who had at first thought that Jess might be Damien's girlfriend.

Stormy just nodded, still holding her face in her hands.

"What does the note say?" Annie asked. Stormy looked up.

Lilly opened the note and scanned the handwritten lines, looking like she'd just melted. And then read it out loud.

" 'I am counting the seconds until I see you walk down the aisle and become my wife. You are my dream come true.' "

They all sighed and cooed and then everyone's attention was firmly back on Lilly. Stormy thought it was one of the sweetest things anyone had ever written—but it made her chest hurt too. She also realized it was time to pull herself together, this was Lilly's big day and all this talk of her and Marcus wasn't appropriate. But she was also feeling gutted. She wished she'd phoned Lilly back. She wished she hadn't had that fight with Marcus.

The rest of the day went by without any other talk about Marcus. They settled into enjoying each other's company. They hadn't all been in the same room for a while now. Not since Annie had flown out to South Africa so they could all meet her baby, Noah. He was the first baby in the group and everyone had gone crazy over him, with his massive blue eyes and head of huge red curls—which he would probably hate as a teenager—as everyone kept saying!

Stormy was trying hard to be completely present, but her mind kept drifting off to Marcus and what Lilly had just said . . .

*Did she want to try and make it past three weeks with him? Did he even want that?*

Her thoughts were suddenly interrupted by a loud bang.

Everyone turned to see Val standing there as if she'd just seen a ghost. She quickly bent down and picked her phone off the floor—that had obviously been the bang. She was staring down at her phone now, her hands shaking.

"What?" Everyone was on their feet moving towards her.

She turned the phone around and showed the room, with a look of someone who had been totally frozen in horror.

Jane was the first to take the phone. "It's a ring. Who's sending you a picture of a ring?" She started reading the message out loud.

"'Do you think she'll say yes to this?'" Jane said thoughtfully.

"He's going to ask her to marry him! He's going to propose to her! Oh my God, he's asking her to marry him." Val's hands covered her mouth, the color drained from her face. "He's going to marry her."

There was a tiny pause and then each and every one gasped and jumped as they got it.

"Bastard!" Stormy said angrily.

"Don't call him that," Val said defensively.

"You know how I feel about Matt. I like most people, but that guy is an idiot, I'm sorry." This was a bone of great contention and had been for years. Val had been hopelessly in love with her so-called best friend and neighbor for years, and he hadn't noticed her. She had been pining for him, drowning in the hell of unrequited love and he'd been going along very happily "oblivious" to Val's feelings.

Everyone kept still for a moment, waiting to gauge Val's reaction before they responded. Val had been a total mess over this guy. When it came to him, her emotions were often very unpredictable. One minute she was swearing blind she was going to move, delete his number and never speak to him again, the next moment she was in tears watching chick-flicks on the floor, while she could hear him and his new girlfriend—soon to be fiancée—having sex next door.

"I'm fine!" She threw her arms in the air. "I'm fine, guys. In fact, maybe this is a good thing. Maybe this needs to happen so I can finally move on! I'm fine."

But everyone could see that she was not fine. *Not at all.*

"I'm totally fine. Besides, it's Lilly's wedding. Let's not talk about Matt. I'm fine. We need to get dressed soon! I'm fine." She was trying to smile. Trying to put on a brave face; Stormy knew how she felt. But everyone backed off and all agreed with her that it probably was a good thing. That she could finally get over him and move on to someone who saw her for how amazing she was. But the looks everyone was giving each other when Val wasn't looking meant that they all knew what was going to happen. That this would kill her again and she would land up doing something stupid and masochistic like helping him organize his upcoming wedding.

Finally, it was time to put the dresses on and Annie brought them all out carefully in their garment bags. She unzipped them all one by one. They were pretty; pale pink in color with thin dove-gray waistbands.

"They're pretty," Stormy said.

Annie looked at Stormy, rolled her eyes and then opened the last bag. "Did you really think we would make you wear that?" Annie pulled out another version of the dress, but this one had a bright pink belt that was almost luminous.

"Oohh!" Stormy clapped excitedly. "It's amazing." She got up and took the dress happily.

They all started slipping their dresses on and the make-up artist put the final touches on everyone's faces. Stormy stared at herself in the full-length mirror in shock; she'd never seen herself this dressed up before. And she had to admit, she kind of liked the effect.

Then it was Lilly's turn. And she looked incredible. Her wedding gown was perfect, echoing the timeless romance of their setting: beautiful, strapless and tight-fitting, adorned with vintage lace and a thin pink ribbon around the waist. Lilly glowed with happiness as it was lifted carefully over her head and the delicate pearl buttons fastened.

The final touches were added: a flowing, lace-edged veil and a pair of droplet ruby earrings that Damien had given to her as a gift, to remind her of the "burning moon" that had brought them together.

Everyone looked at each other and fell into a giant group hug, before heading out the door.

# CHAPTER FORTY-EIGHT

## DESTINY. MAGIC

~

**Marcus**

*T*he flight finally took off. He'd told Damien to let the ceremony go on without him and that he'd catch up at the reception,
because he might be as much as two and a half hours late, but
Damien had insisted they would wait. The guests would be more
than happy to do some more sightseeing or relaxing at the hotel,
he'd said, and he suspected the ladies would love the extra time to
get ready. Besides, he was secretly grateful, he'd confessed—he was
still trying to get his vows perfect, and had been practicing them
with Jess. Plus, with any luck, Lilly's mom would have passed out
by then!

Marcus remembered what had happened the first time he'd met
Lilly's mom. Damien had warned him about her, but the warning
hadn't adequately prepared him. It had been at an engagement dinner; she'd got up and made a terribly inappropriate (and totally

unplanned, unsanctioned and unexpected) speech about the "terrible difficulties of marriage"—such a great thing to say to a newly engaged couple in love. And after that, she'd fallen off her chair. Obviously accustomed to this, Lilly's family had just dragged her to the other end of the room, given her a pillow and put a blanket over her. Marcus had found the whole thing pretty shocking. He'd left soon afterwards. At the time he remembered them all talking about Storm running late and he'd thought they were talking about the weather—in retrospect, they had been talking about Stormy.

He suddenly imagined what it must have been like for Stormy to have lived with her. His stomach twisted as he thought about her childhood and how terrible it had been. But that wasn't his concern, was it? He shouldn't even care about that. Stormy was going to Greece after the wedding, and he was going back home to his life. They'd probably never see each other again. Which was better. When they were around each other, things had a tendency to become very unmanageable very quickly, and by that he meant that they were either fighting or fucking!

Marcus settled back into his seat and closed his eyes. He was about to drift off to sleep when he wondered if Stormy had been okay flying alone. The thought caused him to flick his eyes open again. *Shit*. He tried again, closing his eyes once more, but another thought of her popped into his head; she'd banged her head on a table and he'd been a sarcastic jerk. He tried to close his eyes for the third time and another thought hit him. This one made him sit up dead straight. Last night it had honestly felt, for the first time in his life maybe, that he'd made love to someone. It wasn't sex, it had been something else entirely, or so he had thought. Marcus flagged the air hostess down and called for a drink, there was no way he was going to get any sleep on this flight. Might as well lubricate the discomfort he was feeling.

By the time Marcus arrived in Prague and caught a taxi outside the airport, it was already dark. He knew that it was meant to be one of the most beautiful cities in the world, but he hadn't been expecting this—lit up against the night sky, it was utterly breathtaking. Everything had a golden glow to it, which reflected in the waters as he drove past the iconic Charles Bridge and into the main part of the city. Huge, glowing steeples and towers loomed above him. This had to be one of the most romantic places in the world, and he was here, and so was Stormy. This time the thought didn't make him feel good. He felt so empty. Like a part of him had been ripped out. *But how could he feel that way after such a short time?*

"You made it." Damien greeted him at the door of their hotel room once Marcus had finally arrived.

"Sorry, it was touch and go there for a while."

"It's okay. You're here." Marcus and Damien gave each other one of those manly, back-patting hugs.

"Hey." Jess got up and walked over. Jess was Damien's best and longest friend. Marcus had never really bonded with her that much over the years, but he'd gotten to know her fairly well; the straight-talking lesbian that had no filter when it came to speaking her mind.

"So, I hear you and Stormy are, like, getting jiggy with it?"

*Just like that!*

"Crap, Jess!" Marcus exclaimed and turned to Damien. "Does everyone know?"

Damien made a face like he was thinking. "Pretty much."

"I bet she's a demon in the sack," Jess said matter-of-factly.

"Jess!" Marcus exclaimed again. She was worse than Stormy when it came to saying inappropriate things. And he wasn't used to hearing that kind of statement coming out of a woman's mouth. Maybe a frat boy. "I'm not talking about it."

"Are we not there in our relationship yet?" she asked, rolling the sleeves of her tuxedo jacket up, exposing both arms which were covered in tattoos.

"No. I don't think so," Marcus said. "I don't think I'm there with anyone."

She shrugged, totally unoffended. "It's cool. But I bet she is, though."

"It's not like that . . . I swear. And don't talk about her like that." Suddenly, he felt very defensive. Suddenly, he wanted to protect her and protect what they'd shared. It was not for public consumption. It had been special. Just for them . . . *even if it was over.*

"Oohhhh." Jess made a playful girly noise, which was so not her usual style. "Someone's got it ba-aa-d!"

Marcus hung his head, trying to look away. Trying not to let the million conflicting emotions he'd been feeling for most of the day show.

"Oh my God! You *have* got it bad!" Jess suddenly said.

"Just *how* bad have you got it?" Damien asked.

"There's nothing going on between us, guys. It's over," he said quickly, trying to regain his composure. Marcus tried his hardest to look up at Jess and Damien with a look that portrayed him as cool and back in control. He could see it wasn't working though, judging by the way they looked at him, and then exchanged glances with raised brows.

"Damien, you need to get married," Marcus said, hoping that

reminding him of that might end this terribly uncomfortable conversation.

"True!" Jess said, her voice taking on a tone of urgency. "We don't want her to think she's been left at the altar again. Time to get this show on the road, guys."

Marcus went to the bathroom and changed into his suit, brushed his teeth and sprayed on some cologne. In a few moments he would be seeing Stormy again. And he wasn't sure he liked that idea. He tried to push that from his mind. This was his cousin's wedding, today was about Damien and Lilly. Not Stormy and Marcus.

"Ready!" Marcus declared, coming out of the bathroom. Damien inhaled a long breath, and suddenly started looking tense.

"Nervous?" Marcus asked his cousin.

Damien shook his head. "Just so excited to see her."

Jess put her arms around them both and started walking them out the door. "Okay then, let's go get you married."

\* \* \*

Marcus wasn't sure who was more nervous—him or the groom? The thought of seeing Stormy again was more than nerve-wracking. He wasn't sure how to be, or how to feel in front of her. A sense of nervous anticipation for the unknown gnawed at him.

He, Jess and Damien were standing front and center in one of the most beautiful buildings he'd ever been in. The wedding ceremony and reception was being held in an old chateau, and they could not have found a better venue. It was night-time, and everything was drenched in the warm glow of candlelight. The atmosphere was mystical, almost ethereal. Large, intricate golden chandeliers hung from high ceilings that were painted with murals dating back centuries. The walls were a deep red, with subtle gold accents everywhere. It really was like stepping into another world.

Next to him, Damien stood wringing his hands, until Jess pulled his nervous fingers apart and held onto one of them. She gave it a reassuring pat, and Damien looked up at her with a grateful smile.

"Totally love you, dude," she whispered and winked at him.

"Me too." Damien bumped her playfully with his shoulder.

Marcus was also wringing his hands; he was just trying to hide it. At one point he had to shove them into his pockets to keep them still. It didn't really work, though, because he just landed up fingering the material at the bottom of the pockets. He felt like he was going to explode, like a ticking bomb getting closer and closer to the end of its countdown. He raised himself up and down on his toes a few times. His feet felt like they wanted to run in the opposite direction. He wanted to see her, he didn't want to see her. *He didn't know what he wanted.*

And when the wedding march filled the air, he had to stop himself from jumping out of his skin with a feeling he'd never had before. Lilly entered first—as she glided down the aisle, Marcus turned to look at his cousin's face momentarily. Damien was glowing, beaming from ear to ear at the sight of her, and the deep love visible in his expression was touching. Marcus had never felt so sentimental before, and he suspected his new-found sentimentality had something to do with Stormy. He glanced back at Lilly. She looked beautiful: blonde, perfect, groomed. She was the type of woman he would have usually gone for in the past.

The bridesmaids were walking behind her, which only served to torture him further. And then he saw her . . .

Never had he felt his heart beat so fast. She looked incredible. The golden glow of the candles made her even more so. Her hair was up, looking more sophisticated than he'd ever seen it. Some pink tendrils had escaped from the intricate knot on top of her head, and when he saw her scratch her scalp as if the tight up-do was making her itchy, he smiled. Only Stormy would do that while walking down the aisle at a wedding. Her scratch loosened a few more strands of hair, and when she was done, the fancy style looked decidedly lopsided and messy. He had to hold down a laugh, especially when a clip fell out and she bent down to pick it up off the floor, crawling on all fours, before pulling it from under a pew with a "Sorry, coming through, nice shoes by the way!"

She was wearing the perfect dress, too. Pale pink. He decided that he adored her in pink. It blended into her pale skin, which he loved. She got closer and looked directly at him now. Her lip quivered in the corner, as if she were trying to hold back tears. *Fuck*, his heart broke. And then she looked away quickly. In that moment he regretted what had happened between them. He wished he could change it. But he wasn't sure if it would be enough to change her mind; Greece, her three-week cut off. Despite the current feelings he was experiencing, they were still in the exact same place they had been in Mombasa.

## Stormy

Stormy had no words for the emotions welling up inside her as she looked across at Marcus standing at the top of the aisle. She was walking towards him—much like a bride might do. She'd had to look away from him quickly the second their eyes had locked, because the feeling she'd gotten had made her want to burst into tears.

But even as she stood there, *purposefully not looking at him*, she could still feel his presence. It was all she could feel, all she could concentrate on. The invisible string was back, it hadn't been severed when the plane took off. It was still there, connecting them across the aisle and pulling them towards each other. But she was resisting. She could see he was resisting too, his stiff body language told her that, and the way he was anxiously rocking back and forth on his heels.

The priest started talking but his words blended together and the monotonous drone washed over her. She barely heard them over the thumping of her heart and the anxious buzz filling her ears. Then the invisible string tugged, hard, and she couldn't help it, it seemed to happen without her permission, but her head tilted up slowly, eyes lifted and they connected with his.

The moment of connection was palpable. An instant physical jolt stiffened her body from head to toe. Her skin tickled, the hairs on her arms and the back of her neck stood up and she shuddered as a strange hot and cold shiver ran through her. And once their eyes locked, she couldn't tear them away from his.

Marcus looked incredible. The warm, soft candlelight really brought out the dazzling golden color in his eyes. She sighed loudly. So much so that Jane nudged her to keep quiet. Marcus gave her a tiny smile at this, which only caused a longer, louder sigh to escape her lips. This time Lilly turned around and looked at her.

"Sorry," she quickly said, looking away from Marcus. "Carry on, carry on. Don't mind me."

A few people in the audience chuckled, probably those that knew her. Her eyes drifted back to Marcus again, but his smile was gone now. Instead, it had been replaced by something that looked like sadness. Her throat tightened as she looked at his face and they fell into another long, silent stare.

The sound of Damien's voice was the thing that finally broke their gaze, and Stormy looked over at him. He'd taken out a crumpled piece of paper from his pocket and with nervous, shaking hands began smoothing it out. He held it up and started reading.

"Lilly, I've been trying to write the perfect vows for days now. But nothing I've written has been good enough, and it's all just landed up in the bin." He smiled a little and looked at Jess, who smiled back knowingly. "But then I realized that the reason I couldn't write anything is because my feelings for you cannot be put into words on a small piece of paper. They are far too big to be restrained by that," he said, gazing adoringly at his bride. "So, I guess I'll throw this one away too," he crunched the paper up and tossed it over his shoulder, "and I'll just speak to you from my heart, the one that you've stolen, well, stole from the first moment I laid eyes on you."

A few "ooohhhs" and sighs rose up from the audience and Lilly looked like she might dissolve into a puddle of emotions on the floor, Stormy wasn't that far behind either. Damien continued.

"I'm in awe of you, Lilly. And when you walked into my life, much like the Big Bang created the entire universe and everything we see today, you created me. *The new me.* The me that is totally complete now, because I have you by my side. I've traveled, I've adventured, I've seen and done and explored and I always thought that settling down meant having my wings clipped, but now I know, it's the opposite. Because you've given me new, better wings that have taken me to places I never even knew existed."

At that, Stormy looked back at Marcus. And as if perfectly choreographed and timed, he looked at her at the exact same moment too.

"Wings that have allowed me to soar higher than I've ever soared before, and from up there, have given me a totally new perspective on life and what I want out of it—and that's you. *Only you.* Today, tomorrow, ten years from now and when we're both old and have probably forgotten each other's names, I'll still want you. Lilly, you're the brightness to my darkness. The yin to my yang, and the missing puzzle piece I didn't even know I was looking for. You make me whole and you make me a better, fuller person than I could ever be on my own."

With her eyes still glued to Marcus's, Damien's words suddenly took on a whole new meaning for her.

## Marcus

He couldn't take his eyes off Stormy as Lilly began her vows.

"Well, I wrote my vows on a piece of paper, Damien," Lilly smiled at him, "and I typed them up too and I've folded them neatly." She took the piece of paper out and unfolded it on its perfectly straight folds. "Damien," she started, "when I first met you on the plane all those years ago, my first thought was that you were terrifying, despite what I looked like at the time." Everyone laughed, the story of Damien and Lilly's first meeting was rather legendary, so much so that it had gone viral and become something of an internet meme.

Marcus finally broke eye contact and looked down at the floor, away from her.

"You were dressed head to toe in black and had more tattoos than I'd ever seen on anyone before. You were just so odd, and strange and mysteriously frightening and you were every single thing I never knew I wanted in a person."

Another laugh rose up from the crowd and Marcus flicked his eyes up at Stormy again. She was looking at him and before he knew what he was doing, he gave her a tiny nod. She responded as the smallest smile flickered in the corners of her mouth. Lilly's words were resonating deep inside him, and they seemed to echo everything he was thinking and feeling. Except, instead of someone dressed in black, he'd been met by a burst of bright sunshine.

"I'd lived my entire life by a plan. A road map that I'd carefully worked out. I knew where I was going. What I wanted. Who I wanted and who I wanted to be . . . until you came along and changed everything. *Everything*." Lilly paused as her voice cracked and trembled with emotion.

Marcus and Stormy's eyes were still locked, and now something else was building inside them both. Something that felt big and uncontrollable. Lilly kept talking, but Marcus heard nothing as he and Stormy looked at each other—into each other. He could feel a force pulling them together, it was so strong that he took a step forward because it felt like he would fall over if he didn't. He noticed that Stormy did the same thing. The pull got stronger. An uncomfortable, burning urgency was rising up inside him and it felt as if it was about to explode out of him if he didn't do something with it. *But do what?* The feeling was so overwhelming it was making him feel sick and unsteady on his feet. It was only when he heard those words, that he realized what he had to do . . .

*"You may now kiss the bride."*

It was like an instruction turning him on. He knew what he wanted to do, *needed to do.* And she knew too, because suddenly they were standing right in front of each other. Marcus cupped her face, and without saying a word to her, he kissed her. Stormy took his hands in hers and wrapped his arms around her as they kissed each other—the most important kiss of their lives. It was a kiss of promise. One of hope and possibility and excitement. Destiny. Magic and—

"Excuse me!" Damien tapped Marcus on the shoulder, and he and Stormy broke apart. Stormy looked around in surprise; Marcus too glanced around, and his eyes widened in shock. Wrapped up in their own private bubble, they'd forgotten where they were.

Stormy burst out laughing, as did half of the guests.

"You're stealing my thunder here," Damien said to Marcus.

Jess stepped forward. "Leave it to me, I'll deal with these two." She took them both by the hand and pulled them aside so that Lilly and Damien could have their moment. "Down!" Jess whispered to them with a smile. "Keep your pants on until after the ceremony, please."

"Okay. Shall we try that again?" the priest said, looking rather amused. "In all my years of doing this, I've never seen *that,*" he chuckled. "Right, I now pronounce you husband and wife. You may now kiss the bride."

"Don't you dare," Jess hissed in their ears.

Lilly shot Stormy a quick warning look in jest, before she

turned to Damien. Damien pulled his new wife towards him, and like he'd done with the first kiss they had ever shared (which had also happened to be on a stage at a strip club in Thailand, of all places), he dipped her unexpectedly and kissed her.

The crowd clapped and Marcus turned to Stormy. "I missed you," he whispered.

Stormy smiled. "Yes, I missed you by a mile," she replied.

"I'm sorry," Marcus said.

"Me too. And I won't go to Greece. Can we put trying this back on the table?"

"Consider it on!" Marcus said.

"I can't make any promises, I can't make any—"

"Ssshhh." Marcus put a finger over her lips. "Let's try our best and see where it goes," he said. "That's all we can do."

Stormy nodded. "I can live with that," she said wrapping her arms around his neck.

"Me too," Marcus said, pulling her in for another kiss.

# EPILOGUE

~

## 3 Weeks and 1 Minute Later
## Stormy

*I*t was dark and the flicker of the streetlights made it all somewhat eerie, like something out of a horror film. Stormy had brief visions of men wearing human skin masks, with hooks for arms, jumping out of the bushes, but she quickly pushed that away. She needed to focus. Because she was currently trying to climb over a fence, in the dark, without alerting all the neighborhood hounds or the security guards that patrolled at night. The fence was high, the night was cold and Stormy was not really *au fait* with the finer points of breaking and entering, especially while trying to hold a cake, her guitar case and a backpack.

She'd baked the cake earlier that day. Let's just say she was no Martha Stewart. It had only risen on one side—how does that even happen?—and when she'd taken it out of the oven, the middle kind of caved in, so now it was more like a large donut.

She'd filled the middle with cream to try and disguise the culinary Grand Canyon that had been created, but forgot to add sugar, so she'd poured it on top, and threw some cherries on in hopes they would distract from the disaster that lurked below the white fluff. So, at this point, she was just hoping it was vaguely edible. She also had something very special to add to the cake too, something that Marcus really wanted, and had wanted for a while now . . .

After a tentative start, and a near tumble, she finally managed to climb over the fence and looked around suspiciously like a cat burglar . . . she'd never understood why they were called cat burglars. Did they steal cats? Or look like cats when breaking in? Or did the cats do the breaking and entering? Cats were sneaky things—she wouldn't put it past them.

She tiptoed up to the front door and slid the key in. She actually hadn't needed to tiptoe, but she just loved the drama of it. At least it wasn't full-on breaking and entering, she thought—she'd "borrowed" the spare key the day before and had a copy made. In fact, she hadn't really needed to climb the fence either, but hey, it was fun.

She slipped into the house unseen and closed the door quietly behind her. She was really getting the hang of this breaking and entering thing. Hey, maybe she could become one of those professional international burglars, those cool ones that do cartwheels and yoga moves through glowing security beams, cut holes through glass and climb up the side of buildings wearing leather cat suits. (*Mmmm*, curious—why was it called a cat suit? What was it with cats and burglarizing? Suspicious.)

The house was dark and Stormy didn't want to turn on the

lights. She was counting on the element of surprise, and she couldn't wait to see the look on Marcus's face when he found her. She snuck inside his bedroom, and found him fast asleep and snoring! Not those skin-crawling snores that large, hairy men make, but a cute little snore. Mind you, she thought everything he did was cute. He could probably burp and scratch his balls and she'd still find it adorable. He was just as cute as a zipper.

And the more time she spent with him, the cuter he'd gotten. He'd actually purchased a vegan cookbook the other day, and attempted to make her dinner—and he was a good cook. He was good at other things, too . . . she bit her lip just thinking about it. You would've thought that the insane sexual attraction might have fizzled out a little by now, but *oh no*. It had escalated. *They* had escalated, and they were currently doing things that Stormy was pretty sure were illegal in parts of the world! Or if not, should be.

She stood there in the doorway watching Marcus for a moment. His face was squished into the pillow and he had the slightest bit of drool in the corner of his mouth. Adorable! Even his drool was cute, that's how stupidly in love she was with this man.

*In love* . . . she just hadn't said it to him yet. It had been on the tip of her tongue so many times, but something had always stopped her. And when Marcus had said it for the first time a week ago, a part of her had wanted to shout it back. But she was ready to do it now. So ready. More ready than she had ever been for anything in her entire life.

She'd tried to figure out what the most surprising way of doing this would be. What would generate the most shock value? She could jump on his bed and yell *surprise* and then start strumming her guitar. She could lie down naked on the floor with the cake on her, like one of those sushi girls, and shout "*konnichiwa*"—she wasn't sure how she would strum the guitar like that though! Or she could just slip in next to him and wrap her arms around him—that was currently her favorite thing to do. And they'd been doing it almost every night since returning from the wedding. "*Taking it slow*," they'd said, "*not seeing each other every day*," "*not sleeping with each other every night*." Yeah, right! That hadn't happened. They had spent almost every waking moment and free bit of time they had together.

Lilly had been so right. He was the yin to her yang. The jelly on her peanut butter, the sprinkles on her vegan ice cream, that last missing puzzle piece that you can never find no matter where and how hard you look, and then when you do finally find it, everything is complete and you can finally see the full picture. That's how it all felt with Marcus.

Stormy crept closer to the bed. She decided that the best approach would be to jump on top of him, so as to wake him with a fright and get the most out of this moment. She wanted to make this a moment he would never forget. She glanced down at her watch—*yup, she owned a watch now*. Marcus had bought it for her when he realized that she always ran late. It was neon pink and full of polka dots at least, and not a gold housewifey watch. The watch confirmed it: it was exactly three weeks and one minute since they'd started dating!

This was cause for a celebration indeed. Stormy put the cake and her backpack on the floor, picked up her guitar and hurtled herself through the air . . .

## Marcus

Marcus woke with a fright as he felt something pounce. His immediate reaction was to fight back, which he did. He pushed whatever had pounced on him off and immediately saw a flourish of color rush past his face, followed by a loud squelching noise.

"Storm?" He sat up, guessing that the flourish of color belonged to his girlfriend. The squelching sound, however, he wasn't so sure about. "Are you okay?"

"Umm . . . sort of?" The room was in total darkness, and Marcus reached for the bedside light. When he flicked it on, the sight before him was nothing like he'd ever seen before.

Stormy was sitting on the floor—luckily unhurt—but her face, hair and upper body were now covered in a sticky-looking white goo. And then he saw it, and his heart fell into his stomach. Lilly's words were suddenly ringing in his ears . . . *and she always breaks up with them by writing a song and singing it to them* . . .

He looked at the clock beside his bed. 12:02. It was exactly two minutes past three weeks. He swallowed hard and stared at the guitar, waiting for her to start. Waiting for his heart to be broken.

"Goddess, you look like you've seen a ghost," she said, looking around the room.

"If you're going to do it, please get it over with quickly." He looked at her, sitting up in the bed. He was fully awake now.

"Do what?" she asked, her face scrunching up into a total look of confusion. And then, slowly, it changed. "Do you think I'm going to break up with you?"

"Are you?" Marcus asked cautiously.

At this, she burst out laughing. "You're so cute!" she squealed in between laughter. "NO! I am not breaking up with you. At all."

"You're not?"

"No, silly!" she said with the sweetest smile on her face. His shoulders relaxed, he let out a deep breath and felt like he wanted to cry tears of absolute happiness.

"What the hell is that, by the way?" He pointed at the mess that Stormy was covered in.

"It *was* a cake," Stormy said as she stood up slowly, wiping the cream from her face. "That *so* did not go as I'd imagined."

Marcus was still not a hundred percent sure what had happened, exactly. "If you're not here to break up with me, then what are you doing?"

"Happy anniversary!" Stormy shouted in a happy, singsong voice. "Well, not really anniversary, but happy *making-it-through-the-three-week-vibe-thing!*"

Marcus watched as she did a kind of jump, swooshing her arms around and coming to land in a kind of "ta-da" pose. He smiled broadly at her. This perky, cake-covered, rainbow-haired woman standing before him—she was *his* perky, cake-covered, rainbow-haired woman. And God, he loved her.

Marcus climbed out of the bed and walked over to her, a little hesitantly. He loved her, but he wasn't so sure about being covered with cake. "Thanks for the anniversary surprise!"

"Sorry about the cake, but you can lick it off me if you like," Stormy offered, sticking her face closer to him, where the majority of the stuff seemed to be.

"As tempting as that sounds, I'd rather not." He reached for her hand. "But . . . might I suggest a shower?" He gave her a naughty smile, which wasn't lost on her. She gave him one right back and started leading him to the bathroom.

Marcus turned on the shower and checked the temperature with his hand, and when it was perfect, he stripped his clothes off and stepped into the cubicle. Stormy put her guitar down and followed him in. And although he had seen her naked at least twice a day for the past—he still couldn't quite get over it—three weeks, he was sure he would never get bored of seeing her like this. (And he was still finding adorable tattoos in odd spots from time to time.)

They wrapped their arms around each other under the gush of warm water. Marcus had been mulling over something in his head for the past week that he had been too scared to bring up, but this seemed like as good a time as any.

"So, I've been thinking," he started tentatively. He didn't want to scare her away—he knew what a big deal crossing the three-week mark was. "We basically spend every night together. And you're staying at Lilly's mom's house while she's on tour, but she'll be back tomorrow and then you'll have nowhere to go and I know it probably seems really soon but . . ." He paused, making sure he sounded casual and nonchalant. He didn't want to come across as too desperate or needy—which he kind of was, to be honest. "So I was thinking that, if we made it past the three-week mark then—"

"Yes, I'll move in with you," Stormy cut him off with a smile.

"What?" Marcus felt his heart do some strange backflips.

"You were going to ask me to move in with you, weren't you?" she quickly asked.

"Yes. You don't have to do it right now, we can wait a little while if you want—"

Stormy shook her head. "Oh no. I'm moving in tonight. I've already packed my bag, it's in your room, and I also got myself a key made. Hope you don't mind." She winked at him playfully.

"You don't mess around, do you?" he chuckled, feeling stunned and elated all at once. Now that the cake had washed away, he pulled her close and kissed her. "Thank you for moving in with me." It was the best sort-of-anniversary gift Marcus could have ever wished for.

"It's a pleasure." She smiled.

"I've also got you a gift," he finally said, after a bit more kissing. He knew she wasn't going to like it, though; in fact, she was probably going to hate it, but it was time, and she needed it for what he had planned for her. Her face lit up, and he felt slightly bad, because he knew when she saw it her face would not be doing that.

They got out of the shower and wrapped themselves up in towels. He led her by the hand to the lounge, where he'd left it. But as predicted, when she saw it, she stopped dead. Marcus went over and picked up the box . . .

"Here." He was trying to sound cheerful. "It's—"

"I know what it is, Marcus," Stormy eyed the box suspiciously. "It's a lap computer." She looked like she was trying to size the thing up.

"Laptop, but close enough." He smiled to himself—that never got old. Ever. And the more he got to know her, the more extensively she had revealed this unique, Stormy-style English. It knew no limits, either—some of the things that came out of her mouth were priceless. He loved that about her.

"It's very sweet of you, but I'll use my typewriter if I need to write anything." Yes, she had a typewriter, an actual old-fashioned typewriter. And not in an ironic sense, like a Hipster might have; in a genuine, honest-to-God "use a typewriter" sense. He hadn't believed her at first, until she'd shown him "Tilly Typewriter" (she named practically everything).

"Well, for what I have in mind, you're going to need it. Because without it, you won't be able to do all this, and I've already signed you up." Marcus put the computer down and pulled out the booklet he'd downloaded from the internet. He'd researched for ages until he'd found the right one for her. He handed it over and she gazed at it, and started reading out loud.

"The Universal Center of Knowledge? What is this?" She looked up at him.

"Read on."

She opened the booklet and started reading. "The Universal Center of Knowledge is an online college for the study of holistic practices and alternative healing."

Marcus jumped in. "I thought it was time to make all the things you do official, and they have this really great course in something called Vortex therapy. It sounds interesting, although I didn't understand a word of it. And there's also a course in homeopathy— which I know you love—and also on aromatherapy. But you can enroll in whatever you want, and it's correspondence so you can take your time doing it. There's no hurry or anything. And then I thought, one day, when you're ready, we can always convert the cottage outside into a space for you to see clients, and I know you also said you want to teach drama to kids, so you could do that there too, and—"

Marcus felt Stormy throw her arms around him, cutting off his stream of nervous chatter. She held onto him tightly and he wrapped his arms around her. He'd been hoping for this reaction; he'd been thinking about a way to help her do this for a while now, ever since he had sensed the sadness in her when she'd told him she'd dropped out of school, that day in Mombasa. He didn't want to be some great knight in shining armor, swooping in to rescue her, but she deserved this chance. And he was the guy to give it to her.

"I love it. Thank you." She looked up at Marcus with that expression that totally melted and annihilated him. And it probably would for the rest of his life—hopefully.

"But you're going to have to help me with that thing," she said, pointing her finger at the dreaded computer. "Is it even safe?"

"What do you mean, *safe*? It's not going to bite you or anything like that."

Stormy placed her hands on her hips and looked at Marcus with that look he had become very familiar with over the past three weeks; he steadied himself and waited for it, no doubt it would be good. It always was.

"Marcus, I *told* you, I've seen the *Terminator* movies, I know what can happen with those . . ." She pointed again. "Those machine-computers and all that artificial intelligence stuff. I know!"

Marcus burst out laughing and grabbed Stormy, picking her up off the ground just a little. "I love you," he said, kissing her again. He'd first told her that he loved her three weeks ago, she still hadn't said it back, but he knew it wasn't easy for her and he hadn't been able to hold it in any longer.

"Oh my gosh!" She pulled away quickly. "I almost forgot your main, main, big present!" She ran into the bedroom, emerging a minute later with her guitar.

"Okay, stand there," she said to him excitedly. "I wrote you a song, well sort of, actually not really, but I just thought it would sound really good if I said it with background noise."

Marcus's heart skipped a beat.

Stormy readied herself to strum, and as she did . . .

"*I love you!*"

She half sang it, half shouted it.

"I love you too," Marcus quickly said, feeling a rush of joy like no other. He ran over to her and hugged her.

## 12 Weeks and 1 Minute Later

Still together!

## 18 Weeks and 1 Minute Later

Yup, still together . . .

# ACKNOWLEDGMENTS

It's a bit of a miracle this book actually happened, all thanks to the thieving burglar who broke into my house and stole my computer with this book on! I hope you enjoyed reading it while I had to rewrite large parts of it, whoever you are. So a massive, big, enormous thank-you needs to go out to all the people that made the rewriting process a little easier and brought me energy drinks and snacks and encouraged me when I thought I couldn't take it! And of course, my publisher, for giving me the much-needed extension . . . I am now much more vigilant with backing up my work. Lesson learned. Big time.

I write books because I want my readers – you – to laugh and have a blast and get swept away in a story that sometimes requires a certain amount of suspension of disbelief. I have been so overwhelmed by my sales lately, and am so thankful that you are all buying my books and enjoying them. This is the best gift any reader can give to an author because it means that I can carry on doing what I love doing; dreaming big and crazy and not limiting my imagination as to where my stories can go. So thanks to everyone that has picked this book up to read. I hope you enjoy Marcus and Stormy as much as I enjoyed writing them (the second time around)!

Read on for a sneak peek at Val's story in

**The Great Ex-Scape**

Coming soon from Headline Eternal!

# CHAPTER ONE

*Crappiest*, crap day of my entire effing life!

I'd been perching on the closed toilet seat for so long, that parts of my body had gone numb. The feeling had started in my feet, worked its way up into my ankles and was slowly numbing my calves. Maybe if I stayed here for long enough, everything would go numb? (Wishful thinking.)

My new—and ludicrously overpriced—pink cardigan was officially ruined from the mixture of mascara-stained tears and snot bubbles I'd been pouring into it for the last hour. But it was all I could do to stifle the undignified sounds of my uncontrollable sobs. This was a public restroom after all!

I had a headache from hell; possibly from tear-induced dehydration, possibly from the now-half-empty bottle of wine I'd been sipping on for the last hour. But I knew I had to leave at some point. I couldn't hide in a toilet cubicle for ever, as much as I wanted to. People would start to wonder. *He* would start to wonder.

This had been one of those monumentally bad ideas from the

start. *No*, what was I saying? This wasn't just a "bad idea", this was the worst idea ever conceived of. On a scale of one to worst idea ever this would be right up there with DIY open heart surgery (something I was seriously considering, since the pain of it breaking was almost too much to bear).

Going to my best friend's engagement party.

*Sounds perfectly benign.*

Making a speech at my best friend's engagement party.

*Totally normal.*

Toasting my best friend and his beautiful new fiancée.

*Absolutely acceptable.*

That is, until you replace the word "best friend" with "*the man I've been hopelessly, devotedly and excruciatingly in love with for the past three years.*"

I glanced at my watch; ten minutes before I needed to make the speech. Ten minutes until I was due to take up position in front of friends and families and deliver the old thrilled-and-couldn't-be-happier-for-them speech.

I gulped down another more-than-a-mouthful of anaesthetizing wine as my phone beeped. I rolled my eyes when I saw whose name was lighting up the screen. It was my friend, Lilly. Recently married Lilly. She'd been on my case for the last week, insisting that this was my last chance to tell him how I felt—even if he didn't feel the same way—I needed to get it off my chest. *And what if he did feel the same way, she'd said?*

She'd thrown around those phrases that get your hopes up, only for them to be later dashed, and downright shattered in the flaming pits of friend-zoned hell. I glanced at my phone; another one of those dreaded phrases was splashed across it.

*You have to tell him how you feel before it's too late. What if you are meant to be?*

Meant to be? Yeah, that's what I'd thought too. All that hanging out together. Pizza and beer evenings. Staying up all night chatting on the phone. We'd even gone to a friend's wedding together, for heaven's sake. Surely that was date-y? My friends had all agreed . . . it was date-y!

I'd certainly interpreted those as very clear signs. We were meant to be together! It was only a matter of time before he confessed his true feelings for me. But as time passed . . .and passed . . .and passed, nothing happened. And then *she* came along. And everything changed.

I needed to snap out of this. I needed to get a grip. I needed to go outside and pretend that everything was totally fine. *More than fine.* I needed to pretend that I couldn't be more thrilled for my BFF. I'd written a speech drenched in a smorgasbord of hideous romance clichés that I'd plucked directly from the internet. Every one of them repulsed me, and I wasn't sure how I was going to manage to say them out loud.

*Why had I agreed to this in the first place?* But this was only the appetizer; the main course was yet to come . . .

And let me tell you, it is a turducken of tragedy. One horrific idea rolled into another equally dreadful one and then stuffed into the mother of shitty ideas. Grilled, basted, tenderized and deboned!

Agreeing to help him pick out his wedding suit.

Agreeing to emcee his wedding.

Agreeing to help him choose his romantic honeymoon destination—where they'd have lots of romantic honeymoon sex.

Clearly, I was a sadomasochist hell-bent on torturing myself. But I had to do this. I had no other option. There was no way out.

*So I stood up . . .*

Pins and needles in feet. Kneecaps crunching. Dead legs. Stomach lurching. General revolting creeping feeling.

I took my first step, the first step I'd taken in ages, but as I did . . . *Whoosh!* It hit me all at once. The alcohol raced through my body, spiking the blood in my veins and making me buzz. I took another step and the buzz gave way to a much more unpleasant feeling.

Suddenly, I felt woozy. *Very woozy.* And this wasn't the kind of establishment for wooziness. The engagement party was being held at *her* parents' restaurant on their award-winning wine farm in the beautiful Cape Wine lands; no expense spared. Very fancy. It was the kind of upper-crusty party that people with surnames beginning with *Vander* and ending in *Child* went to. Many of the guests had been flown up from Jo'burg to be here, including myself.

I stared at myself in the bathroom mirror holding on to the sink for added support. I looked hideous. What was my mother's favorite saying? "I look like the wreck of the Hesperus." I'd never known what a Hesperus was, but for some reason the word seemed to describe perfectly how I looked and felt right now.

"Hesss Perrr Russs." I hissed it out loudly as I leaned towards the mirror and then almost laugh/cried out loud.

I grabbed some paper towels and made an attempt at wiping my tears away. I blew my nose quickly when I realized it was making a

I froze. A deathly pause followed as people turned and looked for me.

"Val!" he said it a bit louder this time. "Val?"

*What the hell was I going to do?*

**WARNING: Being jilted at the altar in front of 500 wedding guests can lead to irrational behaviour, such as going on your honeymoon to Thailand alone. Recovery will lead to partying the night away at Burning Moon festival – and falling in love with the person you least expect . . .**

**Don't miss *Burning Moon*, the first book in the Destination Love series.**

Available now from

**Newly single.**

**Holiday of a lifetime.**

**Bumping into 'the ex'.**

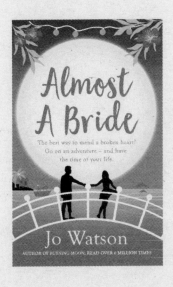

For more laugh-out-loud, swoon-worthy hijinks,
check out *Almost A Bride*, the second book
in the Destination Love series.

Available now from

**HEADLINE**
ETERNAL

When you go to Greece to meet your family but end up snogging your smokin' hot tour guide. #sorrynotsorry

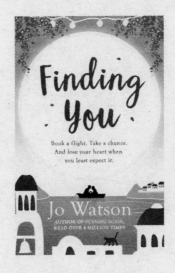

Get ready for a rollercoaster of a rom-com on the beaches of Santorini with the third Destination Love book, *Finding You*.

Available now from

**One night can change everything . . .**

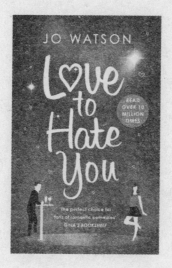

Love funny, romantic stories? You don't want to miss *Love to Hate You*

Available now from

**HEADLINE**
ETERNAL

# HEADLINE
# ETERNAL

## FIND YOUR HEART'S DESIRE...

VISIT OUR WEBSITE: www.headlineeternal.com
FIND US ON FACEBOOK: facebook.com/eternalromance
CONNECT WITH US ON TWITTER: @eternal_books
FOLLOW US ON INSTAGRAM: @headlineeternal
EMAIL US: eternalromance@headline.co.uk